■ □ ■ □ ■

MOCKING DESIRE

Writings from an Unbound Europe

■ ▢ ■ ▢ ■

DRAGO JANČAR

MOCKING
DESIRE

Translated from the Slovene by Michael Biggins

NORTHWESTERN UNIVERSITY PRESS

EVANSTON, ILLINOIS

Northwestern University Press
Evanston, Illinois 60208-4210

Originally published in Slovene in 1993 under the title *Posmehljivo poželenje*.
Copyright © 1993 by Drago Jančar. English translation copyright © 1998 by
Northwestern University Press. Published 1998 by arrangement with Drago
Jančar and the Copyright Agency of Slovenia. All rights reserved.

Grateful acknowledgment is made to Therese Kerze for her support of this
translation.

Printed in the United States of America

ISBN 0-8101-1553-0 (cloth)
ISBN 0-8101-1554-9 (paper)

Library of Congress Cataloging-in-Publication Data

Jančar, Drago.
    [Posmehljivo poželenje. English]
    Mocking desire / Drago Jančar ; translated from the Slovene by
Michael Biggins.
    p. cm.
    ISBN 0-8101-1553-0 (cloth : alk. paper). — ISBN 0-8101-1554-9
(pbk. : alk. paper)
    I. Biggins, Michael. II. Title.
PG1919.2.A54P6713 1998
891.8'435—dc21   98-15527
                                                       CIP

■ □ ■ □ ■

MOCKING DESIRE

CHAPTER 1

THE TEXT

THE FIRST THING HE SAW WAS A DETAIL: AN EMPTY EYEGLASSES frame on the desolate landscape below.

In the next instant the plane tilted dangerously, and he caught sight of tablets of ice and heard the sound of a trumpet. All along the ocean's surface, as far as the horizon: the frozen surfaces of floating islands, collecting here and there in massive clumps, the razor edges of their peaks barely discernible. Up above, somewhere very close by, at first the isolated, jagged sound of a single metal instrument, followed immediately by a disharmony of hundreds, perhaps thousands of them. And when the huge beast boomed and then shook from beak to tail, he felt that familiar hollow thing above his stomach, not quite pain, an ache in his empty breast, a prickly shell around his genitals, the dispoportionateness of objects and space, as in distant childhood awakenings. The airplane's gigantic wing reached all the way from his window high above down to the blurs of land and sea far below. Elongated beyond comprehension, it almost touched the jutting, icy razor edges and snowy sticking points. At this, the plane should have righted itself, but in defiance of common sense it maintained its dangerous attitude; it should have banked away from the dangerous seascape and begun descending toward the thin layer of dry land. But it continued to shudder, and its long left wing was now probably scraping the ground. That was on the left. On the right side, through windows that were now far, far above, the orange light of the setting sun poured in. "Is it from there?" he wondered. "And is that where the trumpet bursts come from?" He felt a thud: the wing had broken off the top of an iceberg, and now it was making hopeless, wavering attempts to right itself. But the icebergs were still beneath him to the left, the fiery sky up above. The white-frothed ocean surface was now practically in front of his eyes rushing in the opposite direction—dirty snow on the frozen configuration of the lower world, tin cans, somebody's empty glasses frames. The enormous attractive force of earth's gravity, the horrible uneasiness in his empty breast, a familiar-looking empty glasses frame, the landscape rushing beneath his feet, the shuddering of the airplane. This was no longer a flight over a level surface searching for power to lift off; this was a fall. All right, he said, let's fall then.

As he looked around him one last time, he found himself suddenly all alone in the huge aircraft. Only the video screen in front of him flickered with the image of a stewardess, her graceful movements, the oxygen mask in her hands, her fingers, breasts, her smile, and all of this in the fiery light that flashed through the windows onto the screen. He tried to burrow into the fold in his seat, and now beneath his feet he caught sight of the same rushing landscape. Was the machine all at once flying horizontally over alternating marine blue and dirty snowy surfaces again? But if that's the case, where is the floor of the aircraft? Why can he see through it? Why are there things flying in the opposite direction over the ocean's glimmering surface: images, aluminum cans, a glasses frame, faces? Letters, a text? That's a text, he tried to say, but his voice caught in his throat, in his chest, or somewhere. That's a text running at top speed in the opposite direction, a text with images, and a trumpet blast. The text runs at top speed over the surface. He can easily read it, and he notes each word in his memory in order to write them down immediately afterward: The sky's dark cupola lies over the water. A ray of light falls athwart the water from a distance, out of the breach dividing heaven and earth. Crows caw from a field; but out of the huge rift, as he flies into it, there comes a crystal silence. He's surrounded by that silence as he flies between heaven and earth somewhere into its inner reaches. A bell tower rings. He can hear it now. He knows, he sees this sound of his, motionless for an instant. For an instant it hovers in the air, and then its echo washes away toward the bright rift on the horizon.

"And never," Fred Blaumann says, his fingers drumming on a book, "never start a story with a dream."

That's what's happening here, he thought, that's what's happening here. It's drawing the huge bird and me, together with the slanting ray of light and the crystalline peals of silence—not toward the earth, not toward the icebergs, not with the ocean into the earth's recesses, but into something that's already taking place, something that I'm both writing and reading at the same time. Reading, hearing, seeing, and feeling. But not understanding. Professor Blaumann understands it. He understands everything. And he can explain it all, too. He knows how the story ought to start. Never with a dream! Never! "And if at all possible, never use exclamation points!"

He can clearly see Fred Blaumann's face before him, surrounded by sweet, attentive, obedient, talented faces. He can see beads of sweat under the wisps of hair on the crown of his head, on his shiny, incipient bald spot. Around it the faces with their inquisitive eyes are arranged as though around a baroque altar. That's happening here, and the trumpets abruptly fall silent. The rushing landscape has stopped. The text stops, the surface calms down. He closed his eyes.

He opened them. A gigantic fan was droning over his head. It shuddered at regular intervals. He had forgotten to turn it off before he went to sleep. He knelt on the bed and pulled the cord. The wings of the big bird beneath his ceiling came to rest. He listened to the unaccustomed silence and tried to collect himself. He drew a sharp line between his dreams, which dare not start the story, and reality, which wasn't particularly believable, either. Trumpets. The piercing sound of brass instruments. Drums! What about that, Professor of Creative Writing? Can the story start with drums? With a parade contingent of young black people marching up and down the street, practicing for their performance? Thirty-odd black youths marching in even lines along both sides of the street, with trumpets, drums in the first row, drums in the last: will that do? And with a multitude of black girls in red and white blouses marching down the middle, a caterpillar of black legs keeping time to the music beneath their short skirts. And an ample—fat, let's say—a fat, black teacher with a whistle clenched in her teeth and balloonlike flesh stuffed into her sweatsuit, above and below the waistband a rippling of flesh. And the high-pitched wail of all the wind instruments, a penetrating sound that can't be described, a sound that ricochets off their brass-studded uniforms like the rays of the morning sun. A young, black, incessantly moving, playing, drumming—let's say teeming—dancing centipede with a big banner over its head. The banner is fringed and sways over them as they come closer. In its center the silhouettes of two horseback riders are embroidered in gold and red. Above them are the words:

Andrew Bell Junior High School Band

and under the horses' hooves:

New Orleans, Louisiana

CHAPTER 2

A SERMON ON THE FALL

I

He closed the window and stared at the grime on the panes for a while. It hadn't rained in a long time. When he first arrived, this place was being drenched. In New York it snowed, and he had walked through the city's filthy slush, but down here where the sun always shone, it had been raining. His sponsor was waiting for him at the airport, together with one of his students, a dark-haired girl with perpetual chewing gum. They were loud and welcoming, and the whole time it rained. They went looking for his apartment, dodging streams of water coming off the roofs: St. Philip Street 18. In an office with a sign that said REAL ESTATE they settled on his rent. From under his umbrella the view was always restricted: the sidewalk and above it green verandas. A few store windows, a small office, the signing of a lease. Then suddenly he was here. The professor and his student ran off down the street, hand in hand, with one umbrella for the two of them. Here he was, suddenly.

But now there had been no rain for quite a while and dust had collected on the windows. Through the smudges he could see the Spanish facades across the street. The horns, drums, the entire ruckus had retreated into the next street, and only now could he make out a melody. Before it had been sheer noise, the shrill blare of trumpets, but now it was like the gentle music that washes through an airplane cabin after the wheels have hit the tarmac. When he first arrived it had rained, but it had been dry and warm for several days now. Everyone was waiting for a breeze from the river. It might bring more rain, followed by spring, for sure. Now and then a man in an undershirt, with a beer can in his hand, would walk up to one of the windows across the street. His heavy flesh rippling beneath the fabric. He keeps wiping the sweat from his forehead. Sometimes a blond woman gets up from the bed. She used to be pretty. Now strands of hair hang down limply over her face. Both of them have grown old and never leave their room. He's never seen them outside yet. Kowalski and Stella. They're waiting for spring, too. Spring comes early to this city, earlier than it does anywhere else.

His room had become quiet and dark again. Tangled bed-sheets, crumpled sheets of paper he had lain on in his sleep, bottled water at his bedside. Things arranged in peaceful, watchful disarray. After all that ruckus and sleeplessness, suddenly the perfect peace of things. Alone at this early morning hour, flung into this expanse where he can only conceive of himself as a dot at the continent's lower extremity. Every morning he has to conjure up a geographical image of the world if he wants to know where he is and what all this means. Above him is the brown mass of the American continent, scrawled over with mountains and rivers, sectioned off into perfect rectangles of states, with white splotches at the top, a blue gulf at the bottom, and here at the base of America's soft, warm underbelly, etched with the capillaries and the delta of a great river, here he was. Hurled here from afar, and all else had been left above, behind, somewhere else. Within the dot that designated the city above the delta, he was an invisible, moving dot. An unseen observer. An inaudible eavesdropper. An unknowing sage. A dot.

2

With a few quick movements he turns his folding bed back into a couch. The bed is okay when it's a couch. Now it's okay. It's not okay when it's a bed, because it takes up too much space then and tilts over to the left. It's not okay when the faucet drips in the bathtub, and he pulls the stopper out of the wall together with the chain that's supposed to keep it there. But when he takes a shower, it's okay. This place is humid and you have to shower a lot. Or turn on the air conditioner. But this air conditioner is very old, and it rattles even more than the ceiling fan on its elliptically wobbling axis. The ceiling fan is entertaining and unusual, it reminds him of Humphrey Bogart in a movie set in some sumptuously exotic locale. The ceiling fan is a perpetual reminder to him that he's somewhere else. The ceiling fan is okay. His fellowship, the university, the students of creative writing, and Professor Fred Blaumann are okay. Professor Blaumann is a writer. He writes about melancholy and is reluctant to talk about it. He likes to talk about jogging and exclamation marks. Sometimes the class has a visit from Peter Diamond, whose friends call him Pedro. Diamond is his nom de plume, in fact his name is supposed to be something else, maybe Juarez. Peter Diamond rides in on his bicycle. Peter Diamond lives with Irene, both of them are artists and they live an artist's life in New Orleans. His neighbor is a photographer and an eccentric. His name is Gumbo. Gumbo is something like jambalaya. Both of them are okay. In fact, everything is okay, except for the gay bar across the street where there's lots of screaming and loud music every night. Now, suddenly, he was here, a character in some other story, and everything was fine. Except for the landlord. His landlord owned lots of houses in the area and this one, unfortunately, was least okay. At his age he could have come up with a better landlord.

"You had your chance to check all that out," the landlord said after listening to the complaint about the air conditioner, the ceiling fan, the shower, the bathtub stopper, and the gay bar. "You should have checked it out before you signed the lease."

But back when they were in the dimly lit office signing the contract, with the torrential rain pouring off the roofs onto the pavement, they just smiled. The price was high, but then, Mr. G—r—a . . . ?

" . . . d—n—i—k. Gradnik."

"Grand . . . Nick?"

"Gregor Gradnik."

"From Pennsylvania, you say?"

"Slovenia."

. . . but then Mr. Grand Nick, being a writer himself, should know better than anyone just where he was living. This was the Vieux Carré, this is where Tennessee Williams lived. The Streetcar Named Desire, you know. And all that other stuff. So Grand Nick who comes from Pennslovenia and may be the next Dostoevsky had better know that the French Quarter has its price. Besides the basic price there were certain extra expenses. And just one hour later the smiling landlord was in his room, letting himself in without even knocking. If he didn't write a check exactly on the first of the month, he told him, he'd have his electricity shut off. He owns a lot of buildings, and he owns them precisely because he doesn't let anybody who comes from over there trick him out of his rent. He speaks loudly and threateningly, mercilessly reminding him of a certain landlady from his student days who had her sons pick up his furniture and put it out in the rain.

The art photographer gives his door a kick, his way of saying good morning.

"Did you see the parade? Did it scare you?"

3

I'm an observer, he tells himself, I observe what happens to me here on the other side of the world. If he ever tells anyone about all of this, the hardest part will be conveying the smells, the scents of all the rooms, streets, the green patios in backyards, the wooden frame suburban houses, the waters of the great river, the marketplace, the dives where drunken sailors bring their women in the morning. Colors can be easily represented, as can sounds. Everyone has some blues and Dixieland tunes he can replay in memory, or some unctuous country melodies. The staccato of the American audio scene is universal. Likewise, the colors of the southern sky could be described. But the smells. How could he describe the smells that accompanied him everywhere? Maybe he should try describing smells with colors: a patio could be blue-green, the smell of a hallway could be a warm, wet dark gray. The smell of a morning street could be a washed-out yellow and the smell of the bars where black musicians play could be pink, or maybe violet. But everywhere a gently shifting, rainbowlike spectrum.

He lived in the square test pattern of streets that the French had founded two centuries before—La Nouvelle Orleans. About the city one need say nothing. It's all been said before. Here he was at the beginning of some story of his and everything was at his disposal.

He had wanted to go to New York like everyone else, but only New Orleans had an opening for a writer's fellowship. It has cockroaches, a friend of his who had sailed the world had warned him. And rice and beans. He had said nothing about jazz. For the birthplace of jazz, jazz was so self-evident that unless you were a tour guide it was inappropriate to say anything about it at all with respect to New Orleans. After a binge, his traveler friend had told him, if you want to sober up before you get back on the boat, they sell good coffee in the marketplace. He wasn't sure why he would want to get back on a boat when there wouldn't be any boat to begin with. A library, a university, these there would be. There would be something for him to learn, and he would have to give something in return. That part of the trip looked like it might be the most dangerous of all. At the thought of having to lecture American students about literature and, worse still, analyze their writing, his hands began to sweat, just as though he were facing a difficult test himself. Even at home he disliked talking about literature—literature was to be written and read, read and written. But if the Americans had invented courses and whole schools of creative writing, then they probably knew what for. The twentieth century had proved that they knew everything. And if fortune in the form of a fellowship competition for writers had chosen him, then he would just have to lecture about literature. Eat rice and beans. And drink black coffee in the marketplace before he got back on the boat.

And one day, when he comes to observe himself and his life during this one-year segment, it will seem as though it were somebody else who spent his days wandering around some city in the American South. The things that will happen to him in that story will have hardly anything to do with reality. They'll become part of the story, together with the colors, sounds, and scents. Blurred and iridescent. A part of waking in the morning to the shrill blare of trumpets, to slow-moving black people and their loud colors. A segment of something. A journey around some axis, like the fan above his head. His friend had sailed around the world on a steamship. He had been thirty-five years old, and had eaten rice and beans in this town.

A painter whom he knew had once thrown his canvases in a heap, doused them with gasoline, and ignited them. He should have moved on, should have shifted his axis into some new space. If you don't go to America at thirty-five, you could end up hanging yourself. Or sailing around the world. Burning your paintings. Or standing at the train station each night, watching the departing trains as they follow Thomas Mann to Venice. Then drinking yourself stupid with the riffraff. Of course, there are countless other possibilities, all of which are linked to some form of self-torment or free fall, willful vegetating, deterioration, agony in your marriage, prestige-bearing agony at work. And the time is not that far off when you'll blame it all on the day you were born. On Slovenia, for being small and having nothing but small people in it. On Europe, for being a grotesque, powdered hag. On the fog that blankets the valleys, or on the garbage men for not picking up the trash.

But America is great and all of us are her smiling children.

4

How art thou fallen from Heaven, O Lucifer, son of the morning! How art thou cut down to the ground! he cried out in a voice that trembled slightly.

Fifteen heads fell silent immediately, and he could feel their curious gazes trained on him. That was what you had to do—pique their curiosity. Even Professor Fred Blaumann, sitting in the back row, smiled and waited for him to go on. He was going to let him swim, and his smile was saying, "That was a pretty risky dive into the water, now how's he going to swim out?" Gregor Gradnik said nothing, put his hand behind his back, and slowly extended his fingers one by one. Count to five, count to five. An actor in Ljubljana had taught him that. Let them think you're lost and don't know where to go from here. He was afraid he didn't.

I beheld him as lightning fall from heaven.

Isn't that nicely put? It reminded him of a comic strip. American TV evangelists had fascinated him from the day he arrived. He had traveled six thousand miles to the land of computerized brains, and who were the very first people he discovered here: Methodist preachers straight out of the seventeenth century. Straight out of times when the world was still pathetic, when the world was still *of the heart.* Preachers who had come straight from some muddy marketplace where pigs and chickens got caught underfoot, and who settled right into America's flashing TV screens. Where an electronic ticker tape keeps track of donations from the faithful. *And in our souls settle fallen angels whom God has thrust away.* Did they think that the sermon was a literary genre? Demons and angels observe the struggle between good and evil in the human soul. All of us have both hovering above us whenever we make moral decisions. Just like a writer observing his protagonist. Who will be victorious—the fallen angel who drags the soul downward? The fall and struggle of both angels: the allegory of it is horrible, graphic, dramatic. Or will the good angel win and carry the soul off with him upward, off of the screen and into a realm of pure radiance? There is a sequel to the story in every Sunday-morning TV sermon. And yet we all know that that isn't literature. Why?

A male student with a huge number 9 on his T-shirt kept staring at him as he chewed his gum. Number 9 was the most gifted one of all, Professor Blaumann had told him. So that meant he was washing out. A good-looking blond girl who worked in a posh art-supply store on Royal Street said she liked what he said because it had ended with a question mark. Blaumann's seminar was death to exclamation marks. Professor Fred Blaumann was staring straight ahead. He wasn't happy. Professor Blaumann didn't care for heavy subjects. You have to understand the difference in methodology, he had explained to him on the first day. We don't teach literature here, we teach them how to write. No heavy subjects. Life experience, genuine self-expression. It always worked like this: during the first hour the instructor lectured, and during the second they discussed the students' literary products, their attempts at self-expression. This is when Professor Blaumann would pounce on every exclamation mark and shout: no exclamation marks! And every time he would then discourse eloquently on the subject of exclamation marks. But Gregor Gradnik was certain that life experience, the essence of America, was to be found in televangelists' sermons. God sits with the Israelis in their tanks, and that's why they win. The devil lives in Hollywood. The perpetual battle between clearly delineated Good and Evil.

Of all misfortunes the greatest is the wish to contain both God and Satan in one's heart at once. Sermons aren't literature precisely because they're exclusive, they recognize only the one or the other. But literature wants to embrace both good and evil *in one's heart at once.*

"Sure, no argument," Professor Blaumann said. "That's very basic: Raskolnikov. Dostoevsky." He had wanted to say, sure, no argument, but this business with the televangelists is pretty obscure. It occurred to him that the professor might be ashamed of televangelists. Of the bank account numbers flashing across the screen while the sinful fall to their knees and the audience sings, "Sing, brothers and sisters, sing!" For him TV evangelists were as far removed from literature as America was from that muddy European marketplace with pigs.

"Falling in your sleep," he added in an attempt to rescue the class, "falling in your dreams is nothing other than a recollection of the falling angel. This is rooted very deeply in man's genetic makeup."

"But more importantly," the professor exclaimed, "there are too many novels that begin with dreams.

"And sermons, too," he shouted out, "sermons just have too many exclamation marks."

And here began a discourse on exclamation marks. His students listened carefully.

5

Ah, greatest of all lands on earth! The land to which he had flown in the midst of an ugly winter. When the heavy bird soared over the ocean, over frozen islands which later appeared to him so many times in dreams as empty eyeglasses frames. The filthy slush of New York City's streets. The homeless warming themselves in the steam that billows out of its manholes.

Ah, Professor Blaumann and his students! He wanted to explain to them how he had fallen into this story and how on that first Sunday morning a preacher had howled at him from the television in his room at the Hotel Edison. He wanted to tell them that this was a real story, that the com ponents were all there. That they should take a look at Gustave Doré's picture of the angel falling. That stood at the beginning, at the beginning of everything:

From out of the night sky strewn with stars, a swath of light falls onto the earth. The light falls through clouds onto part of the earth's curved surface. Between heaven and earth, in the midst of the sheathlike light that dissipates toward its edges, a falling body that agonizingly draws our attention. The head is lowermost, beneath it the hands are crossed as though in an attempt to shield it from its inevitable collision with the bottom. Dark, billowing robes, and helpless legs, bent slightly at the knees, extending upward out of them. But especially the wings, black as though singed, as if a fire through which the body has already fallen had seared them. The tempter of man approaches us inexorably in his precipitous flight. Cast downward onto us from heaven. And this, this is always at the beginning, professor. Always. The discourses on exclamation marks come much later; the genetic makeup, too. Isidore Ducasse comte de Lautréaumont once had this vision: as the angel rises up to the dazzling heights, and as he, Maldoror, descends into the vertiginous abyss of evil, the two catch sight of each other. And what a sight! Everything that mankind has thought in the past sixty centuries, and everything it will think in the coming sixty, is encompassed in that image. And that is just one fleeting moment. In fact, the good and bad angel exchange their very long stories. We hear them both, and their words become confounded in a single, incomprehensible tale.

CHAPTER 3

MADEMOISELLE
AND THE ARTISTS

I

Across the way a runner was limbering up beside a brick building. Gregor Gradnik sat on his bench and watched the runner's determined, regular movements. The noonday sun illuminated the building's red facade, dotted with gleaming windows and open doorways. The southern sun flooding the humid landscape, the white paths leading through the sodden grass, the students' bright-colored clothes, their white and black faces, the flurry of white tennis shoes at the entrance to the cafeteria. It's February and snowing at home now, he thought, and the streets are probably full of black slush. Ana is wearing her rubber galoshes, and there's the fusty smell of too many sweaty bodies on the buses now. At this point the runner's buoyant figure disengaged itself from its blaze of light and made its way at a bob toward Gregor Gradnik. Streams of water from the wet grass splashed against the runner's shins and calves. Not until the jogger was about twenty strides away did Gregor recognize him as Professor Blaumann. His jogging stride wasn't as graceful as it had seemed from a distance. His lips bobbled, spraying out gusts of spittle. He paused in front of him like a snorting horse, though he kept running in place. Water kept squishing out from under his tennis shoes and his mouth sprayed saliva.

"Spleen!" the professor exclaimed. "Spleen! The vapors exhaled by the mouth serve to dissipate spleen!"

Professor Blaumann wasn't just a professor. He was a writer. He had spent a long time getting ready to write a book about the substance of melancholy. Something between fiction and an essay. Something that would be fiction and nonfiction. Both at the same time. The essence of melancholy had everything in the world to do with spleen.

Gradnik stood up. It struck him that his colleague had begun the kind of disquisition that requires you to stand.

"Sit down," his fellow writer said and continued to thrash the grass beneath his feet. "I mustn't stop, you understand."

Gradnik understood: he could get a chill, his body could harden, his blood could coagulate, it wouldn't be good for the heart. Even so, he remained standing. He couldn't sit with his colleague standing and delivering a scholarly discourse. He remembered how he had greeted him in his office. After all that scurrying around under umbrellas, the next day he had stood in the middle of his book-lined office. Wearing a professorially tweed sportcoat. And a red tie, in a tranquil room that breathed of knowledge and furniture, of furniture that breathed. Gradnik learned that the furniture was done in Chippendale style, or, rather, in imitation Chippendale style. They spoke amid long silences, with a sudden commotion now and then out in the hallway. The hallways breathed through the doors. Melancholy matter, Gradnik learned, is related to spleen. Spleen was to be understood literally, in its biological sense. Spleen was just that: spleen. It was where the refuse of the bodily fluids collected. Bodily fluids were humours. And humour, in older English, referred exclusively to bodily fluids and nothing else. As melancholy matter is produced, the blood becomes thick as tar. "You see the connection, don't you, between spleen and spleen, between the biological fact and the literary concept? This is going to be a brilliant text," he said. "When I finish it, I can die.

"Spleen produces vapors that poison the brain. Physical activity dilutes them, thins out the tar. The melancholy matter can't reach the brain. Don't you see?"

Large drops of sweat were collecting amid the sparse hair on the professor's ruddy scalp and sliding down his face. His bowed legs kept flexing at the knees. His hands were wringing out his wet cap.

And there was something white jutting out from under his running shorts. Gradnik didn't dare look to see what it was—a loose piece of fabric or whatever. In any case, the thing sticking out of his shorts, pressing against his thigh, made Gradnik uneasy.

"Now excuse me," the professor exclaimed. "That's Meg Holick running over there. What a gazelle! I think I'll join her."

Meg Holick was a student in the creative-writing class. She was the dark-haired girl who had met him at the airport with Fred Blaumann. The two had run off down the street under the same umbrella. The professor turned and sloshed through the wet grass after his carefree gazelle.

"If you're free we can continue this at lunch," he called out.

"Right," Gradnik called back, "that's just what I was thinking."

2

That's just what he wasn't thinking. He was thinking how to avoid precisely that. He didn't want to be trapped slurping soup in silence with his colleague, who would be wearing that red necktie again and holding forth on melancholy matter. During his first days he had had lunch in the students' part of the cafeteria and from a safe, camouflaged distance observed the faculty dining room, where it was the rule to speak of oneself, constantly oneself. He had nothing to say about himself. From the students' part of the cafeteria you could see the light blue wallpaper on the faculty dining-room walls and the subtle nodding of heads skilled at both asking questions and listening to answers. The raucous world on this side was divided from that world—Blaumann's world—by a door that was always left wide open. Yet it was still so quiet there that you could hear the clinking of utensils. On this side you shouted across tables and slammed trays down. The silence in there and the racket out here complemented each other. Whenever a student crossed the dividing line between clatter and silence he would lower his voice. When faculty members crossed through the students' cafeteria they would shout to each other, pull the tabs off of soft-drink cans, and pour down the beverage as they walked. The feeding ritual, Fred Blaumann would say, was a manifestation of a *differentio specifica*. Students, you could say, were an example of *fluctuatio,* whatever you imagine that to be. Faculty, staff—this is the *institutio,* the establishment, *die Stiftung.* Professor Fred Blaumann has entirely different problems from a student like Meg Holick. The professor has scholarly problems, creative problems with melancholy matter, where a student has fluctuational problems. This doesn't prevent them from running together, but neither does it mean that she could ever be initiated into the complexities that govern the silent world over there. It's not just a matter of the age difference or disparate knowledge bases; at bottom it was a fixed quantity and the complexity of the world that the professor carried on his bowed legs and which, in the student's case, were reduced to various issues of a transitory nature.

Here Gregor Gradnik caught himself in the midst of an impossible thought—something had reminded him of his year in the army. On the face of it the comparison seemed unlikely: in some fusty, high-arched, small-windowed Balkan stable that had been turned into an army mess, a huge herd of young males in rumpled green overcoats jostles for food. They hold plates filled with beans in a starchy sauce. Steam rises up from enormous kettles. In a corner of the mess, sitting at tables covered with white cloths that have goulash spots on them, are the officers. Their gun belts are draped over the backs of their chairs, so that they don't have to keep shifting their rears while they eat. So they don't have to fish their pistols out from between their legs, where the weapons tend to slide. With jackets unbuttoned and cigarettes between their fingers, they hold forth on the mysterious organizational and professional problems of their complex world.

"You've been invited to a party," Fred Blaumann said.

"The artistic demimonde should be there," he said.

"If I'm not mistaken, you should hear a great deal about alienation. Alienation still gets talked about here a lot."

3

"Alienation," the young lady said. "Is that some kind of cheese? It sounds French."

The young lady was popping hazelnuts into her mouth. She had a self-replenishing handful of them.

"They told me I could find you under the cloud of cigarette smoke," she said.

The young lady had watery blue eyes and a smattering of freckles on her white skin.

"Of all kinds of alienation," she said, "I think my favorite is Beaujolais. Californian is good, too."

The young lady was not an artist. Her friend, though, was an artist and had written a successful book about bicycling.

"But I'm drinking bourbon now," she said, "because they don't have that kind of wine here."

Two wet spots were spreading around the young lady's underarms. She was dressed in a light fabric, but in this crowd it was hot.

"Why don't you take your jacket off?" she said. "You must be hot."

The young lady was lightly dressed, like everyone else.

Only he was wearing a thick, woolly jacket, only he had a cloud of smoke billowing up above his head.

"Do you like garlic?" she asked. "Garlic has become incredibly popular in this country in the last few years."

The young lady was leaning against a bookcase; in the crowd they were virtually pressed up against each other. He could feel her warm bourbon breath.

"You watch!" she exclaimed. "I'm going to invent a garlic that doesn't give you bad breath."

The young lady's name was Irene Anderson. Irene Anderson, Madison, Indiana. New Orleans for the past five years.

"A discreet garlic," Gregor Gradnik offered.

Irene Anderson was overjoyed and clapped her hands.

"That's it exactly. Discreet garlic."

4

Before the blast she introduced her friend to him. Peter Diamond was a writer and he had written a hit they referred to as *Cycling New Orleans.* The name for the garlic, she said, the name for the garlic. A name for the garlic? he said. Discreet garlic? Interesting. You're a writer, too? he said. How interesting. Around here—and this has been statistically proven—every third person is a writer. We've been approaching that ratio ever since creative-writing workshops started up. I'm involved in one. Are you? Writers aren't made, though, don't you agree? They're born. There are more and more of these mechanical workshops. The Russians tried it with their engineers of human souls. That was something like a creative-writing program, don't you think? Yes, yes. Absolutely. There's rice and beans being served in the kitchen. Interesting. With garlic, lots of it.

Before the blast they ate rice and beans, pressed up against the bookshelf. It turned out that they lived close to each other. That the two of them lived on St. Peter Street. They had a magnificent balcony like a Spanish veranda. When Mardi Gras came there would be a balcony party. He would be invited. It also turned out that Peter Diamond sometimes attended Fred Blaumann's workshop. A writer has to be curious about things. There's always something to learn. Fred's expertise on the use of exclamation marks was first-rate. Highly restrictive, you might say. But now he's writing something new. About melancholy matter. Nonfiction that's actually fiction. Or the other way around. Vice versa. These beans are excellent. Do you think Faulkner ate them? Not in his later years; in his later years he cycled. There's even a play showing about it: *Faulkner's Bicycle*. By Wont Dalk. That's a pseudonym, it comes from Don't Walk, you can find his anagram on every stoplight in town. Interesting. Really. The rice and beans are good. Spicy, Miss Anderson said. Sherwood Anderson must have eaten rice and beans. And vice versa.

Irene Anderson knew how to laugh well, so that occasionally she choked on her laughter and Peter Diamond affectionately thumped her on the back. He promised Gregor a copy of his book, the hit they referred to as *Cycling New Orleans*. He would inscribe it to Gregor.

Before the blast they introduced him to Popescu. He was the only other person wearing a thick jacket, with a cloud of cigarette smoke billowing above his head. Also to Lee Dong, from Korea. And to some Russian who was the owner of the house. Before the blast Fred Blaumann arrived. Wearing a wide grin on his face he plied his way through the crowd, with his blond wife, who was a head taller than him, in tow. Fred waved to him. Meg Holick, the jogging student, was nowhere to be seen. Then came the blast.

5

"Merciful heavens!" a woman's voice cried out. "He's not really going to do it, is he?"

Silence spread from the next room in a broad wave. It wasn't the noise that spread; after that outcry silence flooded the house like a rising tide. He pushed his way through the overheated bodies to the doorway. On a huge screen in the corner of the room was the image of a definitely nervous young male. His eyes were darting in all directions, and the camera kept zooming in on his hands, which were grasping the back of his chair.

"He announced he's going to shoot himself," said his Russian host, tossing a handful of peanuts in his mouth. He began to grind them so fast that his double chin shook. "I can't help it," said the quiz show emcee in his iridescent suit on the iridescent screen. "I can't help it, you said that Delphi is in Egypt." The camera panned across the studio audience as it burst out in laughter. Clearly, everyone knew where Delphi was except Bill. "Delphi, Bill," he called him by name, "Bill, Delphi is in Greece." The young man on the chair muttered something and seized more firmly onto the back of the chair. "If you'd said Greece," the emcee said enticingly, "the two thousand dollars would have been yours. Two thousand, Bill. Sorry." Music. A word from their sponsors.

"He won't do it," the Russian said.

"Even if he does, he's an idiot," someone called out from the crowd.

"He won't," the Russian said.

"Ever since we've had TV there's been some killing or war going on every day," a woman's voice said.

"This is something different," the Russian said and propelled another handful of nuts down his gullet.

"It's TV shit is what it is, not something different," said a man standing in front of the television pushing its buttons.

The picture on the screen returned to the studio. The alluring emcee quietly and slowly approached the man in the chair. "In our last round," he said, "a week ago, Bill, you announced that you were going to do something. If you didn't win, you were going to do something that the world had never seen." Bill fidgeted nervously. Silence. "And I'll do it, too," he said. The emcee looked into the camera. "Why would you do that, Bill? Why?" The young man's eyes started to dart around again and he muttered something inaudible. "You need money!" the emcee exclaimed, spread his arms wide and turned victoriously toward the audience. "Who doesn't?" he exclaimed, and the audience roared with laughter. "But only the winner gets it!" he said. "Only the one that knows where Delphi is." He paused for a moment and then added sympathetically, "In Greece, Bill." The young man's hands let go of the back of his easy chair, he leaned back, bowed his head, and watched the emcee's feet flutter across the wobbling studio floor. "Next week," the emcee began, "next week . . . " At that instant there was a ruckus, several spectators jumped to their feet, and the camera lurched back to focus on the stage. Bill had pulled a gun out of his pocket and his shaking hands were fumbling with something on it. Someone ran toward him from behind the stage curtain. He shoved the chair back. He aimed at his head. Then came the blast. Some later claimed that there had been no blast. But there was one; there had to be one. The camera danced all out of control and then forced its way through the crowd to the man, who was lying on the floor. He seemed to be moving.

He noticed Fred overturning a bottle. He saw Irene Anderson cover her face with her hands. The Russian swallowed a whole fistful of peanuts.

"Shit," he said. "He really did it."

CHAPTER 4

MELANCHOLY MATTER

I

What?

Melancholy.

What did you say?

Melancholy. The anatomy of melancholy.

That's nothing but rubbish.

In 1621 the famous work of the Protestant cleric Robert Burton, *The Anatomy of Melancholy*, was published in England. There were those who held it to be a piece of charlatanry from the very beginning, and others who thought it a work of genius. The dispute over it has continued to this day. Fred Blaumann was convinced that the latter faction was right. In fact, it was an incredible, grandiose work. In three weighty volumes the author explores the causes and etiology of melancholy, describes its symptoms and effects on the individual, and investigates in detail the possible cures for this age-old disease of mankind. Following the definition of the word, which begins with divine cause and man's being cast into the world and sin—with his fall—*The Anatomy of Melancholy* develops into a finely articulated, complex system of cause and effect. Symptoms of the soul and symptoms of the body, natural and supernatural causes, melancholy of the head and melancholy of the liver, melancholy caused by demons and witches, thoughts and sex, food and book learning, the melancholy of knowledge and the melancholy of love, consisting of the body's humors and of sinful thoughts, symptoms of the malady of love, symptoms of jealousy, hypochondriacal or windy melancholy, the melancholy of desire, and of loneliness. It was a global, cosmic work. Fred Blaumann was convinced that the modern age with its rationality had been wrong to neglect it. What's more, he was convinced this had been due to a misunderstanding that he would set to rights. There was no more rational book than this. No other book so full of imagination and brilliant argumentation deriving from *the thing itself.*

"The thing itself, don't you see! When you say spleen, what do you think of? Well, what do you think of, Gradnik?" Fred had already mastered the pronunciation of his name. "You think of Byron, of Baudelaire. You think of Weltschmerz, good God, what a wonderful word. Now if you say the name Trakl, Georg Trakl, what occurs to you?" "Violent disharmony," Gradnik answered. "Dark, musty Salzburg streets." "Of course," Fred Blaumann exclaimed. "And that's melancholy. A mood. Something completely intangible." He hit a few keys on his computer:

Melancholie

> Bläuliche Schatten. O ihr dunklen Augen,
> Die lang mich anschaun im Vorübergleiten.
> Gitarrenklänge sanft den Herbst begleiten
> Im Garten, aufgelöst in braunen Läugen.
> Des Todes ernste Düsternis bereiten
> Nymphische Hände, an roten Büsten säugen
> Verfallne Lippen und in schwarzen Läugen
> Des Sonnenjünglings feuchte Locken gleiten.

Melancholy

> Bluish shadows. O, you dark eyes
> Gazing at me, gliding past.
> Guitar chords accompany the autumn
> Dissolving, leaching in the garden darkly.

Nymphean hands unfold Death's sullen
Twilight, and withered lips feed at crimson
Breasts. And in the black recesses
The sun god's sodden tresses flutter.

"But no," Blaumann corrected himself. "No, Trakl didn't realize he was expressing just one of the symptoms of matter, of melancholy matter."

Fred Blaumann had something in common with Robert Burton. He spent most of his time in study, just as Burton said of himself. He lived a "quiet, fixed, and private life," *mihi & musis* on campus, with his books, his jogging, his learned and witty conversations, as do all people who live with melancholy substance.

2

"What did you say?"

"Melancholy. The anatomy of melancholy."

"Oh, that's nothing."

Maybe it really was nothing, as his landlord said when he asked him what he was studying up there at the university. Gradnik signed the check.

"Well, what isn't nothing? What is something?"

"Real estate."

No doubt. But that doesn't make the study of melancholy rubbish. For Fred Blaumann it was everything. His expertise with exclamation points was fine for students of creative writing. But Blaumann's big issue was reserved for solitary hours, for vigils at the computer screen. For preparing the magnum opus that had preoccupied him for seven years. The work into which he tried to initiate Gregor Gradnik with all his professorial zeal. "You'll understand," he exclaimed one evening as they sat in his Chippendale office after hours of creative writing. "I knew from the beginning that you'd understand." His landlord's real estate was something for sure, while the things they study at universities these days often weren't anything at all. Curiosities, a waste of time and taxpayers' money. Perhaps, but Fred Blaumann's specialty was melancholy and nothing else. An empty thing. For what else are we to understand by that word but some intangible sorrow, perhaps even fear. *Void of sorrow and void of fear.* Fred Blaumann would establish the link between that void and matter. At first, and in a brilliant style, he would let the poets speak; then he would set them firmly on legs of reality—alchemy, medicine, physics. It wasn't nothing and it wasn't empty, as the landlord said. Quite the opposite, it was just as tangible and fixed as his real estate. Robert Burton wasn't the only one. For centuries people had tried to prove the existence of a special substance circulating through man's universe and possibly through the entire cosmos. Proof of the existence of melancholy matter had been as important as discovering the philosopher's stone. Today the world is familiar with the black sun and sorrowful angel of Dürer's *Melancholy,* the *Melancholy* of Lucas Cranach the Elder, the *Melancholy* of Cornelius Antonisz, Heemskerk's *Melancholy* or the *Melancolia* of Thomas de Lee. But many physicians had proven that melancholy was just an artistic representation of a real, if uncomprehended, state of things. For a time there was a firm conviction that melancholy derived from the spleen, the organ where so much of the waste of the body's fluids (*humours!*) mixes with the blood. Books have been written about this, too, and a whole bibliography rolls across the screen. Therefore: melancholy matter is a thick fluid, a dark, sticky pitch that slowly circulates through the organism, causing a gloomy disposition. At times to such an extent that a person takes leave of his senses. In the past they used vinegar to dissipate melancholy matter, mixing it with various other remedies to bring about a change in the patient's physical state. Those remedies eased the pressure from deposits of bile, without actually moving them.

But most frequently of all, melancholy matter collected in the intestines, where it mixed with bile. This then gave rise to vapors that poisoned the brain. And there we have it.

This brings us back full circle to the poets. Back to Baudelaire, with all due respect, and even, with your indulgence, to Trakl and his *Bläuliche Schatten.* Sometimes these vapors escape through the mouth of the melancholic and bring the risk of infection to others.

3

Gregor Gradnik was speechless. It had never occurred to him to link poetry to bilious vapors. He stared at the computer screen, with endless rows of names, comparisons, quotations, authors, and titles. Blaumann fascinated him even more than Sunday-morning TV evangelists. The professor who corrected his students commas by day and urged them to approach writing as *self-expression* spent every night at his computer, engrossed in the great and even cosmic Blaumannian thesis. A jogger by day, at night he researched his great alchemical book, which would explain melancholy *in substantio* to the world.

Blaumann's computer was linked to databases at various English universities, and it was there, in England, that he discovered the case of a man living in the seventeenth century who had arranged to have confession and the Eucharist administered in his house during Holy Week, because he was afraid of the excess quantities of bilious vapor that the crowds of contrite and downtrodden faithful would produce in church.

Vapor! Fred Blaumann had reached a fevered pitch of recognition. Vapor! Not, however:

> All my griefs to this are jolly
> Naught so sad as melancholy.

And when he wrote his book, he wouldn't just deal with melancholy as an Elizabethan disease; he would plumb its historical depths. From Constantine the African—he struck a key and the date 1087 flashed onto the screen—to Robert

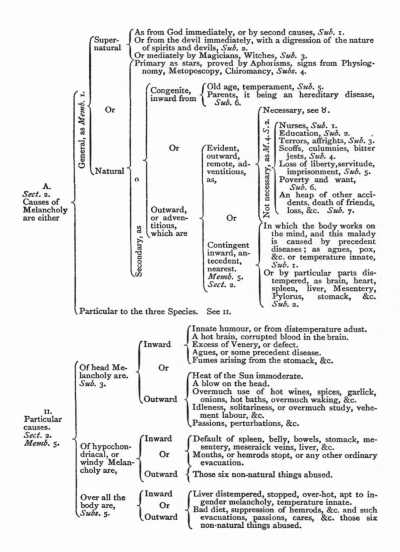

A.
Sect. 2.
Causes of
Melancholy
are either

General, as *Memb.* 1.

Supernatural
- As from God immediately, or by second causes, *Sub.* 1.
- Or from the devil immediately, with a digression of the nature of spirits and devils, *Sub.* 2.
- Or mediately by Magicians, Witches, *Sub.* 3.
- Primary as stars, proved by Aphorisms, signs from Physiognomy, Metoposcopy, Chiromancy, *Subs.* 4.

Or

Natural
- Congenite, inward from
  - Old age, temperament, *Sub.* 5.
  - Parents, it being an hereditary disease, *Sub.* 6.
- Or
- Outward, or adventitious, which are (Secondary, as)
  - Evident, outward, remote, adventitious, as,
    - Necessary, see ♉.
    - Not necessary, as *M. 4. S.* 2.
      - Nurses, *Sub.* 1.
      - Education, *Sub.* 2.
      - Terrors, affrights, *Sub.* 3.
      - Scoffs, culumnies, bitter jests, *Sub.* 4.
      - Loss of liberty, servitude, imprisonment, *Sub.* 5.
      - Poverty and want, *Sub.* 6.
      - An heap of other accidents, death of friends, loss, &c. *Sub.* 7.
  - Or
  - Contingent inward, antecedent, nearest. *Memb.* 5. *Sect.* 2.
    - In which the body works on the mind, and this malady is caused by precedent diseases; as agues, pox, &c. or temperature innate, *Sub.* 1.
    - Or by particular parts distempered, as brain, heart, spleen, liver, Mesentery, Pylorus, stomach, &c. *Sub.* 2.

Particular to the three Species. See II.

II.
Particular
causes.
Sect. 2.
Memb. 5.

Of head Melancholy are. *Sub.* 3.
- Inward
  - Innate humour, or from distemperature adust.
  - A hot brain, corrupted blood in the brain.
  - Excess of Venery, or defect.
  - Agues, or some precedent disease.
  - Fumes arising from the stomack, &c.
- Or
- Outward
  - Heat of the Sun immoderate.
  - A blow on the head.
  - Overmuch use of hot wines, spices, garlick, onions, hot baths, overmuch waking, &c.
  - Idleness, solitariness, or overmuch study, vehement labour, &c.
  - Passions, perturbations, &c.

Of hypochondriacal, or windy Melancholy are,
- Inward
  - Default of spleen, belly, bowels, stomack, mesentery, meseraick veins, liver, &c.
- Or
  - Months, or hemrods stopt, or any other ordinary evacuation.
- Outward
  - Those six non-natural things abused.

Over all the body are, *Subs.* 5.
- Inward
  - Liver distempered, stopped, over-hot, apt to ingender melancholy, temperature innate.
- Or
- Outward
  - Bad diet, suppression of hemrods, &c. and such evacuations, passions, cares, &c. those six non-natural things abused.

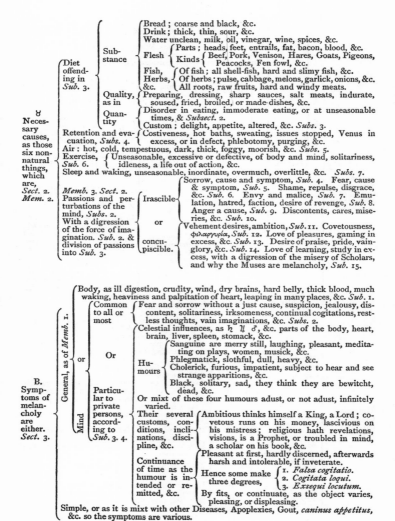

ੂ Necessary causes, as those six non-natural things, which are, Sect. 2. Mem. 2.

Diet offending in *Sub.* 3.

- Substance
  - Bread; coarse and black, &c.
  - Drink; thick, thin, sour, &c.
  - Water unclean, milk, oil, vinegar, wine, spices, &c.
  - Flesh
    - Parts; heads, feet, entrails, fat, bacon, blood, &c.
    - Kinds { Beef, Pork, Venison, Hares, Goats, Pigeons, Peacocks, Fen fowl, &c.
  - Fish, Of fish; all shell-fish, hard and slimy fish, &c.
  - Herbs, Of herbs; pulse, cabbage, melons, garlick, onions, &c.
  - &c. All roots, raw fruits, hard and windy meats.
- Quality, as in { Preparing, dressing, sharp sauces, salt meats, indurate, soused, fried, broiled, or made-dishes, &c.
- Quantity { Disorder in eating, immoderate eating, or at unseasonable times, & *Subsect.* 2.

Custom; delight, appetite, altered, &c. *Subs.* 3.

Retention and evacuation, *Subs.* 4. { Costiveness, hot baths, sweating, issues stopped, Venus in excess, or in defect, phlebotomy, purging, &c.

Air: hot, cold, tempestuous, dark, thick, foggy, moorish, &c. *Subs.* 5.

Exercise, *Sub.* 6. { Unseasonable, excessive or defective, of body and mind, solitariness, idleness, a life out of action, &c.

Sleep and waking, unseasonable, inordinate, overmuch, overlittle, &c. *Subs.* 7.

Memb. 3. *Sect.* 2. Passions and perturbations of the mind, With a digression of the force of imagination. *Sub.* 2. & division of passions into *Sub.* 3.

- Irascible
  - Sorrow, cause and symptom, *Sub.* 4. Fear, cause & symptom, *Sub.* 5. Shame, repulse, disgrace, &c. *Sub.* 6. Envy and malice, *Sub.* 7. Emulation, hatred, faction, desire of revenge, *Sub.* 8. Anger a cause, *Sub.* 9. Discontents, cares, miseries, &c. *Sub.* 10.
- or
- concupiscible.
  - Vehement desires, ambition, *Sub.* 11. Covetousness, φιλαργυρία, *Sub.* 12. Love of pleasures, gaming in excess, &c. *Sub.* 13. Desire of praise, pride, vainglory, &c. *Sub.* 14. Love of learning, study in excess, with a digression of the misery of Scholars, and why the Muses are melancholy, *Sub.* 15.

B. Symptoms of melancholy are either. Sect. 3.

General, as of *Memb.* 1.

- or
  - Common to all or most
    - Body, as ill digestion, crudity, wind, dry brains, hard belly, thick blood, much waking, heaviness and palpitation of heart, leaping in many places, &c. *Sub.* 1.
    - Fear and sorrow without a just cause, suspicion, jealousy, discontent, solitariness, irksomeness, continual cogitations, restless thoughts, vain imaginations, &c. *Subs.* 2.
  - Or
    - Celestial influences, as ♄ ♃ ♂, &c. parts of the body, heart, brain, liver, spleen, stomack, &c.
    - Humours
      - Sanguine are merry still, laughing, pleasant, meditating on plays, women, musick, &c.
      - Phlegmatick, slothful, dull, heavy, &c.
      - Cholerick, furious, impatient, subject to hear and see strange apparitions, &c.
      - Black, solitary, sad, they think they are bewitcht, dead, &c.
    - Or mixt of these four humours adust, or not adust, infinitely varied.
  - Particular to private persons, according to *Sub.* 3. 4.
    - Their several customs, conditions, inclinations, discipline, &c.
      - Ambitious thinks himself a King, a Lord; covetous runs on his money, lascivious on his mistress; religious hath revelations, visions, is a Prophet, or troubled in mind, a scholar on his book, &c.

Mind

- Continuance of time as the humour is intended or remitted, &c.
  - Pleasant at first, hardly discerned, afterwards harsh and intolerable, if inveterate.
  - Hence some make three degrees, { 1. *Falsa cogitatio.* 2. *Cogitata loqui.* 3. *Exsequi locutum.*
  - By fits, or continuate, as the object varies, pleasing, or displeasing.

Simple, or as it is mixt with other Diseases, Apoplexies, Gout, *caninus appetitus,* &c. so the symptoms are various.

Particular symptoms to the three distinct species. Sect. 3. Memb. 2.

Head-melancholy. Sub. 1.

In body — Headache, binding, heaviness, vertigo, lightness, singing of the ears, much waking, fixed eyes, high colour, red eyes, hard belly, dry body, no great sign of melancholy in the other parts.

Or

In mind — Continual fear, sorrow, suspicion, discontent, superfluous cares, solicitude, anxiety, perpetual cogitation of such toys they are possessed with, thoughts like dreams, &c.

Hypochondriacal or windy melancholy. Sub. 2.

In body — Wind, rumbling in the guts, belly-ache, heat in the bowels, convulsions, crudities, short wind, sour and sharp belchings, cold sweat, pain in the left side, suffocation, palpitation, heaviness of the heart, singing in the ears, much spittle, and moist, &c.

Or

In mind — Fearful, sad, suspicious, discontent, anxiety, &c. Lascivious by reason of much wind, troublesome dreams, affected by fits, &c.

Over all the body. Sub. 3.

In body — Black, most part lean, broad veins, gross, thick blood, their hemrods commonly stopped, &c.

Or

In mind — Fearful, sad, solitary, hate light, averse from company, fearful dreams, &c.

Symptoms of Nuns, Maids, and Widows, melancholy, in body and mind, &c.

A reason of these symptoms. Memb. 3.

Why they are so fearful, sad, suspicious without a cause, why solitary, why melancholy men are witty, why they suppose they hear and see strange voices, visions, apparitions.

Why they prophesy, and speak strange languages, whence comes their crudity, rumbling, convulsions, cold sweat, heaviness of heart, palpitation, cardiaca, fearful dreams, much waking, prodigious phantasies.

C Prognosticks of melancholy. Sect. 4.

Tending to good, as

Morphew, scabs, itch, breaking out, &c.
Black jaundice.
If the hemrods voluntarily open.
If varices appear.

Tending to evil, as

Leanness, dryness, hollow-eyed, &c.
Inveterate melancholy is incurable.
If cold, it degenerates often into epilepsy, apoplexy, dotage, or into blindness.
If hot, into madness, despair, and violent death.

Corollaries and questions.

The grievousness of this above all other diseases.
The diseases of the mind are more grevious than those of the body.
Whether it be lawful in this case of melancholy, for a man to offer violence to himself. *Neg.*
How a melancholy or mad man, offering violence to himself, is to be censured.

In diseases
consider
Sec. 1.
Memb. 1.

- Their Causes. *Subs.* 1.
  - Impulsive; { Sin, concupiscence, &c.
  - Instrumental; { Intemperance, all second causes, &c.
- Or Definition, Member, Division, *Subs.* 2.
  - Of the body 300, which are
    - Epidemical, as Plague, Plica, &c. Or
    - Particular; as Gout; Dropsy, &c.
  - Or of the head or mind. *Subs.* 3.
    - In disposition; as all perturbations, evil affection, &c. Or
    - Habits, as *Subs.* 4.
      - Dotage.
      - Phrensy.
      - Madness.
      - Extasy.
      - Lycanthropia.
      - Chorus Sancti Viti.
      - Hydrophobia.
      - Possession or obsession of Devils.
      - Melancholy. See ♈.

♈ Melancholy: in which consider

- Its Æquivocations, in Disposition, Improper, &c. *Subsect.* 5.
- *Memb.* 2. To its explication, a digression of anatomy, in which observe parts of *Subs.* 1.
  - Body hath parts *Subs.* 1.
    - contained as
      - Humours, 4. Blood, Phlegm, &c.
      - Spirits; vital, natural, animal.
    - or containing
      - Similar; spermatical, or flesh, bones, nerves, &c.
      - Dissimilar; brain, heart, liver, &c. *Subs.* 4.
  - Or Soul & his faculties, as
    - Vegetal. *Subs.* 5.
    - Sensible. *Subs.* 6, 7, 8.
    - Rational. *Subsect.* 9, 10, 11.
- *Memb.* 3.
- Its definition, name, difference, *Sub.* 1.
- The part and parties, affected, affection, &c. *Sub.* 2.
- The matter of melancholy, natural, unnatural, &c. *Sub.* 4.
- Species, or kinds, which are
  - Proper to parts, as { Of the head alone, Hypochondriacal, or windy melancholy. Of the whole Body. } with their several causes, symptoms, prognosticks, cures.
  - Or Indefinite; as Love-melancholy, the subject of the third Partition.
- Its Causes in general. *Sect.* 2. A.
- Its Symptoms or signs. *Sect.* 3. B.
- Its Prognosticks or Indications. *Sect.* 4.
- Its Cures; the subject of the second Partition.

Burton—another key, 1621. And beyond, to Fred Blaumann.
"Can you imagine?" he said. "Six centuries of melancholy, and more."

CHAPTER 5

- ■ □ ■ □ ■

THE LONELINESS OF
THE STREETCAR BELL

I

Across the street, on the second floor, the man in the undershirt and the woman with blond, limp hair stand at the window. She unwraps a cut of meat and proffers it to his nose so he can sniff it. The man pushes her away. But the woman persists, and now the man sniffs the cut of meat. Both of them burst out laughing. Stella and Kowalski.

The bar down the street is a lot like most others in the Quarter: a cross between an English pub and a southern tavern, the atmosphere somewhere between the primness of a private club and sweaty insouciance. And yet, it's also something completely different. The people here are different from the clientele of any other bar around.

Every night at Rigby's Bar a huge-headed dog sits in the doorway eating ice cubes. The customers at Rigby's Bar are neither artists nor melancholics. In fact, those types never come here. The language here is unlike anything they speak, and the tattooed arms belong to a different world. Artists and melancholics, inventors of discreet garlic and best-selling cycling books stand around at parties, holding glasses, eating rice and beans and vice versa, and holding forth on alienation. At Rigby's Jesus sometimes plays. Jesus is black, and sometimes he plays the harmonica. When he plays—and that seldom happens—everyone listens. For Jesus plays divinely. At Rigby's the waitress Debbie, who wears green suspenders, is constantly laughing. The green suspenders are so that people will notice what's between them. Bob and Martin sit behind the bar. Bob is sly and muscular. Bob is the law here. Martin is old and wise, and he dispenses pearls of wisdom. Gumbo thinks, Jesus plays, and Liana, a pretty blond, waits for tourists from Texas. Bob is a procurer, Martin a former actor, Liana available, and Gumbo an art photographer. Rigby's Bar is open twenty-four hours a day. Martin's dog sometimes snores and everyone laughs.

Gumbo doesn't know what melancholy is. Not even Debbie knows. Martin probably knows but prefers not to hear about it, and Bob is too sly to take notice. Nobody at Rigby's knows what melancholy is. In fact, the whole Quarter avoids it like a demon shuns the cross. Jesus might know what it is, but only when he plays. Martin's dog is the only melancholic creature here, lying in the doorway night after night, now and then raising his huge, Oblomovian head. He only comes to life when Martin throws him an ice cube. Then he blinks and starts crunching. If Gumbo knew about Professor Blaumann's research, he'd become involved in melancholy matter on the spot.

"Did you see that poor shmuck who shot himself?" asks Bob with an eagle tattooed on his arm.

"A shmuck is a shmuck. What can you say about a shmuck?" Liana says.

"If he'd already decided to do it," Gumbo says, "then he should have opened a business for suicides beforehand. He could have gotten a trip to Delphi out of it."

"Gumbo, always the thinker," Debbie says and laughs. "I won twenty dollars on it. I knew he'd do it."

Martin says nothing and throws his dog an ice cube. Gregor Gradnik sits at a round table in the corner, where the tourists sit. Rigby's inhabitants sit on tall bar stools. Two gentlemen in neckties stagger in. Bob and Liana exchange glances: Liana smiles, Bob nods.

They remind him a little bit of cockroaches.

There's a poker game going on in the back room. Whenever a policeman walks past outside, Bob whistles and the poker players hide their cards. Even though the police don't care much; they could send a plainclothesman if they wanted. Still, according to old habit they hide their cards. Mitch is one of the players. Several times Gregor can hear Blanche, her laughter . . . she must still be somewhere close by.

2

He only had one cockroach, but one that he could be proud of. Perhaps it had been living there before him, or perhaps it came with the torrential rains and humidity of the same hurricane that had marked his arrival. Maybe it had crept into his apartment with him. The hurricane had grazed the city with its tail, bringing heavy downpours. This had given way to drizzle, followed by thick, humid air, through which people could hardly move. It got very hot, even though it was barely the end of February. Everyone started talking about cockroaches. As Mardi Gras approaches with its parades, the cockroaches start converging on New Orleans from all directions in huge swarms. In the past they were a sign of poisoned air and yellow fever, but now they marked the insanity of carnival. Universally despised in his country, cockroaches enjoyed greater respect here. They were even an approved topic of conversation for the faculty dining room: the places they'd infested, how they'd tried to get rid of them, and how they showed up again after that.

Gradnik's cockroach was handsome, fat, and quick. Soon after arriving he had wanted to kill it. He was holding the fork that would pin its disgusting body to the floor. Then he remembered that he had witnessed this scene before: the flinging of apples, which penetrated the gaps of its carapace and got stuck there. After that he lost all desire to kill it. But it was then that his cockroach got its name: Gregor Samsa. In memory of the day when when its life was spared. Or of the storm that raged when they moved into 18 St. Philip

Street together. Once he would find him on the floor, another time on a shelf or high up on the wall. He never left the kitchen. The electric lights would send him scurrying madly back into his crack. Flat-bodied orthopterans that flee from the light. They feed themselves on crumbs of bread, flour, grain, anything. And he wasn't a chestnut brown, the way the book said. He was black. He was a special, Louisianan cockroach. His ancestors had lived in the bayous, in harmony with the human beings that had settled there. They crawled over the empty shells of crayfish that were strewn in huge heaps around the beds.

He never crawled into Gradnik's bed. And Gradnik never dreamed about him. At that time Gregor Gradnik didn't yet know that before him lay a life among cockroaches.

3

Gumbo was something like jambalaya. Jambalaya is a dish made of crayfish, small lobsters, rice, and various spices. Sometimes it includes stewed fish; sometimes also beans. Gumbo is the same thing, only slightly different. Exactly how different is something that's known only in the bayous of the great river delta, in Cajun Country, where Gumbo comes from. In fact, his name was Oristide, but they called him Gumbo, and he seemed to be happy with that. Set on top of his round but agile body was a big, Oblomovian head, like the one on Martin's dog. He may have been round, but he rolled swiftly, his thoughts darting around like Louisiana cockroaches. Gumbo's real name was Oristide, and the names of all of his brothers and sisters began with O: Ovide, Oristes, Olive, Onesia, Otheo, Odalia, Octave, Olite, Oristide. He wasn't the last in line: after him came Odette, his favorite sister, and Odeson, his favorite brother. The letter O comes right after N: his father's name was Nicholas. After O comes P, and his mother's name was Politte. Gregor Gradnik wasn't convinced that Gumbo told the truth every second of his life. In fact, it wasn't so much a matter of the truth as of

Gumbo's limitless ability to invent things. If Gumbo had known about melancholy, if he had spent seven years of his life dealing with it, then there is no doubt that something uniquely practical would have come of it. Gumbo was a creator of endlessly new ideas, a philosopher of success. *Enrichissez-vous.* Gumbo was on the trail of some great success. He didn't know what field it would happen in yet, but it would happen.

At the moment he was into art photography. He didn't have any great expectations of it; this was a temporary thing, preparation for his great achievement. Gumbo had an answer to every question. When it turned out that this was art photography of a special kind, that these were photo narratives with balloons for the dialogue, but with original photographs of a very particular kind below, Gumbo pulled the following estimable vindication out of his hat:

"Everyone who creates contributes to our knowledge of life. Historians and poets. And art photographers who take a special kind of pictures."

Nor was the creative exertion a small one:

"You have no idea how you have to wait for the precise moment of penetration to photograph it. The way a poet waits for inspiration."

Maybe the comparison isn't exactly perfect, but come on: this is what the customer wants. A book he can get through fast, a suspenseful movie, and photos that capture just the right moment. But the general level of taste had fallen considerably. Gregor didn't quite understand it all, but Gumbo's superstructures were fresh and unpredictable. Once, laden with cameras, he called out to him across the street:

"Sacrebleu! A whole day wasted. They changed girls three times and even gave him another injection. Nothing."

He signaled this *nothing* with a limp arm. These artistic experiences gave rise to a new train of thought. Gumbo was always thinking. Gumbo came from a Catholic family.

"Augustine writes that Adam had erections at will. Whenever his will said so, he had one. But physical desire is an enemy of the will. Desire is the result of sin. Will, however, is the natural state of things."

It wasn't just that Gumbo was always thinking; he was always trying to make those thoughts useful.

"If there was some way for us to get to the natural state of things," he said, lost in thought, "the state of will, that would simplify our work tremendously. There's very little desire involved here, but there's always a will."

He spent several weeks pondering the elimination of desire and stimulation of the will. A discovery would have produced fantastic results at work. *Enrichissez-vouz, enrichissez-vous.* But a deep abyss separated concept from implementation. Eventually he dropped it and started working on something else. At any rate, he didn't want to deal with the problems attending art photography of a particular kind anymore.

"C'est awful!" he said, and for several days after that he didn't leave his apartment.

4

"C'est awful."

Suddenly it was senseless. Slow. Everything came to a halt, in fact. The ceiling fan stopped. The air conditioner failed. The vertical axis that ran through him and that he carried with him suddenly withdrew. The sense of everything was in a state of flux. Aside from him. "Void of sorrow and void of fear." Venice wasn't the only empty place; all at once, New Orleans could be empty, too. Fred Blaumann studies melancholy and jogs with Meg Holick. Irene Anderson rides Peter Diamond's bicycle. Utensils clink softly in a light blue dining room. Students offer their writing exercises, full of self-expression. Bibliographies flash across computer screens. Tourists walk down Bourbon Street, guffawing. Deals get made on the other side of the Canal. Cyber brains chomp and squeak. Hucksters trundle kitsch down St. Peter

Street. An old jazz band plays in Preservation Hall. On Royal Street a blond coed sells art pictures. Gumbo is an art photographer. Bob and Liana wait for customers. Debbie wins twenty bucks on a bet. Martin's dog chomps ice. Cockroaches creep out of the cracks. From out of the continent's belly, the river slowly funnels homeless men into the warmth of the city. Black men idle by the docks. The river flows, roaches swarm, Debbie laughs, the air is thick and warm, coffee brews, steam rises off of breakfast beans.

Not a streetcar anywhere. Although you can hear its bell at night sometimes, as it heads toward Elysian Fields. As the turquoise sky darkens and from all sides you can hear the solitary sounds of upright pianos. And jukeboxes.

5

During his morning shave he examined the dark rings under his eyes. A ridiculous pimple was blossoming on the end of his nose. The oppressive algae that last night had found its way from the silty river bottom into his lungs weighed down on his heart.

He ran outside and breathed in the cool breeze blowing in from the river and thinning the heavy air. Tousled people came out of their lairs to pick up the day's milk. Somewhere on a patio a fountain splashed. On the riverbank two homeless men disentangled themselves from their sleeping bags. One stuck a pipe into the hole in the middle of his stubbly face and then stared at a boat as it sailed away, at its stern where the gigantic paddle shot forth streams of froth and churned the brown water beneath it. This drifter understood something that Gregor Gradnik suddenly could no longer grasp.

Loneliness.

Not homesickness. This is loneliness. The landscape and city, institutions and people, telephones and door handles, laws and phrases—his curiosity had tried to swallow all of these things, it had devoured and appropriated them. And still he stands completely outside of them. A mere observer.

A living inanimate creature. Involved in nothing. In an inchoate state. Feeling like an abandoned woman who roams her empty apartment after a night of lovemaking.

The sediments that a traveler bears within himself are supplemented with others on his journey. Colors settle onto colors already in the eyes. New faces enter the gallery of familiar ones. Words arrange themselves into meanings. Feelings lie down in layers on top of what was felt before. But this is no journey. A journey is like air going into your lungs, food into your body. A journey is with Ana in Tunisia, to the accompaniment of Arab ululations and vivid colors. A journey is with Ana beneath the low sun of the Adriatic, beneath a pendulous sky as the winter wind whisks clouds across it. Skiing with Ana, with puffs of breath freezing around their mouths. Looking at Matejko's monumental painting in Kraków. Between crumpled sheets in the disheveled room of some hotel in Bohemia, where trucks rumble past in the early morning. Long night watches as a soldier on some moonlit Balkan tableland. A journey is with Italo Svevo, a brief sentimental journey, as he sets off on a wagon, on his belly, for Mars. But here there was nothing but sheer destination. Where a person feels more and more alone in his ever-increasing freedom. Where there isn't even anyone for you to boast to about your freedom. And where you can't assert it, either, since nothing here is enslaved.

This was the point he had reached now. Mars. A cool, humid breeze blew in from the wide river. That boyhood place in the middle of the woods where time stopped. Time, which inheres in all things and people, together with them, and which here, beside this flowing body of water, was beyond him, against him. Wrenched out of his anesthetized passivity, with nothing but river algae permeating his brain and lungs, a primordial state. Where no one runs anywhere, where everything is destination, where all living and dead things hover motionlessly in their pretemporal state. Only he and some lonely woman in her empty apartment this morning know that they've come to a stop, that they're alone and that everything is irrevocably in motion.

In hotel rooms and the solitude of empty trains. How well we knew them, all his traveling life he had gotten to know them. In hotel rooms and in the solitude of empty trains he had sometimes tried to hold onto a feeling that verged on something all-encompassing. But every time he would catch himself in the act of observing himself, and realized he could get no further than that. As though he were outside, looking through the window of the racing train at his own self leaning against the glass. As a boy he had spent hours walking along a spur of railroad track that ended, pointlessly, in the middle of the woods near his hometown. Now he was back there. Here. One day, one day he would go back to that place to see if he had left something of himself here, too.

Across the street Kowalski was standing at the window. His heavy flesh protruded from beneath his undershirt. He slowly lathered his bristly face all the way up to the wispy hair at his temples. From behind, Stella got out of bed and looked at him for a long time. She was asking him something, to which he answered inaudibly. The steamboat *Natchez* sounded its foghorn from the river.

CHAPTER 6

DISCREET GARLIC

I

"I'm not convinced she's entirely loyal to him."

Fred said this as they were taking the ferry across the wide canal. He said it abruptly and thoughtfully, as though he were talking to himself.

"Supposedly, she's not entirely loyal to him."

Fred Blaumann said, and added nothing. Supposedly not entirely loyal, the one about whom he wasn't entirely convinced was leaning against a railing and gazing out over the muddy waves of the wide river canal. Irene Anderson, blond, indeterminate age. Gregor Gradnik guessed thirty, give or take a year. That, in fact, is how old all the women in this country looked. The ones under thirty tried to look a little older, and the ones over thirty made an effort to look a little younger. Fred often surprised him with his Protestant sermons, but he always left them undone. Just as a story should have gotten under way, he would leave it hanging in midair. Perhaps this was his authorial prerogative, something he taught his students in creative-writing class. The one she supposedly wasn't entirely loyal to was holding a camera in his hands. A writer of the new wave, the author of the practical book *Cycling New Orleans,* which had almost sold out, and had gotten rave reviews in the *Picayune.* He was trying for an artistic effect, to catch the reflection of the morning sun off the brown waves of this fork of the river.

Irene Anderson and Peter Diamond: Gregor Gradnik watched them—after all, he was an observer—he watched them and tried to understand. He was on the scent of something that he couldn't quite grasp, something that was invisibly circulating, something Blaumannesque.

2

On Sunday morning they drove out of town to Barataria Bay. Five people in a roomy, old Buick. The southern landscape drenched in sunlight, fleeting past, bright houses decorated in lively colors, occasional trees, well-tended plantations, then scrub, lazy conversations, music in the car, a cinematic pan across the smooth skin of America.

Home, Ana, friends, the quiet of his study, everything was suddenly so far away. It felt as though he'd been here a long, long time. He experienced this change as an infinite flat surface: as far as the eye could see, not just to the end of this level road, but all the way to the horizon, everywhere there stretched new faces, roads, and landscapes. Life was here. Everything else was over the horizon; but even before that, between the horizon and beyond lay the glittering surface of the ocean's abyss. By an imperceptible metamorphosis the spatial separation changed into a temporal one. He had only been here a few months, yet an entire world that had belonged to him body and soul had retreated into the blurry and hollow past. He knew that at any instant it could summon him back, together with all its sounds and images. But he let it wait. Sooner or later it would be his again. Whenever it came of its own accord, a shout from the street, a few notes of music, or the flickering of a live image on the TV screen would shatter it. His new world was as fragile as crystal, and he was careful not to break it. The presence here of a single living witness from the other world would join the two worlds together, and the fiction would collapse. But objects, pictures, or books from over there didn't shatter the crystal. Their presence reminded him of the existence of something else, something from before that continued to live its own life; but this life lacked any human contact and was abstract. That was the fiction. This, here, is the real world. Ana's handwriting, or her voice over the telephone were of course different. Those were real vibrations of the heart, which the hand translated into writing, or the voice committed to a telephone receiver. But still it was so very, very far away. This is exactly what she would say: I feel you're so very, very far away. What else could he be but far away, if that was how she thought.

In a lone store by the side of the road Fred's wife warbled at an unexpected discovery—she had found a bottle of wine from Slovenia, from the Maribor region. Images appeared from the other side of the crystal bell jar: hills overgrown with grapevines, the autumn sun, his homeland through a prism of fragmentary scenes. And the knowledge that this was a living conduit to life over there. For if space distorts the dimension of time, then this bottle put the lie to everything. The life it contained had endured in its independent course. The birth, maturation, and death of this wine, barely living now on an overheated shelf in some store in the southern end of Louisiana, in a nameless place.

Then they continued gliding down the straight road, over the sunny, taut skin of America, to the accompaniment of country music and conversations broken off midway. A moment set in space, measurable on the speedometer. A moment of life enduring somewhere else.

3

In a roadside restaurant—everything happens by the roadside—they ate the reddish flesh of crabs and left behind a huge graveyard of their shells. Gregor ordered glasses and opened the bottle of Slovenian Riesling. He removed the label as lifeless proof that this living wine had existed. Fred praised the wine, praised his textual analysis of Sunday-morning televangelists. "Historical context!" he shouted.

"Historical context! American students don't have that. Joyce has it, context, every sentence, in Joyce. . . . " A second later he and Mary were quarreling over their noisy renters and whether they would have to vacate that part of the house. But Irene had heard the praise—of the wine and the historical context. *Supposedly? Entirely?*

Discreet garlic. Discreet garlic.

Irene Anderson had explained her idea to some biologist. "About business and garlic?" Peter said. "About kissing and garlic?" Peter laughed charmingly. Peter was an artist and had the right to laugh; it was part of being an artist. But supposedly the biologist had been completely serious. The idea wasn't bad, it had business potential, and it could probably even be pulled off. "But!" Irene raised her head and the sweet double chin straightened as she demanded attention. But if they were to extract whatever acid causes the bad odor, they'd be damaging its internal organic balance. And what followed she delivered with emphasis: The world is in a precarious state of internal balance. If you remove or change just one of the molecular bonds in its structure, you damage and change the whole. Including the qualities of the organism. It's true, this thing really wouldn't cause bad breath anymore, but then again it wouldn't be garlic, either. It would be something else. This was exactly what Irene Anderson didn't want. She wanted the same thing, but without the bad breath.

The same thing. Only discreet.

On the way back Fred and Mary sat in the back seat. The famous professor of the famous university was bickering with his wife about their renters, insisting that he couldn't just give them the boot. He wasn't, after all, some tight Jew. Fred Blaumann's distant ancestors had been Jews, so he could talk this way. Diamond was driving and taking delight in every bicycle path along the way. Irene sat in the middle and told about the last case of rape that had come to court. The man had broken into the bedroom through a window while the husband was on a business trip to Arizona. He had held a knife to her throat. Five years was too mild a punishment for a person like that. Although it was a big car, it was close quarters in the front seat for three. Irene sat between Peter and Gregor, talking about the cynical criminal in court. Gregor watched the countryside sprint past to the right, while he thought about her warm thigh under the thin fabric of clothing, which kept touching him involuntarily. The internal balance of many molecules was damaged several times. Every time that happened, Peter Diamond hit the dashboard with his fist, because each time the speedometer started to waver erratically, like the magnetized needle between two poles of a compass.

■ □ ■ □ ■

CHAPTER 7

THE SLAVIC SOUL
AND THE TEMPTER

I

The needle of the compass wavered between two poles, between laughter and despair. The delicate balance slipped away.

There went out a secret decree in the land: there shall be no sorrow, life is joyous. Laughter bubbled forth from throats; it crackled from loudspeakers.

A group of noisy students has gotten onto the bus. An exceptionally heavyset young black man shouts straight in his ear every time he turns around to face someone in the back. "How you comin'? Nicely. Right smart." Laughter. "God don't like ugly." Laughter. "Big I and little you." Laughter. Then he turns to Gradnik, "He's havin' a blood rush." Guffaws. "If I'm lyin' I'm dyin'." The devotions of modern man: laughter. "If I'm jokin' I'm chokin'." The whole bus guffaws and shakes with laughter. How beautiful people are when they cry, Gregor Gradnik thought. Blaumann's computer is full of sobbing and blue melancholy. But this world laughs away. This entire hemisphere was shaking with laughter, with tears in its eyes, a healthy laughter, a laughter unto despair. Laughter had flooded the continent.

It had rolled through the lecture halls, and now it was rolling drunk down Bourbon Street. In this city black people played jazz and laughed even at funerals. Peter Diamond laughed, Irene Anderson laughed, Debbie laughed incessantly.

They laughed incorrectly, as Gumbo later determined, but they laughed because it was required, the same as optimism. Anyone who wanted to cry had to closet himself and lock the door behind him. Tears were forbidden on this continent. The television laughed and the radio smirked. The mornings tittered and the evenings guffawed. Even the devil and the Lord God laughed.

Sorrow had been brutally expelled from this life. In the Quarter, which echoed with hellish shrieks of laughter, sorrow had stolen into the most inconspicuous corners.

2

At the Lafitte an old woman sits at the piano, playing French chansons. Heavy layers of powder cover the deep furrows of her face. The powder is a bright white, her face is white, but her dress is black. Every evening she plays French chansons. This is Lady Lilly. The whole Quarter knows her, and so does Gregor Gradnik. In his creative-writing course he had been handed a short sketch of her, a blurry picture of a *confessional nature.* The confessor had written that you could feel the room awash in Slavic soul. Lady Lilly is Russian. Sometimes she plays a Russian song for Popescu, the Romanian, and this gives wings to his Romanian soul, which is like a Slavic one. There are bar stools all around the huge piano. This is where the tourists sit, and then Lady Lilly has to sing "New York, New York." At those times New York is as far away as the Russian steppe and even the tourists can sense what a Slavic soul is. Lady Lilly can't help but sing with soul.

On Sunday evening after their drive through the bayous the little bar is empty. Inside it, amid the cosmic laughter of the Quarter, sit three Slavic souls. Plus the bartender, reading the sports pages behind the bar. Occasionally Lady Lilly plays something on the piano and sings a bit. She has to play, in order to attract customers. But no one comes. Louisa Dmitrievna Kordachova sips a Caribbean sun cocktail through a straw and brushes away a tear now and then. Louisa also comes here every night. She works as a waitress in a coffee-house by the riverside, and all day long she has to laugh, smile, and grin. This is why she sits here in the evenings and listens to Lady Lilly. Tears aren't forbidden here. Louisa Dmitrievna Kordachova sees something in Lady Lilly that only the confessor in his class at the university had come close to perceiving. She sips her cocktail, brushes away a tear, and thinks out loud:

"Lady Lilly is from the same place as my Mom and Dad. Maybe not exactly from the same place, because it's a huge, an incredibly huge country, even bigger than America. Vast fields of grain. Their boats go up and down wide rivers and they play accordions. The same as in Cajun Country, only different, more gently. They light whole sheaves of candles inside their dark churches. They're like sheaves of skinny, yellow candles. At night they read novels. The young girls are pale and full of longing. Because they're sickly, they have to go spend a month in the country. But even there they start crying for somebody who stayed behind in Moscow. They want to go to Moscow. When they're in Moscow they dance under huge chandeliers. Lady Lilly was there when they still danced under chandeliers. She had a white dress, she told me. I'd go back, myself. All I have here is laughter and tips. But how can I go back if I was born here, in Louisville, Kentucky? Young girls there are sad, not because anybody left them or they're poor, but because everyone thinks they're more attractive when they're sad. They never even have to laugh at all."

On Sunday evening the bar is sadly empty. No one laughs. Gregor Gradnik consoles Louisa Dmitrievna Kordachova.

"Is it really so bad to laugh?"

"Yes, it is. Very bad."

A tear drops into her Caribbean sun. It's close to midnight, and when he glances at the mirror, he suddenly sees someone else standing there. A scene out of Hieronymus Bosch, in which a tempter stands behind a frightened girl and whispers something in her ear.

From Blaumann's computer:

"I haven't the mouth," writes a French poet of the fifteenth century, "I haven't the mouth that could laugh, but that my eyes would deny it. And see how I should like to deny my heart with the tears that pour forth from my eyes." Sorrow, tears, sobriety: in some periods of human history these haven't just been outward marks of distinction and refinement, they have become the very model of a civilized life. It remains uncertain when laughter and abandon were admitted into the higher spheres of human spirituality. The dejection of suitors, frail yet spontaneous femi-nine charm, the pallor of lovers, the winsome eyes of heartsick young girls—these had all been signs of nobility, while laughter and reckless abandon belonged to the vanity of the marketplace, to crude village revelries, to waterfront taverns. Jan Huizinga writes that a sorrowful approach to the world at one point took over the entire European way of life. Devotio moderna. *You could recognize the devotés by their calm and quiet gestures and the way they bowed their heads as they walked.* Devotio *was a unique delicacy of the heart, allowing the devoté virtually to dis-solve in tears.* Fuerunt mihi lacrimae meae panis die ac nocte. *Translation: My tears were my bread, day and night. Of one Vincento Ferrero his contemporaries wrote: "He cried so much that everyone cried with him. Crying was such a passion for him that he was very reluctant to withhold his tears."*

Lady Lilly sings in her raspy, old woman's voice. With her bony fingers she latches clawlike onto the piano's smooth, shiny keys. The bar is empty; it's Sunday night. Tourists go to the roisterous bars full of laughter. A lone, petite girl sits beside the piano that serves as a bar, and she cries. Tears run down her cheeks. Real, forbidden tears. The bitter drops fall into the mixture of liqueurs, Campari, martini and lemon, her Caribbean sun. Louisa Dmitrievna Kordachova cries for someone who never was, for an accordion on some Ukrainian river that doesn't exist, because all day long she has to laugh in a coffeehouse on the laughter-saturated bank of the Mississippi. And behind her stands a tempter from a painting by Bosch. He touches her shoulders, which shudder from her unstoppable crying. Meanwhile, Lady Lilly sings on and on. The old lady plays just as readily for one, or two, or for herself alone. There is no belle figure plopped in front of her, no one demands that she sing "New York, New York," no amateur pianist tries to push her off of the piano bench. From the trembling shoulders that allow themselves to be caressed, a message shoots forth into the tempter's guts, telling him this girl will give in. Pity and desire, old bedfellows, wink at each other. And hovering not far off is the good angel, who exclaims: That's despicable. But the tempter doesn't hear him; he embraces her around the shoulders and gently tries to convince her of something: the tempter as father, as friend. As the wise and understanding one. *Lacrimae meae panis die ac nocte,* he says. Her shoulders stop trembling. She raises her tear-streaked face toward him.

"What did you say?"

The tempter has some miraculous formulas. The tempter knows that when things get bad, there's always curiosity. Curiosity about anything that isn't bad. He translates. Kordachova brushes away her tears.

"What language did you say that in?"

"Latin."

"I thought it was Mexican."

"Another Caribbean sun."

She nods. Now she looks at him gratefully.

"And a bourbon and soda for Lady Lilly."

And a bourbon and soda for Lady Lilly. The young waiter drops his sports section and looks at him spitefully. The tempter is cautious. Perhaps the waiter is a good angel who will interfere. He tries to charm him and says about the weather, "Some humidity, huh?"

"I don't give a damn about the humidity," the young waiter says. "We're closed."

He is. He's inside there, the one who wants to stop him. He's jumped inside the waiter's skin and he's speaking at him from inside there with contempt. "And bring me four beers, too," the tempter says firmly and clearly, with the devil's authority. "I'll take them with me." He roars, "So the young lady and I will have something to drink!" The waiter's face goes white and he smiles timidly. He smells the tempter's stench. It stinks of singed flesh, so he obeys. Whenever the tempter is on the rampage, everyone in his way had best clear out.

5

"I don't go to strangers' apartments at night," Louisa says with dignity.

There are only a few people out walking. Fits of music billow out of the bars that are still open. The tempter walks close beside her. Cans of beer distend his trouser pockets. His bladder is also distended, since he's forgotten to do what needed to be done. His whole being is taut and shivers in agitation. This is how the good angel hovering in a cloud behind them does him harm. He has to be cold-blooded now. "Ana is waiting for you," he says. "Aaaana," he sings in his ear. "Get lost," the tempter says, "beat it." "Let me hail a taxi," he says. "No need," she says, "I live close by." She really does live very close by. For a long time she stands in front of some door. She looks for her keys, looks at him, then looks for her keys again. "I don't know," she says, "I don't know." Two steps lead up from the sidewalk to a tall door, which probably opens onto a large, common hallway. Then she quickly unlocks it and walks in. It's not a hallway; this is the apartment. Apartment?

"Is this where you live? Nice apartment," he says and bites his tongue. Even a tempter can make mistakes.

"You're the first person who's called this an apartment."

He is struck dumb and stares blankly ahead. This is a crying disgrace. It really isn't an apartment, more of a cell. A narrow, walled-in corridor with a high ceiling, reminiscent of a prison cell, and windowless. Breeding ground for cockroaches, to be sure. Only the one door, leading directly onto the street. And a greedy landlady indifferent to where her money comes from. It's intolerably hot, and within an instant he's covered in sweat. The tempter is seized by claustrophobia and the impossibility of escape. Couldn't she at least open the door, he thinks. What, onto the street? The look on her face is cold and hopeless.

"Are you happy now?"

"Why shouldn't I be?"

Why not, indeed? The tempter is right on the verge of his goal. His opposite angel has been proven powerless and left hanging in a cloud at the door. You didn't dare come inside, whiner. The tempter has a right to be pleased. To sit down on the bed beside her and open a beer, still cold. To stretch out and prop his head against the cell wall. To stroke the slender nape of her neck and her hunched shoulders. But he is impatient. Even the tempter makes mistakes, and he is overwhelmed with impatient desire. Louisa Dmitrievna Kordachova wants to talk. She can't get enough of talking. Or of tears. The tempter is impatient, and he forgets about everything around him, about her, and about himself. Even the tempter makes mistakes.

6

"My landlord is a pig."

So it isn't a landlady.

"My boyfriend's a pig."

This is why she cried. One of the reasons.

"The world is piggish."

The world is piggish because it put her in this apartment, which her smiles at the café all day long barely pay for. Her boyfriend is a pig because she's been waiting for him at the Lafitte for three days. Every evening she waited for him, and now here she is with someone else. Someone who keeps reaching under her sweaty cotton T-shirt to stroke her smooth back, while she talks about her boyfriend, the son of some big shot. To whom she'd been faithful for the whole two months she'd been sleeping with him. But now he's nowhere to be found—now, when he ought to rescue her from this pit. This hole, this cockroach nest. Her father went on an all-out binge and now he's practically lost his mind. She had to get out on her own, she couldn't bear it otherwise. Her mother calls her at the Café du Monde every day: Louisa, you've got a head on your shoulders, you weren't meant to be a waitress. But she's not going to quit, she just won't. Neither will the tempter quit, he kisses her eyes and the mouth that won't stop talking. Something tells him he should stop, that in a case like this one you stop. But not the tempter, not him, they'd have to chop off his hands, which can't stop, which convulsively stroke her skin, smooth, so utterly smooth and damp as it is from the humidity and sweat. He unfastens her buttons and strokes her tiny breasts. Don't do that, she says, but devoid of all will. Don't do that, she says and leans back against the wall, which is covered with damp stains, and lets him run his sweaty hands across her warm belly. Then she falls silent and closes her eyes and again she says don't do that when he pulls open her zipper and with a gentle undulation slips his hand under the delicate fabric, don't do that, but she does nothing to stop it. She does nothing to stop the undulating manipulations as they creep under the almost invisible edge of the delicate fabric and over the skin, the fine hairs. She does nothing to stop it. She even starts breathing faster, and gently spreads her legs.

This thing is mine, the tempter says.

He stops and draws back. Louisa opens her eyes and stares motionlessly at the ceiling. The tempter can feel that something is wrong with him, something painful and severe. He reaches for the beer can, which is empty. And only now does a horrendous pain shoot through his midsection. The thought of beer turns the unbearable desire at belt level into unbearable pain. My bladder's going to burst, he thinks. I forgot, he thinks. Calm down, he says, calm down. This night is yours. Still, he thinks, this was quite a mistake. Even the tempter makes mistakes.

7

To continue this story, we should first say something about American toilets, where flushing technology is entirely different from what it is in Europe. American toilet bowls are half-filled with water, and when you flush them the water drains out and is immediately replaced with fresh liquid. Peeing into an American toilet is like peeing into a lake: it's very close to nature.

At this point he was met by the one he thought he had left hanging in a cloud outside the door.

"I need to," the tempter said in extreme embarrassment, "I ought to have sooner . . . it's all the beer, you know."

She pointed a limp arm at a door without taking her eyes off the ceiling. It was the first time he had noticed this door. It was unfinished and covered with the same peeling wallpaper as the walls around it. "I'll be just a minute," he said with the same kind of soothing voice he might use with a lover of many years' standing. But Louisa Dmitrievna Kordachova was not his lover. She was unhappy and she stared at the ceiling. He went inside, unfastened his trousers, and gazed at the pool of water in horror, as though he were looking into a dark lake. With an immense effort he managed to hold back. This pissing is going to wreck everything, he thought. The stream that falls in there can't help but be loud. This loud, unavoidable pissing, which is going to be unavoidably audible through the wooden door, will be humiliating for her. It would be merciless. It was instantly clear to him that this unavoidably impending humiliation would be the end. Good night. He had left her there on the bed with her legs slightly spread and her blouse unbuttoned. Staring at the ceiling. And right in the midst of this vile apartment which she hates, she'll have to listen to an intolerable pissing sound more suited to a whorehouse. She, whose mother tells her every day that she's got a head on her shoulders. She, who sits in the Lafitte every night waiting for her boyfriend to rescue her from this place, she is now suddenly going to listen, in the middle of this wretched apartment, as a stranger whom she just met this evening pisses into her toilet. After telling him everything about herself, after yielding to him, after all this the person goes and pisses? After everything that's just happened, on top of this whole, piggish world.

The tempter's mind started working feverishly. No longer containing himself, he spun around and hit the sink attached to the wall with his incipient stream. With the other hand he flushed the toilet and then quickly turned the water on in the sink. He heaved a sigh of relief. This had been both clever and practical: she would think that he was washing his hands, maybe even his face, sweaty in this hot room with no air conditioner, no fan, and no windows. He had never pissed so long in in his life. Not only had he been clever and practical, he was also good: he would spare her difficult thoughts. It flowed out of him as though he contained a reservoir of beer—one minute, ten minutes, an hour? With his head bowed he gazed at the damned yellow fluid as it splashed against the sides of the sink, the flow of tap water insufficient to rinse it all away, churning it instead into a disgusting foam. It started to smell like urine, like horse piss on hot asphalt.

He jumped. He hadn't noticed the door opening. He didn't know when it had opened, how long it had been open. In any case, there was Louisa standing in the doorway. She was buttoned up to the neck and her eyes gazed vacantly, the way they had stared at the ceiling. The way you stare at cockroaches. But in the tempter's eyes there was some distress and some horror at his miserable and irreparable state.

In these circumstances pissing in a sink is infinitely more shameful than pissing audibly. And naturally, into a lake.

She closed the door and said nothing.

He leaned on the wall.

This thing is lost. And forever, at that.

When, in ignominy, he returned to the hapless hallway with its peeling wallpaper, the only thing remaining in her eyes was what she had known about the world all along: piggishness.

8

He thought he might explain something to her. He would begin his explanation with the difference between American and European toilet bowls. He thought he might make an offer to help. Maybe he could turn part of his stipend over to her. The door banged. The tempter scurried out onto the street. Only a wretched and unhappy Gregor Gradnik remained. Unable to set anything right anymore. Whatever he might say or do now could only fit into its predetermined place in the mosaic of the world as piggishness. As he walked down the empty street past the Lafitte, he saw a shaft of light falling through the crack in the door. He went around to the other side of the building and slipped on something slimy on the pavement, perhaps the vomit of some tourist. He looked through the window. Lady Lilly was bent over the piano, motionlessly, as though she were dead. She started and looked toward the window, as if sensing that someone was watching her. Her wig was off, and her sparse hair stuck to her scalp. Then, with shaking hands she scrabbled around in her purse for a long time. She pulled a watch out of it and brought it right up to her eyes. It was four o'clock in the morning.

CHAPTER 8

THE SCHOOL OF
CREATIVE LAUGHTER

I

Trumpets! Drums!

The next morning trumpets and drums woke him up again. Black youths were thrashing away at drums strapped around their waists and blowing, cheeks distended, into the mouthpieces of flashy brass instruments. Amid them swarmed a centipede of young black girls in short skirts. Their director was there, too, with a whistle in her mouth and bloated, rippling flesh beneath her clothes. It's a parade! It's a parade! Everyone was talking about the parades that were already practicing in every corner of the city. Did you see the parade? Did it frighten you? Gumbo said that the upcoming days were worthy of a person's fear. These are dangerous days, he said. This is a very special time, Fred said as he cut his steak amid the silence of the faculty dining room. I would even say, he said as he stabbed his salad, I would say that some old European Christian elements have been preserved here. But then each group added something of its own: blacks, Creoles, the local French population. I would say that one shouldn't lecture about Mardi Gras. You simply have to jump into it all and swim.

Spring was also coming. Gregor Gradnik spent a Sunday afternoon with Peter, Irene, and their friends. They stood in a circle in the park, ate rice and beans, and toasted each other with cans of beer. This is the only state in America, Peter's friend boasted, where you can serve alcohol in public. And in the next few days there'll be more of it flowing than water. N.O. doesn't have its own water, all the drinking water is brought in by truck and sold in stores. Irene ran through the grass in her shorts. Peter talked about the second edition of his book *Cycling New Orleans*. Everyone listened attentively. Irene clapped her hands, they formed a circle, and Irene announced, "From one writer to another!"

Diamond autographed his book—the first edition, last copy—and offered it to Gregor with a bow. Everyone applauded. Gregor thanked him. He'll never write a book like this, at least not such a successful one, he said. Oh, come on, now, why not? Peter said. Because he's cursed with a Slavic accent. Ah, Diamond said, paper is very patient, you can't hear a thing from it. But mostly, Gregor said, because he's not too good on a bicycle.

On the book's cover the author was shown standing next to his bicycle, in a bow tie and tennis shoes. The bow tie, the author explained, suggests that the book has to do with academic matters—history, botany, ethnography. The tennis shoes suggest that our approach will be unconventional—sporting. But handsomest of all was the bicycle. There it stood in the picture like a stallion. It was a woman's bike, Irene's at first, then shared by both of them. It was an old, chrome bike, the kind they don't make anymore. It was even handsomer in person than in the picture. They stood around it, stroking and admiring it.

Then Gregor tried out the famous bicycle that was featured on the book cover.

There were no birds chirping in the park: there were huge transistor radios booming everywhere, and the smell of barbecue pork ribs that black people with gold rings on their fingers would set onto grills. Most of them crowded next to the piers of a concrete viaduct. Cars rumbled by up above, while down below the black people grilled their sweet ribs. A cloud of sweetly redolent grill smoke blocked out the sun.

But the sun shone away. It warmed the streets and with every day there were more people in the city. Bands of wandering bums streamed into the city via the river bottoms, into America's soft, warm underbelly, and made camp in the abandoned warehouses and factories of a city quarter slated for demolition. Merchants and peddlers, revelers and pickpockets, male and female prostitutes, rich people in their big cars all came into the city. The bars were full. Lady Lilly played "New York, New York" every night.

Mardi Gras was approaching and New Orleans made ready for its big moment.

Barely ten days before the insanity erupted, Gumbo announced a totally original plan. Before events began spinning in their crazy, unstoppable gyre, Gumbo founded an unusual business. He may not have chosen the best time for its inauguration.

2

"Oh, give me a break with these bookish professors."

"And these blabbering writers. It's all of it either rotten or in deep freeze."

Gumbo was in a bad mood. His Oblomovian head was dizzy and drooped over the bar. The tall bar stool he was sitting on tottered dangerously. Martin's dog raised its head several times and growled slightly.

"Nobody invents anything anymore."

"Somebody ought to give it all a good disinfecting."

Debbie said that someone ought to disinfect him. Or deep-freeze him. A gob of French curses rained down on her. When he recovered, he went on. The problem was that there just weren't any writers anymore. The writers were walking around in neckties and blabbing nonsense at the universities. Ever since they'd lost Tennessee, there hadn't been anyone left in these parts. Tennessee with his dolls and studs—it all smelled of sweat and perfume and blood and bourbon, all at the same time. Nowadays all you can smell is deodorant, the underarm kind. Nobody knows how to slug or cry or bite. Or, least of all, how to laugh.

"What a lot of shit that kind of life is."

He banged on the table, and Martin's dog raised its heavy head and rose up on its front legs. Gumbo was sick of everything: sick of Debbie and Martin's dog, but most of all he was sick of professors and writers. That same morning he went home and in front of his building he put up a sign that had been ready for a long time:

Dr. Oristide's
internationally renowned
SCHOOL OF CREATIVE LAUGHTER
St. Philip St. 18, apt. 3, N.O.

3

"There are all kinds of schools in the world," he told Gregor Gradnik that morning, "but there isn't anybody who can teach people how to laugh. And that's just what people in this country desperately need."

Gregor thought that it wasn't; clearly, what they needed most desperately was creative-writing courses. Laughter had already been taken care of in a secret decree, "On Laughter and Optimism," that the Sunday-morning evangelists had signed. But it was still possible that people weren't laughing *correctly,* as Gumbo thought.

The biggest challenge facing the new business on the block was its sign. Gumbo had quite simply nailed it to Gregor's window, because his own windows looked out onto the courtyard and the sign had to face the street. He had nailed it so low that, unused to the obstruction, pedestrians started knocking their heads against it at night. It had been installed roughly at eye level. By night it banged and reverberated like a gong. Judging from the force of the blow, Gregor could predict how many fuck yous and offs would be directed at each word inscribed on it. He was afraid for the windowpanes, since it was highly probable that sooner or later someone would not only attack the sign with the guffawing jaws that engulfed the inscription, but the window, too. Or the owner.

"Do you really not understand?" Gumbo said. "That's exactly the way it needs to be. Who's going to look at a sign hanging way up high somewhere? Like that voodoo advisor a few blocks over. The sign has to be at eye level. Any marketing textbook will tell you that a sign has to hit a person straight in the eye."

Gregor understood. He only doubted whether this was really intended literally.

"It isn't. But if it literally hits them, so much the better. Don't you think so?"

Sure. There was almost no arguing this. He only wondered why they shouldn't hit it back. It was entirely possible.

Gumbo shook his Gumbovian head.

"You really don't understand anything. Private property in America? If somebody damages that? You shoot first and ask questions later."

Gradnik was curious about the curriculum of the school that was starting here.

"The curriculum? Well, for instance, you can't walk into an office and act like your mother just died. This is something you learn, it takes practice. If the person can't be bothered, let them go to acting school. There are as many of those as you like. Then comes the theory."

Ah, Gumbo! Gumbo had long since worked everything out. Gumbo, ya-ya, as the black people of Louisiana sing.

4

He got up and pulled out from under his desk a cardboard box filled with papers and books. *Laughter Through the Ages.* Sushchenko: *Do Animals Laugh?* Bergson: *An Essay on Laughter.* Clippings from newspapers, photos of laughing people, Eskimos, Bantus, Good Humor men, and presidential candidates. Clark Gable laughed one way, John Kennedy another,

Marilyn Monroe yet another way, and Ella Fitzgerald a fourth. All of laughing America was here, and the rest of the globe with it. But a person never laughs with just his face alone, he said, and he pulled another folder out of the box. Here were bodies in a variety of risible poses, heaving shoulders, arms seizing onto a stomach that aches from laughter. And a person rarely laughs alone; laughter is agreement: a theater filled with a laughing audience; Bavarian beer drinkers with their mugs, flush with laughter; a squad of soldiers whose rifles keep dropping to the ground as they laugh; patients in a hospital ward laugh at someone who has just been wheeled in on a gurney; Parisian prostitutes with missing teeth; soldiers in the Boer War standing over a dead native, grinning; Brazilian headhunters with trophies in their hands; mountain climbers at the summit . . . The broad grin of triumph and the bitter grimace of defeat, toothpaste smiles and smirks of gluttony. Interactive laughter: the simultaneous laugh of the vanquished and the victor, of a doctor and an epileptic, of an old man and a young girl, sorrow and laughter, anger and laughter, labor and laughter. Gesture and meaning. Laughter and success. Anderson's *Dark Laughter*. Mark Twain. The Mona Lisa's smile. All of it arranged in file folders, systematized and annotated. The school had been *fascinatingly* well prepared.

5

At 5 p.m. the warm sun shone into the empty bar through the front windows. Gumbo explained the role of laughter in the work of an art photographer, in petting and penetration. Various phases of intercourse are linked, in a variety of ways, to laughter as a more advanced form of human expressivity. The camera tries to capture the harmony of the upper and the lower, of physicality and spirituality—and a good camera will catch their *interference*. As long as interference lasts, there is no laughter. Laughter comes before or after. If there is laughter, it's unconscious, like the wail of a cat, or the spout of a whale. A whale? Why not a whale? Gumbo had pondered many a thing while photographing. Liana pulled up a bar stool and listened for a while. She said Gumbo had no idea what he was talking about. Gregor caught sight of Fred's car driving down the street. He remembered that he was supposed to be at the creative-writing workshop. Attendance was down the week before Mardi Gras. He hadn't missed a thing. This was at 5 P.M. Some customers with briefcases walked in, and Bob called to Liana. Liana left.

At eight o'clock Martin's dog lay down in the doorway and started crunching ice. His master sat at the bar. At eight o'clock Gregor suggested to Gumbo that he include Martin. Perhaps Martin, who was an actor, could take over the workshops, and Gumbo, as the thinker, could lead the discussions. No, Gumbo said, no retired actors. Liana came back.

By nine o'clock the bar was full of tourists. Their table was full, since Debbie had no time left to clear away their empty glasses. Gumbo said that this thing could bring in millions. Imagine opening creative-laughing workshops all over America. Publishing textbooks. *Laughter Over Heart Disease, Cooking with a Smile.* Gumbo asked if they could expand into the East European market. Gregor was skeptical, laughter didn't yet have the same currency there. Maybe he could translate one of their textbooks. Sure, but it would be hard to find a publisher. Very significant, Gumbo said, everything is doubtful with you. At nine o'clock Liana left.

At eleven Gumbo started vomiting a little bit, and Gregor remembered that he needed to call Ana in Ljubljana. Ana wasn't in, so he called Irene. He told her there was someone here who had an even better idea than discreet garlic: maybe she'd like to meet him. Please not so loud, she said, Peter was writing. Maybe he only imagined her saying this. In any case, she said that she couldn't understand what he was saying. Then she asked if she should try to interpret what he was trying to tell her. Liana came back, cursed, and sat down with them. She announced she wasn't going anywhere else. At eleven Tonio Gomez sat down on a bar stool.

6

Tonio Gomez called him *dottore*. Most likely because Gumbo was always thinking. And out loud, at that. Dottore Oristide. He never called him Gumbo. Tonio Gomez was a small, dignified man. He always wore a white suit and a colorful necktie. His thick, black hair fell in handsome waves down over his collar. He would frequently come to Gumbo's apartment carrying a briefcase, and sometimes he had a package under his arm. Tonio Gomez was the manager of the art photography studio. Tonio Gomez always smiled correctly. With a correct smile he walked up to the table and asked professionally when Gumbo would be returning the goods. *Vederemo,* Gumbo said. You can say *vederemo,* and I can say screw you. So say screw me, Gumbo said, I'm my own man now. Tonio Gomez's handsome face darkened. Bob fidgeted on his bar stool. He sent Debbie over, who escorted *vederemo* behind the bar. Liana, who had been applying makeup, practically fell off her bar stool.

7

Around midnight Gumbo burst out crying. Around midnight Gregor in a haze caught sight of Martin's dog standing in the doorway and staring at him. His eyes were as big as mill wheels. Dottore Oristide's face was soaked with tears. Most of all he'd like to make Odette laugh. But it's impossible—he struck her and nothing will fix that. He had struck Odette on a poor Cajun farm in the middle of the bayous. Odette is his youngest and favorite sister. Ovide, Oristes, Olive, Onesia, Otheo, Odalia, Octave, and Olite are older, and he doesn't like them. Odette and Odeson are younger, and he likes them. As long as they don't go bad. Like Odette went bad. He struck her because of the oysters. Because they were bad. Actually, the oysters were only a pretext. In fact, he struck her because she had slept with a friend of his, who was also an art photographer, now he's living somewhere in Arizona. If she were here, he'd make her laugh. Odette laughs real nice. But now she's in Arizona, where there aren't any oysters at all. Only snakes. At two in the morning Liana was asleep, and Deborah said this was enough. Bob said the same thing, enough, Dottore Gumbo. They stood up and headed toward the door as best they could. Martin's dog was asleep, everyone was asleep, everything was resting before the remarkable days ahead that were called Mardi Gras.

At two in the morning Gumbo banged his Oblomovian head against the gong that bore the inscription:

Dr. Oristide's
internationally renowned
SCHOOL OF CREATIVE LAUGHTER
St. Philip St. 18, *apt.* 3, *N.O.*

■ □ ■ □ ■

CHAPTER 9

THE GOOD ANGEL'S
LAUGHTER

I

For the last few days before the big holiday Gumbo lurked behind tombstones. Parades—very colorful ones—had already started rolling through the suburbs. Trumpet and drum music resounded everywhere.

The business hadn't met with much success. In fact it was an utter fiasco. Over the weekend Gumbo sat in his apartment waiting for customers. There were none, and he consoled himself with the fact that it was the weekend. On Monday he hung out on the sidewalk, walking back and forth in front of his sign and inviting passersby to join his school. No one joined. Instead of customers, only Martin and dog, Debbie, Liana, and Bob stopped by to check things out. Dottore Gumbo defied their ill will and envy.

On Tuesday, just as he had given up all hope, an elderly man knocked on the door. He was interested in this school of his, he said. It had been ten years since his wife had died, and in all that time he hadn't laughed. Gumbo looked at him askance at first, but then he saw that it was for real. His visitor was crushed with sadness. He wasn't ready for cases like this one. Still, he decided to take him in. But he insisted on payment in advance. It turned out that the man's sadness wasn't just on account of his wife's departure, but also because he was penniless. He had put all of his savings into the purchase of a stone monument. His debt was deeper than his dear wife's grave. This was definitely not how Dr. Oristide had imagined his internationally acclaimed school. He wouldn't give his talent away for philanthropic ends. Let the gentleman apply to the Salvation Army for help. And without hesitation he showed him the door. If he could build a monument like that, if he's prepared to invest in the beyond, then that's his decision. But if a person chooses laughter, then he's investing in life and he'd better have a bank account to match. And anyway, how can you teach a man to laugh who's apparently going to stay in debt twenty years after he dies. Gumbo wasn't naive, and neither were his prospective clients.

By Wednesday there still weren't any customers, and nobody noticed the sign anymore except the people who crashed into it with their heads at night. A profound depression overcame Gumbo. He had driven away the only person to have put his hopes in his knowledge. Now he wouldn't even be able to test his abilities. And besides: the kind of people that talk about their mortgages for sure have something else that you could take—that they could pay with. He dropped everything and raced off to the cemetery.

2

He roamed through the long passageways of New Orleans's cemeteries, which are like small cities from a dream. The ten-foot-high tombstones are like light gray facades, the walkways between them like streets. He lost himself among them, asking people about Joseph. His customer didn't even have a chance to leave a calling card, so abruptly had he dismissed him. But he remembered the name. For two days he roamed through the labyrinths of Necropolis from morning to night, but Joseph had been swallowed up by the earth. Maybe he, too, had died in the meantime. Yet Gumbo didn't give up. He would find her—her image, that is, on the porcelain portraits that were attached to the fronts of the tombstones. That's impossible, Gregor said. Don't worry, Gumbo said, a husband and wife who have lived together for that long, who love each other so much that the unhappy widower is unable to laugh for a full ten years after she dies—a couple like that has to look alike. Not just in the way they walk, which is a commonly known fact, but their facial features start to merge. He had memorized the widower's face. He rushed back to the cemeteries. And at last on one of the porcelain ovals he found the face of a pudgy woman who was the spitting image of Joseph, his customer. He decided to wait for him.

He lay down on the grave and dejectedly listened to the sounds of spirited music that the wind wafted into the stillness of the cemetery, and he waited for his customer.

3

On the last day before Mardi Gras, when tension started rising in the city like a tide, Gregor Gradnik had no time to deal with Gumbo's sorry business. His apartment had been broken into. That afternoon, when he came home from Blaumann's computer filled with melancholy matter, the firefighters were already gone. So was the door to his apartment. Fragments of shattered wood still held to the hinges. Neighbors stuck their heads out the doors up and down the hallway.

"It was a gas leak," said one of the heads. "Insurance should cover it."

Strewn about the floor lay dishes, books, articles of clothing. An overturned bottle of milk.

There was his typewriter, too, which was undamaged, and his radio, which was broken. An army of giants had rampaged through here. To judge by the tracks they had left: on some of his notes for creative-writing class there was a gigantic footprint from a rubber traction sole. He stared at the footprint like Friday first spying the track of cannibals, or a sherpa discovering yeti footprints in the Himalayas.

He sat down on his bed and buried his head in his hands. Then he picked up the phone and started dialing numbers.

4

By evening they had managed to rig a temporary door for him. Not much more could be done right before the holidays. And then Gumbo walked in. He had come directly from the cemetery. He didn't bother to knock. He walked through the devastation straight to the refrigerator. He took out a can of beer and poured it down in one swallow. Bottoms up. The look on his face was full of anger and reproach.

"So now you've managed to completely ruin me," he said, opening another can with a pop. "There's so much." This meant: he had so much to tell him.

"Ruined you?" Gregor looked around the apartment in despair.

"Fire victim. You've ruined me with this."

Beer sweat had soaked his shirt, and beads of perspiration clung to his temples. His face was wet and filled with ominous reproach.

"But there wasn't any fire."

"Makes no difference. You've ruined me."

"You?" He could feel some fluid bubbling through his body. Blood, it was his blood starting to boil.

"That's right, me. You've ruined my business. Who's going to come into a building that's plagued by misfortune? Where firemen go on the rampage and break down the doors? Who's going to come in here to laugh?"

Now Gregor Gradnik could feel the blood rushing to his head. It wasn't enough for this oversized imbecile with the oversized name and oversized kinfolk that he listened to his endless babble; now he was standing in the middle of his ruined apartment telling him with a perfectly serious face, a face full of reproach, that he had ruined him. It wasn't enough for this Švejkian idiot who didn't even know who Švejk was (otherwise he would have incorporated him into his infantile system), who spent whole days spouting quotations he'd misread, who blabbered about the natural state of things, who continually contrived abortive enterprises, on account of which Blaumann wouldn't just send him home, but would commit him to an institution if he only knew that he was spending his time on them, too; it wasn't enough for this distributor of pornographic photos, who any minute risked being nabbed by the police or having that gangster Gomez show up at his front door; it wasn't enough for him that he could sit here anytime he felt like it, that he could open the refrigerator whenever he felt like it, consuming whole cans of beer, that he could walk in the door whenever he felt like it . . . he looked at the boards nailed over his door, and at the thought that anyone who felt like it could walk in now, his vision blurred . . . He grabbed him by the shirt and started to shake him. The huge head bobbled from side to side and two buttons on his shirt popped off. A male scent assaulted him: the odor of sweat, alcohol, and despair. Suddenly he noticed that among the beads of sweat there were also tears streaming down his face.

He thought that this person really was abject, the same as himself. His business had failed and now it would be back to waiting for penetrations and delivering mysterious parcels for Tonio Gomez. And just what did he, Gregor, really know? Why was Gomez standing outside the door? And his favorite sister, Odette, had run off with another penetration artist, with a man he had introduced her to, himself.

He took the beer out of his hand. Despite the shaking, Gumbo hadn't dropped it. He lit a cigarette.

"The landlord was here, too," Gumbo said calmly. "Insurance isn't going to cover the damage. You left the gas on. He ripped my sign off your window. He's going to report us because we were working without a license."

"*We* were?"

"Well, yeah. Technically."

Gregor started to laugh. He was seized with a fit of helpless laughter. Gumbo started explaining how he had lain in wait behind a tombstone. While he was waiting he'd had a good idea having to do with funerals. The deal with funerals was that . . .

5

That evening the two of them were sitting in the Lafitte listening to Lady Lilly. The Blue Piano. The bar was full of tourists, who were crowding around the piano. Louisa Kordachova was also there. They drank Caribbean suns, and Gumbo told her the names of his brothers and sisters. He showed her how they dance at the Maple Leaf. He would invite her to visit there and teach her Cajun dances. Louisa laughed. Gumbo winked at him and said, "You've got to make a woman laugh, that's the whole secret. Everything else follows from that." He described how they ate crawfish and oysters where he came from: with heaps of shells lying around a Frenchman's bed afterward. Mountains of them, and the Frenchmen can't get out of their houses anymore. Black folk walk past their windows and sing:

Poor crawfish ain't got no show,
Frenchman catch 'em and make gumbo.

Go all 'round the Frenchmen's beds,
Don't find nothin' but crawfish heads.

That was funny. Louisa's resonant laughter filled the bar, inciting the tourists to bellow "New York, New York" all the more boisterously. All night that laughter rang in his ears, and the bellowing, too.

6

In the morning he swept up the pieces. He was down on his knees when Gumbo walked in again without bothering to knock. And why should he have bothered, with the door barely holding together? He was wearing shorts and he was all aglow. His school of creative laughter had finally taken root.

"She has an amazing gift for laughter," he said.

"Really," Gregor said. For crying, too, he thought.

"And she's just like Odette."

"The one you hit?"

"That's the one. But the oysters really were bad. I don't regret it. I'd hit her again."

Gregor was silent. You could never find this guy's soft spot. He was as self-renewing as an earthworm, as invulnerable as Achilles, and in all probability immortal, too. Then he found out that Louisa had been impressed by the patio, but thought the apartment would have to be redone. And that the air conditioner would have to be cleaned.

"Laughter just gushes out of her. It's the laughter of a good angel," Gumbo said looking up at the ceiling, expecting to find something there. "Her laughter is like the jingling of angels."

Gregor didn't ask what the jingling of angels was supposed to be like, hoping to avoid an exhaustive answer. Besides, he knew a little bit about the good angel, himself.

No doubt about it, he still hovered over her in his invisible cloud. Now he was the good angel of laughter.

CHAPTER 10

WRESTLING WITH
THE DEVIL

I

Mardi Gras!

Mardi Gras is wild and swift and hot with sin. This is
what a local ethnographer wrote when trying to explain why
Mardi Gras wasn't simply Shrove Tuesday or Latin Carnival.
Mardi Gras was black and white, Creole and Cajun, boastful
and criminal. It smelled like perfume and sweat, like whiskey
and urine.

"Once a year," Fred Blaumann said, stabbing a piece of
steak, "once a year everybody here goes crazy."

Outside St. Aloisius Cathedral, dressed in topcoats, the
footsoldiers of Jesus sit and doze. On the eve of battle multitudes of them gather here from every corner of America. But
even more numerous are the multitudes of revelers who
swarm through the streets and taverns and whose hearts are
open to everything that comes, absolutely everything.

What is lacking in your heart? says the sign that a young
woman dressed in black has hanging around her neck.
Indeed, Gregor Gradnik thinks, what is lacking in my heart?
And what's lacking in Irene Anderson's heart, if she supposedly isn't completely faithful to her writer?

One of Jesus' advance parties walks down Royal Street.
Some of them hand out flyers that warn of perdition. Others
pick up a drunken black man who has passed out too soon.

At Rigby's there are several new women. Two leggy blonds

who look like twins, and a chocolate-colored mulatta with white teeth. Bob sits with them holding a cigar in his bejeweled hand, flexing his tattooed muscles.

There is a ruckus under the Spanish balcony. In the old days this is where they sold black cargo from Africa. Now a beauty walks up and down the balcony, provoking the already wobbly crowd below with red-painted sneers. Across the street stands a stony-faced female foot soldier of the Holy Army. She holds a sign that reads: *For many will seek to enter in, and shall not be able.*

Indoors it is stifling; everyone rushes outdoors. Gregor Gradnik is on the riverbank, where there is a cooling breeze. Fragments of music waft out from the city. Human flesh has already started wriggling on a riverside bench.

In his sleep that night he hears the wailing of police sirens. Amid wailing and screeching sounds the door to a hellish abyss opens. But once it's open, he hears coming from inside jingling laughter and boyish whoops. The Spanish beauty on her balcony gabbers with her red lips, incessantly licking them. Some cowboys yodel.

2

An enormous phallus charges into the crowd. *Trashy*, says Irene, standing next to him with a glass in hand. Irene Anderson is a *mimosa pudica*. They stand on the balcony watching the growing insanity of the street. *Trashy*, she says, but laughs even so. Everybody laughs, Popescu guffaws. The entire street guffaws as the phallic caterpillar butts into people. Some twenty pairs of legs swarm underneath it. The clumsy contraption slowly turns around and its red club goes after women, who run away from it shrieking. Black masks dance around the bloated worm and guide it. A woman in chaps suddenly jumps up onto it and starts riding it just behind its flushed head. Somebody from the crowd throws her a hat. Now it's a rodeo, the phallus starts to buck, and the woman latches onto it tightly with her legs. She strokes it with her hat, then suddenly jumps off. Guffaws and shouts. The phallus butts a policeman, who drops his cap and sunglasses. It shoves him into a doorway as the crowd shouts its enthusiasm. On the balcony Popescu writhes with laughter. Popescu is a Transylvanian vampire. Irene is some sort of fading violet, a *mimosa pudica*, Peter is a French cyclist, Meg Holick is wearing a shockingly short skirt à la Pretty Baby, Fred has a top hat on, and his wife a beehive of white hair, and she's whining. A river of people runs though the apartment and onto the balcony, an SS woman keeps thumping a whip against her boot and reaches its handle out under Lee the Korean's chin. Dixieland sounds come from the street. No one is quite sober anymore.

3

Then there is her sweaty palm. Amid the crowd on Canal Street Irene holds onto Peter the cyclist's T-shirt with one hand and with the other latches onto his hand, which is sweaty. Her hand is sweaty. They stick together so that the crowd won't pull them apart. Mary, with her white hair and long body on high heels, shines over the heads of the crowd. Fred's top hat maneuvers somewhere close by. From the Quarter and elsewhere, from South Carrolton Avenue, from the Rampart, from every street and square there comes surging a buoyant, untrammeled crowd of white and black faces, masks, fleshy likenesses of some mad fantasy. The crowd surges past balconies from which clusters of real and paper flowers hang, toward Canal Street, toward the sound of trombones, trumpets, and the dull thump of countless drums. Her hand is still in his when they reach Canal Street: there is a heart feverishly beating in that hand, in this feverish crowd. With royal flourishes, in imitation of the triumphal pomp of Roman times, plastic gold pieces and necklaces go flying out from the parade floats among clusters of grasping hands. Black faces painted white with full, red lips; white faces painted black and yellow, a centipede of majorettes, dancing backsides, swarming feet, drums, Andrew Bell Junior High Band.

"These are mine," he calls out, "these guys wake me up." But in the wild whirl of dancelike motion, alcohol breath, the swelling din of music and shouting, no one can hear anybody. The hand holds on to him tightly, it doesn't let go.

Next, they're beneath a viaduct where black Indians are dancing. They remind him of the folkloric "runners" in his own country, the harbingers of spring. Black faces with halos of rainbow-colored feathers, someone starts singing a long song, chanting "Tu-way-pa-ka-way-be-prepared-to-die," a rhythmical, conspiratorial, steady trance. Irene feels ill. Peter draws her out of the crowd. Mary trips, Fred has lost his top hat and is taking endless photos. Some blacks gather around Popescu: his bloody teeth and the hook where his hand should be. This has ceased being a masquerade. Someone shoves him, and in the air there is the smell of something profound and dangerous.

Then they're standing with Fred on Bourbon Street. Up on the balconies women are unbuttoning their blouses and showing their breasts. *Show your tits, show your tits.* It's upbeat, but also frightening. A roaring male mob chants, demands, throws coins up to the balcony, show your tits. One of them raises her undershirt and the dark male crowd below roars. Another takes off her blouse and brandishes it, and the excited crowd tries to break down the front door. Beside a wall across the street a dark-skinned man drops his trousers and shakes his veined flesh in his hands. Fred has gone pale and his eyes show dizziness. "Did you see Meg?" he says. "Did you see Meg Holick?" Gregor shakes his head. "Up there," Fred points to the balcony in despair, "she's up there. I saw her." A lone woman dances on the balcony now, a fat woman dancing alone, snaking her arms and snapping her fingers. "I don't see her," Gregor says, "you've got to be wrong." Fred is beside himself. Fred has forgotten who F.B. is. A wave of bodies presses him to the wall. Gregor pulls him out of the crowd, using his elbows to force sweaty bodies aside. Fred is pale. "Out of the way," Gregor shouts, "this is

Professor Blaumann. College of Liberal Arts." Fuck off, someone says, fuck liberal and fuck arts. When they pause to catch their breath and Gregor lights a cigarette, Fred shakes his head. "I've drunk too much," he says. "No, you haven't," says Gregor, "they had you pressed up against the wall." "This is insane," Fred says, "I saw her on the balcony." "It just seemed that way," Gregor says. "I have to find her," Fred says, "I have to find her tonight." Beneath the balcony there is utter chaos. A phalanx of the Holy Army drives into the crowd like a wedge. They're wearing hockey helmets with face guards. A megaphone blares: *Repent! Judgment will be severe! Do you want to burn in hell?* A tall man grabs a crusader by the face guard and starts yanking him around. Suddenly they find themselves amid a snarl of bodies. Gregor shoves and extracts himself from the tangle. Fred runs down the street past Jesus' foot soldiers. He doesn't see the images from his book, residing in his computer. He can't see the Middle Ages or his Elizabethan ailment.

Sin! Sin! Sin!

It's night and torchlight illuminates the banner of the Holy Army. With hockey masks on their faces and crosses in their hands, the foot soldiers work their way through the frenzied, drunken crowd.

Hellfire! Hellfire! Hellfire!

Some yield to them, others taunt them. Most of the crowd doesn't even notice them. The drunken and unbridled crowd rolls through the streets of the Quarter.

You won't escape hell's fury! the megaphone shouts, and its sound merges with a thousand musical instruments, shouts, and whistles.

From Blaumann's book:

The fear of hell caused such severe melancholic symptoms that people died from them. The images of hell were terrible: P. Segneri of Avignon describes it as the blaze of embers and chill of spring water combined, as the bite of a snake, the pouring forth of dragon's bile, the snapping of nerves, and the dislocation of bones, all at once: chains on one's legs, gallows, the wheel, and horses for drawing and quartering at a gallop. But whoever believes this lasts a single moment is in error. That moment is as long as eternity. One must imagine the sphere of the earth, and a bird pecking out just a single grain of it every thousand years. That is how long it will last.

Fred Blaumann doesn't have his computer or his top hat. Even Fred Blaumann, who sees all and knows all, has lost all self-consciousness now and is running. He's running after his student, who is nowhere to be found. He's running after his talented and anxious student, Meg Holick, who has to be, simply has to be someplace else. He runs after a hallucination, if that woman on the balcony pacing up and down the walkway, contorting her body and showing her bare breasts to the deranged crowd of males, to the black man shaking his veinous flesh, isn't a hallucination. Fred Blaumann trips and falls. Gregor picks him up. Once a year everyone here goes crazy.

4

Popescu leans over the balcony and speaks:

"Most of all I enjoy striking at those who don't expect me. I walk into their houses, lay them on their beds, suck the blood from their veins. I drain everything out of them, I dry up all of their life sources, I cause a pallor to spread across their faces, I freeze every part of their bodies, root up their souls, and just as a ravenous wolf drags the prey it has just killed to its lair, so do I drag their bodies off and slowly devour them."

Popescu bellows from the balcony. Meg is inside. Fred has found Meg, but Meg's eyes are vacant. She shares a joint with Number 9. Peter is asleep on the floor, his cyclist's knees touching his chin. With his foot, Gregor touches Irene's leg. "You're not Irene," he says, "you're Irena. I knew an Irena once and loved her." Irena draws her leg back and smiles inwardly. The *mimosa pudica* closes at the slightest touch.

"I rip through their fibers with my teeth, separate flesh from bone, break the thighbones and sip out the soft parts of their skulls," the vampire cries from the balcony. "I suck on their brains, bite off their fingers, spit out the nails."

A placard appears down on the street: *Hell Awaits.*

"That man is disgusting," somebody says.

"I think he's nice," Meg says.

Fred lowers his head. A bottle flies onto the balcony. Peter says something in his sleep. Popescu vomits.

Popescu is leaning over the balcony, the upper half of his body is bent over the railing and rains vomit down on the street. Whistles and bottles fly onto the balcony.

"Somebody stop him," a voice says.

"Take it easy, buddy," Fred says.

"He's not upset," Meg says. "He's sick."

Popescu disgorges whiskey and beer, water and wine, rice and beans, wiggling crayfish, slippery oysters, an entire jambalaya in a magnificent, colorful cascade. When he completely empties, he collapses like a bag. He falls alseep in an instant.

"I had no idea," someone says, "that a person could eat that much."

5

And this is the last sentence that can be put in its proper place. After that Irene vanished—everyone vanished. What followed is what might be referred to as a "film rompu." The film is actually broken and the action lasts three days. It's not that large segments go missing, the way sleep after a night's carousing causes them to do. There was no sleep at all. It was more like a fragmented, crushed world. A kaleidoscope. With sound. Going downhill. Orpheus descending.

Fred Blauman dances at Pat O'Brian's. He sings and dances with Meg among the tourists from Texas. Actually, he hops. They play "The Eyes of Texas." He will be ashamed of this. Mary squeals like a mouse. Fred says: *tagenaria domesti-*

ca, which means domestic mouse. Mary takes her white wig off and throws it into a fountain in the garden. Gumbo appears from somewhere and stands beside the table. Strangely, his round face stretches up into the trees. Gumbo pulls a money clip out of his pocket. There is the roar of a car engine: somebody driving somewhere. Doors slam, some people get out, others get in. He sits next to a black man who swigs from a bottle as though it were water. Somewhere out there is the Maple Leaf. The Maple Leaf is a bar where they play Cajun music and dance. Gumbo dances with Louisa. He promised her. Gumbo is on the stage playing the accordion. Violin, accordion, some French waltzes and polkas. Cajun, Cajun. It sounds Mediterranean and down home, like Dalmatia or Istria.

Back in the car, back with Gumbo. Tonio Gomez is the driver. His face is smooth shaven, almost to the point of bleeding; his wavy hair falls over his collar. He demands that they stop. "Where are you going now?" Gumbo says. Tonio Gomez smiles, there's a woman sitting next to him, he saw her in one of Gumbo's photographs with her tongue stuck out. He demands that they stop at once. Where do you think you're going, you're drunk. "Leave him, let him go," Gomez says. Gomez stops the car. "Be careful," he says from the window, "take care of yourself, *dottore.*" Gumbo is the *dottore,* not him. He walks down some empty street. A dim, orange light shines down from on top of rough-hewn wooden poles. He trips on the ripped-up asphalt. He hears noise at the end of the street, where the light is also better. Like a moth, he scrambles out of the darkness into the light. Somebody runs after him. They wrestle: he wrestles with the devil fiercely. Then he's back among the crush of bodies, which squeezes him. The devil isn't stored in Fred Blaumann's melancholy computer with 6 megabytes of central and 666 megabytes of peripheral memory. He is in the multitude, because he *is* the multitude. *Thy name is legion.*

From Blaumann's book:

A sixteenth-century author (J. Maldonado) describes the devil as a horrible beast. The veins of his testicles are plaited like branches, his bones are brass pipes, his joints are like steel, his jaws are like shields always tightly pressed together so that the wind cannot pass through them. The Breton writer P. J. Helias holds false the claim that he is a red animal with a long tail that vexatiously bites the damned so that they howl with pain. No! He resembles a good-natured Breton from Lower Brittany who has squandered his fortune, or a wandering Jew dragging his bags from one corner of the world to the other. He is always dedicated to higher causes: arranging marriages, celebrating weddings, encouraging every kind of joy and conviviality. Luther knew the devil: by his own account, he spent long nights trying to chase him away by forcing him to smell the human stench and sulphur out of his rear orifice. The devil is also firmly anchored in American tradition. It is well known that Billy Sunday wrestled with the devil for hours in the hot sun before crowds that watched this spectacle.

6

A bare-assed man with a graceful step flounces down the street. He is accompanied by a group of revolting dwarves. All of them have their genitalia stuffed into black, molded leather. They stand watching an overweight traveling salesman as he grapples with something. A whore stands in the middle of the street grinning at him. The fat man is shoving a second whore toward the door of a building. He drops his briefcase on the ground and tries to open the door, which refuses to give. He wants to get her into the doorway. He presses her up against the door, away from the light. He unbuttons his trousers and fumbles with shaking hands under her skirt. He lifts her legs up at the knees and nails her to the wood of the door. He shoves her, at first with his hands, now he thrusts with his rear. Her back keeps banging and ramming against the door. She moans, most likely with pain, not pleasure. The man writhes and slumps, and over his shoulder she gives a sign with her hand. The other understands, grins, becomes serious, grabs the briefcase and runs. The bare-assed giant, with a strap running between his buttocks, pulls on a chain and the harnessed dwarves follow him. They surround the thrusting couple in the entryway. The man looks over his shoulder, draws his rear back, lets the female sack drop to the ground, buttons his trousers and turns around. Bare-ass turns around, too, and pokes a finger at his buttocks. "Here, too," he says, "here, too." The dwarves rattle their chains, clap their tiny hands, and roll on the ground with laughter.

This is now somewhere in the southern part of the city. He walks a long way down the river. The houses are all wooden, then they become smaller and smaller, with shacks and rugged fences. There is the smell of grilled meat, of burnt pork, drenched in a sweet sauce. It also smells of burnt rags. A black man sitting on the steps before a house plays a harmonica. That's Jesus from Rigby's. Maybe Jesus lives here? When he says hello, the other keeps playing and doesn't answer. A sign on the building reads Salvation Army. The windowpanes on the Salvation Army house rattle. A black child climbs up and tries to pry the grille on the window open. He runs to the left. He should come out onto the Rampart soon.

In a small park a shadow separates from the darkness. He retreats. The shadow keeps approaching, it turns out to be a woman. The woman raises her skirt. "One dollar," she says, "with your mouth." Automobile headlights brush past and illuminate her face. It is the face of an old, toothless hag of indeterminate race. Her gums are black. She opens her mouth and sticks a black tongue out of it. When he turns and virtually runs away, he hears her shouting:

"Some day you'll stink, too! Some day you'll croak, too!"

Again several empty streets and through a yard full of demolished cars. Then along a cemetery wall, past stone grave markers. Some woman's pudgy face. "Joseph," he says: he's found Joseph. Across a broad river road, through a seamless band of automobile headlights. The Irish Channel? St. Charles Avenue? Suddenly he recognizes streets, suddenly he walks as though he had a city map at his feet. Suddenly he has the city map from Diamond's book at his feet. The seven, the number seven. He rides along Barronne Street to Canal Street.

The Rex Parade, for a short stretch he follows the main parade closely. King Zulu, the black monarch arrives. A hail of plastic gold pieces. On Canal Street, a dense multitude of heads. He sees it from above; now he flies across it. He can hear the sounds of parades, of trumpets coming from below. He flies, while below gold pieces glimmer as they slowly fall among the heads. He flies through the night sky—at some point he should meet Maldoror. All around the wings of falling and rising creatures flap and rustle. He flies through the night and over the river. Below stand steamboats all lit up. Organ music, pipes. He flies over the roofs of the Quarter, and at the Hotel St. Charles he slowly descends. For a moment he pauses on its annex and looks out over the heads of the dark, dark multitude for another. How many heads? Half a million. One million vibrating breasts, half a million whirling bellies and buttocks. How many devils? Half a million or just one? He looks through a window: a woman lies naked on the bed in a hotel room. Stella. Her eyes are dark hollows. Her body is an empty shell. He slides down the hotel's facade to the street, back into the anthill, the smell of human sweat assailing his face.

Gumbo's art photography studio, seen through a doorway. Gomez is lying on the bed, next to him is a woman with her back turned to him. Gomez raises his drunk head, where his nose should be there is a bloody scar. He plays with a knife and leans over the woman. Gomez's apartment, seen through a doorway. A woman kneels in front of a man. The man's face is turned upward. His lips are parted and his eyes are wide open. He looks at the ceiling, at the crumbling plaster and the wooden beams. Below, the woman's head is pressed to his genitals, her hands press his sides, her head gently moves. His hands convulsively grab her head by the hair and remove a red-green wig, raising it up in the air, to his eyes. The kneeling woman's greasy, black hair is cut in a butch. The kneeling woman now turns to look toward the door. The kneeling woman is a man in makeup smeared over his badly shaven face. Thin eyebrows. Vacant eyes. Eyes that see nothing.

The creatures gathering outside wear tall wigs. There are more and more of them. A large group of transvestites gathers on the steps beneath the veranda of the Napoleon. They mince around on high heels and their skirts have slits in them up to the thighs. Their mouths have been made up into little hearts. A white-haired, wigless albino, taller than the rest, stands on the steps singing. From across the street a basso buffo answers him.

From Blaumann's book:

A riddle of the philosopher's stone. My name is Aelia laelia Crispis. I am neither man nor woman, neither lass nor lad, neither sinner nor saint. I suffer neither hunger nor thirst, taste neither sweetness nor poison. I live neither in the heavens nor on earth, but everywhere. I know neither sorrow nor joy, neither tears nor laughter. I know neither what is cold nor what is heat. I am neither vegetable nor mineral. What am I?

"Look at you," the basso buffo calls out. The basso buffo stands across the street. He's with a crowd of rednecks, all of them with beer in hand. They whistle and guffaw at the lyric baritone and his friends. The basso buffo is rippling with strength. His rear end is stuffed into blue jeans and the buttons on his checked shirt are unfastened, revealing shaggy patches on his belly. But the white-haired albino turns to him and with a graceful gesture replies, "Look at yourself." "You're a disgrace to America," the buffo says. "That's open to debate," the tall albino in high heels replies. Stocky and stuffed approaches. The crowd laughs, the crowd urges him on, the crowd can smell blood. "What are you anyway," the buffo says and reaches for the other's crotch, "show us what you've got." The albino squats and squeals, and the buffos roar with laughter. But in an instant he straightens up and looks down at the buffo. He makes an elegant flourish with his hand over the other's head: "I would never, ever want to be . . . *that.*" Silence. *That* has been humiliated and is now dangerous. He couldn't be *that,* when the real that is in fact standing before him. "You're a fag," says the buffo, "that's what you are." "I'm not a fag," *that* says, "guess what I am." "Let's see your balls," the basso says. The basso is offended: no one is laughing and he continues talking with *that.* With a disgust verging on nausea. "You're a damned bastard, that's what you are," he shouts and slams his fist into the albino's face. The flock of wigs squeals and scatters to all sides. The tall albino tries to escape, too, but the buffo deftly trips him. He kicks him a few times so that you can hear the dull smack of the shoe against the albino's body. The crowd parts for a parade coming down the street. Plastic gold pieces and flowers start raining down from the balconies. The fair-haired creature crawls along the edge of the sidewalk. His garters are torn, and his face is a bloody mess. The crowd goes streaming after the parade.

From Blaumann's book:

The judicial cruelty of the Middle Ages wasn't a sick perversion, but rather indifferent, animal pleasure. A carnival diversion. The masses fell victim to a melancholic disorder that found pleasure in the suffering of others. The citizens of Mons once bought a bandit so that they could enjoy the act of drawing and quartering him. People gasped and laughed at the same time more than they would have at the resurrection of some holy corpse. For a long time people could not get enough of these scenes of torture, and so they would often delay executions, even though the condemned begged to have them carried out.

7

He stands on the roof of a building—the tile-roofed one with the green balconies on the corner of St. Philip and Royal

Streets. He stands right at the edge, lacking any more strength to fly. He is drawn downward and he is about to fall. A text scrolls across the screen, across the screen of a 666-megabyte computer scrolls this text: *formatus de spurcissimo spermate, conceptus in pruritu carnis.* I've got it, he says, I've got it, Fred, this is the source of melancholic sickness. This is the melancholy matter, the vile semen that gives birth to man, the sperm, the sweaty coupling of bodies. The clotted blood, the sweaty bodies down there among the crowd, the pointless bodily secretions down in the rooms beneath this roof, the senseless mating. And down on the street that gigantic phallus is on the rampage, charging into people, stiffening and rising and spraying out a whitish fluid that drenches the city. The melancholy matter that squirts out of swollen organs and oozes out of exhausted ones all over the soaked bedsheets of the Vieux Carré, in entryways, against walls, into flesh, into mouths. An entire Quarter serving no other purpose than *spurcissimo spermate,* sticky, smeared over bellies, chests, black and white faces, on masks and disguises. Melancholy matter: it was melancholy matter that was overflowing this night through the windows of glittering apartments and filthy dives, out of windowless holes, through doors and down corridors and dark entryways, surging down the streets and overflowing the riverfront square, crossing the banks of the Mississippi and flowing down the levees into the brown water, into the yellow water, into its slow, muddy waves, so that it foams, so that it sticks, all frothy, so that the slimy stuff sticks to the sides of boats, which can no longer move, mired in a fecal filth that is part *spurcissimo spermate,* water and the stuff that fetuses float on, washed in by the canals, black and white, lost in the turbulence as it surges downstream to the ocean gulf and there drains into the earth's viscera, hellish river.

Then he slips, seizes onto roofing tiles, grabs a gutter, hangs, then falls, falls again and across the screen races a text that he tries to repeat and scream out, but he can't open his mouth, *elohim, elohim.*

Pie Pelicane, Jesu domine.
Me immundum munda tuo sanguine,
Cuius una stilla salvum facere
Totum mundum quit ab omni scellere.

(Blessed Pelican, Lord Jesus,
Cleanse foul me with your blood,
Of which a single drop can save
The whole world from its sins.)

The text vanishes. The onlooker continues to fall.

8

The silence woke him up. Suddenly there was no noise anywhere. The trumpets had fallen silent. He even thought he could hear birdsong somewhere close by his window. The first light of morning was falling through the dirty window-panes. He seemed to touch something soft with his shoulder. Next to him lay a black female body, curled up into a ball and covered to the waist with a sheet. She was turned away from him, and her rear end was touching his elbow. He grabbed her by the shoulder and shook. Slowly she turned over, opened her eyes, and squinted into the morning sun. It was a young face, with curly hair over a high, black forehead.

"What are you doing here?"

The woman rose up on her elbows and looked at him.

"What am I doing here? I'm sleeping."

She sat up on the bed and put her shoes on.

"I'm sleeping next to a totally drunk man who shouts and talks in his sleep all night long."

"You slept?"

"That's right. Although you did propose something else entirely."

"I did?"

"No. King Zulu did."

He lay back and tried to think. Yvonne. Her name is Yvonne. She had told him not to sleep with his arms over his head. That brings bad dreams. Her grandma, who knew voodoo, had told her this. She had told him this at Rigby's. He had said that it was even worse to sleep alone. Cut. Film rompu.

Then she had smiled showing teeth like pearls. Now she was ill-tempered. Yes, she's from the other side of the river. He winced when she slammed the door. What did she dream about with her arms not over her head? Why hadn't he asked her? Now she was gone. Outside the birds really were singing. He closed his eyes. He saw her riding a boat across the river. Over the waves that calm and remove everything that's evil. The splashing of the yellow waves. And silence. Silence for a long time. The gurgling of water in the fountain on the patio. Water helps, pearl teeth are calming, the big river is calming. He falls back to sleep.

When he awoke at mid-morning, his body was like a shell, empty and drained. The apartment was a hopeless mess. A garbage truck clattered and roared outside his window. Black workers were calling out to each other.

9

The devil is a turkey with no eyes.

This image had stayed with him. An eyeless turkey bent down over the frenzied crowd. When the crowd retreats, it bends over him, over his bed. It has red, wrinkly skin in the place where its eyes should be and a dangerous beak. The black woman who had been here for a visit left that description, that image behind. Yvonne, the black girl's name was Yvonne. She's disappeared and he'll never see her again. No matter, he thought, no matter. It wasn't so much a thought as the state of things. The hopelessly hollow, natural state of things. For a long time he sat on his bed, a crumbled piece of some ruin. An overturned bottle lay on the floor. All around were strewn pieces of clothing, crumpled newspapers. *Trashy,* Irene would say. Where is Irene? In court. Ash Wednesday's crop of rapists and robbers would be bountiful. Where is Fred? At his melancholy computer. *Trashy.*

When he opened the kitchen door several cockroaches scrambled for safety. Gregor Samsa had company.

A garbage truck rumbled down the street. Whatever happened out in the city was being broadcast live over the radio. A journalist was reporting from Canal Street. He praised the municipal services beyond all measure. The trash collectors were heroes of labor. While you slept, tired from Mardi Gras, they were slaving away damned hard. The streets are clean, and with every minute they become cleaner. Maybe, he thought, the apartments at least aren't getting cleaner every minute. Last night these heroes of labor had removed 1,850 tons of trash. And the number is growing every minute. How many cockroaches? He tried to imagine 1,850 tons of trash, with 1,850 tons of cockroaches crawling on it. In the meantime, between intervals of music, the announcer continued spewing more and more statistics: two killed, twenty-three cases of rape, 137 break-ins, 727 assaults and robberies. The figures were acceptable, this year's Mardi Gras had passed in relative peace, in comparison with last summer. Then the chief of police and a hospital director spoke. The two of them were also relatively pleased.

He needed water, milk, whatever. When he thought of the state of his kitchen, all desire to eat or drink anything passed. In the bathroom he looked at his swollen face with big, black shadows under the eyes. Streams of water on the skin, just the skin, the inside could stay ravaged. He let the water flow from the tap, and this calmed him. He would go to the river-front and look at the river all day. The river is calming, the river is impermanence. He picked up his clothes. In a pocket he found some crumpled cigarettes, an ashtray (so I stole?), some keys (but whose?), a plastic necklace, and a bunch of plastic gold pieces with the coats of arms of the kings of various parades.

At the laundromat there were only broken people. Someone was joking, but the rest stared at the drums as they turned. A young woman had a pile of bloody men's clothes.

When he returned, he uncovered a stack of wadded paper with a red and black crucifix. The Holy Army foot soldiers had shoved this in his hand. *All this he suffered for you.* Who? Senselessly, he stared at the sentence. His head was empty, his body drained. Only a roachlike shell kept him together— inside he was hopelessly hollow. Had Popescu, as a Transylvanian vampire, sucked all the blood out of his veins, drained him of all fluids, dried up his sources of life, caused a pallor to spread over his face? Who? Who suffered? He had. The statistics refused to stop. One thousand eight hundred tons, the announcer proclaimed. One thousand eight hundred.

Slowly he began to read the flyer of the Holy Army:

Be aware, brothers and sisters, that for you he shed 62,000 tears and 97,307 drops of blood. That his body received 1,667 blows. 110 slaps to the face. 107 blows to the neck. 380 to the back. 85 on the head. 43 to the chest. 38 to the kidneys. 62 about the shoulders. 40 on the hands. About the hips and legs 32. They struck his mouth 30 times. Basely and abominably, they spat in his dear face 32 times. They kicked him like a prisoner 370 times. They shoved and threw him to the ground 13 times. They dragged him by the hair 30 times. They tore at his beard 38 times. May your heart be inflamed. The crown of thorns pierced his head in 303 places. He moaned and sighed for your salvation 900 times. He bore 162 torments, any one of which could have killed him. He was at death's door 19 times. From the place of judgment to Calvary he took 320 steps with the cross. And for all this he received only a single act of kindness from Saint Veronica, who wiped his sweaty and bleeding face.

He put the flyer away. He would pass it on to Blaumann for his research. Religious melancholy.

10

The telephone rang. He turned off the radio and picked up the receiver. It was Ana, by satellite.

"I've been calling for three days, where have you been?"

"In hell."

"Is that so?"

"That's so."

"In hell."

"That's exactly right."

There was a click in the receiver and the line began to beep. Ana had hung up. A moment later the phone rang again. It was Irene.

On the morning of Ash Wednesday Peter had left for New York.

CHAPTER 11

A SWING IN SPRING

I

The second hour of creative writing dragged on unbearably. Fred Blaumann had talked for the first hour about tragedy and purification in Faulkner's *Absalom, Absalom!* The entire time he spoke, he looked out the window. Maybe this was the reason no one dared to ask why it was that Faulkner had used the ever undesirable exclamation mark in the very title of his book. Meg was gone. Meg was somewhere else. When he finished, he picked up his belongings and left without a word. Probably for his computer, filled with such a great amount of melancholy. He left the discussion of the students' most recent texts to Gregor. Gradnik struggled. The blond art gallery specialist was hopelessly untalented. He was unable to tell her why. Her text once again told of people walking past the gallery where she worked. They would stop in front of her display window, while she observed them and thought how they must see her as some kind of manikin through the glass. The gallery was home to art, and she lived with it. Yet the passersby couldn't understand that. They walked past her like the transitory shadows of life, and she was like a manikin on display. They were unfeeling, and she was also becoming that way, like a manikin in a display window. She was, quite simply, Blanche from *A Streetcar Named Desire*. Life fleeting past. And beauty. Number 9 was talented, but Gradnik wasn't able to tell him why. In his story a basketball player tries to shoot a basket during the last second of a game. At that instant a memory from childhood flashes past him: his brother falls and he tries to catch him; he runs toward him . . . his arm shudders and the ball goes flying toward the basket . . . he catches his brother, both of them fall . . . the ball dances around the rim . . . Maybe he could fix the beginning. He had spent too much time describing the cheering from the bleachers and the basketball player's worsening nerves, the girl sitting in the auditorium watching him. Had it ever occurred to him, he asked Number 9, that writers experienced a similar fear . . . Or the fear of the writer at his computer, that it might delete his text, the unique and unrepeatable text that has just been created. Then he looked out the window. It really was getting to be spring.

Gradnik struggled. The hour dragged on interminably. His words hung in the air, danced on the rim: he was like a manikin in a display window. He had long since stopped talking about Maldoror. He preferred talking about manikins. And now he also understood why Professor Blaumann talked about exclamation marks. He advised Number 9 to read Handke, *The Goalie's Fear at the Penalty Kick.*

2

Life abruptly resumed its previous course. It was surprising how the memory of so many events could be washed away. The beauty of forgetting. Utensils once again clinked in the faculty dining room. Fred sat at his computer, filling it with quotations and similes, but his book didn't move forward an inch. Meg Holick announced that she planned to move to New York as soon as she graduated. Gumbo and Louisa vanished. The apartment was locked down, and several times he saw Tonio Gomez in his white suit standing outside the front door. Popescu, the Romanian Byzantologist, departed. He had saved enough money from his fellowship to buy a car back home. And a new refrigerator. Gregor Samsa disappeared, too. Everybody disappeared, except for Stella with her unwashed hair sitting at her window, smoking cigarette after cigarette. She had never smoked before, but now she had started. Kowalski paced around in the background like a captive lion. Spring was here. They installed a new door. The insurance was going to pay for the damage. The landlord was pleasant, because he'd gotten his check. Debbie waved at him whenever he walked past Rigby's. She still smiled incessantly, and she still always wore her green suspenders. Now she was wearing a green blouse, too, because St. Patrick's Day was approaching. Martin's dog lay in the doorway every night, chomping on ice.

Ana called. She had been skiing. He wrote her a long, sentimental letter.

Plastic gold pieces and necklaces gathered dust on his shelf.

The days were transparent, and a cool, pleasant breeze blew in from the river. The trees leafed out. Spring came to New Orleans very early.

He called Irene and asked her if he could borrow the famous bicycle. They sat in the twilight drinking tea. The wind wafted the sound of blues from some bar down the street. Blue notes and dirty notes. Swing: a tense, relentless progression. But the whole time she kept turning the conversation to Peter, who was in New York finding an apartment for the two of them. It was time for her to move and find something new. She just needed to finish her apprenticeship in court. Still, it was twilight, and there was swing. As he rode away on the bike, he threw a plastic necklace up onto her balcony. She would find it in the morning.

3

He went to the library every day and read whatever the moment's inspiration led him to. He read Thomas Aquinas and collected notes on the subject of *tristitia*, so that he could enter them on Blaumann's computer. That was his modest contribution to the book that would probably never be finished. For Aquinas *tristitia* was a sorrowful emptiness of the soul. *Tristitia* is most at home in lonely, rainy streets, or above the ocean's dark surface, with clouds pressing down. Music has affinities with it. This last he probably added himself. After a while he couldn't tell what he had copied and what was his. The sullen soul was definitely Aquinas's definition. Sullen soul, sluggish soul, mean-spiritedness. This was fun stuff. It took away your desire to move; mental torpor influenced the body. The sin of inaction drove it to commit sinful acts. Sullen soul.

In Audubon Park, where he would ride the bike in the evenings, the treetops were rustling. Strange conifers swayed with dignity this way and that. Tiny leaves shuddered in the red underbrush. The humidity evaporated, drawn, perhaps, onto the broad surface of the river, or into it. He rode between rows of white, wooden buildings. He stepped into one of the small wooden chapels. He sat in front of the Buddhist Center for a long time and looked at the Buddhists as they inclined their heads, understanding something he couldn't approach.

The days were transparent and a cool, pleasant breeze blew in from the river. The trees leafed out. Spring came to New Orleans very early.

■ □ ■ □ ■

CHAPTER 12

POET AND ATHLETE

I

When some future historian tries to establish what drove millions of Americans to start running at the end of the twentieth century, it won't be an easy task. It won't be easy to find an explanation for that sudden racing through parks and over beaches, through the streets of big cities, under the hot, southern sun or in the stinging cold of the north. Human beings in America suddenly started to jog. Morning, noon, evening, and night, young and old, sick and healthy, all of them forsook their previous habits and set out at a sprint. Some broke bones, others sprained ankles, still others suffered heart attacks or were bitten by dogs. But the mass of them kept on running. Businessmen and -women in the midday heat headed not for the shade, but onto molten asphalt roads and raced down them. Women's handbags no longer contained compacts, but tennis shoes. City buses emptied out. The human race of America ran: in droves it raced across the bridges of New York and through the deserts of Nevada; from Alaska to Florida you could meet sweat-drenched people with their temples throbbing, wildly gasping and moaning, with absent gazes, and wearing headphones. Some biologists attempted, as they always do, to find an analogy among other species of mammal: the hidden genetic program that drives whales through the oceans and up onto sandy beaches, or multitudes of rats through the expanses of Siberia. But a historian will know that the human race of Western civilization had been known to do all sorts of things: multitudes had risen up all over Europe and set forth in the rain and winter, through sand and sun to liberate God's tomb, though few of them knew where the country was they were lurching toward. Processions of pilgrims had staggered under the weight of crosses, people had flogged themselves and bled to the verge of death. The adherents of some medieval sects jumped through flames. In Russia they ran naked through the forests, and in Germany barefoot over stones. At the end of the twentieth century they ran in jogging shoes. More than anything, they resembled the maniacal residents of a certain Alpine valley on the Slovenian border, who once each year raced to the top of four mountains: men and women, children and old folks wheezed with rabid eyes from valley floor to mountaintop, breaking legs on the descent back to the valley, allowing the weakest to lag and, eventually, collapse.

Yet there was something new to this at the end of the twentieth century. Medieval vaulters, flagellants, and racing pilgrims were all concerned with the soul over the body. What they held to be higher reasons drove them to run, moan, and torture themselves in every way: the soul was striving toward something, but the body held it back. What's more, one had to injure the body, since it stood in the soul's way, obstructing it in its higher aspirations. And because, in human history, outbreaks of running, flogging, and leaping through flames have always had understandable spiritual reasons, our future historian will have fearsome difficulties explaining that unusual phenomenon known as jogging. He will observe that, toward the end of the twentieth century, there appeared maniacs who started running through streets and wildernesses for no metaphysical reason, just because. For the sake of the body itself. Of course some claimed it was for health reasons, others for social status, but this was only part of the truth. Reasons appeared that came closest to resembling the medieval ones: while running, but especially afterward, a person passed into a higher state of consciousness. The glassy, not-of-this-world stare was proof of this: the runner no longer perceives the real world. If you get in his way, he'll yell at or collide with you. And all runners, all joggers (as the adherents of this greatest sect of all times were called) spoke of a pleasant fatigue—which is to say, they came close to the state of nirvana known to Eastern philosophies. A French philosopher asserted that running obsessives were signs of the coming apocalypse: with lost eyes and foaming mouths they stumbled mindlessly around in anticipation of an imminent catastrophe.

2

Be that as it may, Gregor Gradnik had to run. He had to run if he wanted to get close to Irene Anderson. He wanted to get close to her. She wanted him to get close to her, as close as possible; everything pointed to this. From the first, both of them had wanted that—since meeting in the Russian house, where someone had shot himself on TV, since the drive to Barataria Bay, when the car's speedometer had wavered between two poles like a compass needle, since the journey into the long carnival night and ash morning, since every single moment and all of them together. That had been decided. But something was lacking: he didn't belong to the sect, he hadn't been inducted. He was an outsider. He hung out in suspicious company at Rigby's, a cloud of black cigarette smoke billowed up above him, and at night he would stagger out of jazz bars, saturated with bourbon. All of this would have been all right. After all, Irene Anderson had experience with artists, of which Peter Diamond was one. But Peter also bicycled and wrote books about it. In short, he would have to do both—be an artist (bourbon, Gitanes) and a jogger, both at the same time. You have to maintain a balance, and this was critical. As proof of his balance he needed to undergo some initiation. In the Middle Ages you leaped through fire, and then your brothers and sisters accepted you as one of them, particularly if you were a sister. You had to run up the four mountains, with bleeding feet and frothing mouth.

This was the same sort of thing.

3

"You couldn't make it," she said.

"Make what?"

"Run from here to Audubon Park, to the zoo."

Mentally he tried to measure the distance. He had been there several times with a car. Once he went there by bike, following Peter's artist's paths, stopping at the colonial mansions, sitting in the shade outside the Buddhist temple and watching the shaven heads bowing in contemplation. Irene Anderson ran that distance once a week. She ran some every day, but her real run was to Audubon Park. All the best runners ran there and then described a kind of triumphal circuit among the throng of joggers that formed a living chain of bodies in the park. Gregor thought of his heart, his smoke-saturated lungs, and his muscles that hadn't lifted anything heavier than a book or a glass in a long time. He thought that this would be an arduous and dangerous thing, if he decided on it. He thought that this park was actually a long way off, and that he might possibly expire along the way.

"Of course I could make it," he said, for if he had said that he couldn't, it would have meant that he couldn't do anything, anything at all.

"I used to train for handball."

She laughed out loud. Women sometimes laugh out loud in the most unpleasant way.

"Not just that I could make it. I *will*."

Fine, then they would run on Sunday. Fine, that's what they do here on Sundays. In some places they go to church on Sundays, and other places they sleep late. Here, in New Orleans, praised in all of literature for its slow pace, where life's rhythm is like that of the Mississippi, or of black spirituals—a mournful, lazy motion; where sweat sometimes drips from people's faces while they're standing still; and from their whole bodies when they lie on their beds naked in summertime waiting for a breeze from the river—here some people go running. He remained seated in the coffee shop and watched her through the window as she mounted the famous Diamond-Anderson bicycle. She turned her skirt up over her knees. Of course he'd go running, although he remained seated, looking absently at the big cup of half-finished French coffee in front of him, at the crumbled croissants and the trembling black cigarette in his fingers. He wasn't convinced this would end well. He thought with discomfort that only two things could happen to him on the way to Audubon Park. Ridicule and humiliation, or death with a foaming mouth. At that moment he didn't know which was worse.

4

Over the next few days he exchanged the bus ride home from the library for a walk. In the evening, when it got dark, he tried to run a bit through the lonely streets. Whenever a car approached, he would slacken his pace. Somehow it didn't fit his image of himself. The poet and athlete of Joyce's *Portrait* are two mutually exclusive personalities. The athlete, with lactic acid circulating in his bloodstream, and the poet, who makes the world aware of "something else"—these are universes light-years apart. He was profoundly convinced that Fred Blaumann could possibly be an outstanding professor but never an excellent writer, simply because he ran. Because of that white thing poking out from under his shorts. How could he reconcile Georg Trakl of the dark Salzburg willow trees with the poet racing through traffic toward Audubon Park? Still, he would run. Back then they didn't. Nowadays even poets ran, American ones even more so. Every morning, even after coming home late the night before, he would do twenty deep-knee bends. He bought tennis shoes and drove to the park. After several laps he noticed a curious change. Whenever he had taken walks here before or sat on a bench, no one had taken any notice of him. Now, despite their lost gazes, the runners started to greet him. It would be a motion of the hand, an indistinct murmur, gestures of solidarity between brothers and sisters in fitness. When, after several hundred yards, he stooped over with his hands on his knees and listened as his heart pounded in his head, he could hear shouts of encouragement from the other runners. My heart, he said, my heart's going to burst.

On Saturday he held the telephone receiver in his hand. Irene, he wanted to say, wouldn't it be possible for us to go to bed without this ordeal?

The initiation took place on a Sunday in March, beneath low, foreboding clouds, between the French Quarter and Audubon Park.

5

A—B—C—Č, A—B—C—Č. A—B—C—D, A—B—C—D. The alphabet has twenty-five letters, a sentence for every letter, at least one sentence, and that will get me to the park. A. Audubon Park, that's where the zoo is, from Audubon to the zoo, did I really need that? B. Boy, I could have lived without this, no bone breaks yet, I'm running beautifully for now, the letter B, but this is just the start, I'm moving gracefully, legs carrying my heavy body, we're running abreast, I can hear her breathing, though mine is heavier, I'm all out of shape and involved in this adventure even so, adventure is A, the letter A, now we're at B, but I'm going to belie what they think, belie it, belie it . . . every fourth step I'll belie it. The cigarettes, she said, that's what she said right at the start, your chain-smoking, have you got any idea what it means to smoke so much in this country, God knows what people think of a person who smokes so much, who smokes at all, the cigarettes will do you in after the first five hundred yards. But I've already covered five hundred yards and I'm still running, the trees are green, no fatigue yet, no rush, watch her, the way she wisely parcels out her strength, she runs every morning, every evening, maybe even that judge of hers, the wise man she considers so highly, she considers the letter C, maybe he knows what she can do, she's got short legs, didn't notice until now, but they're nice, but they're nice, her breasts move beneath her T-shirt, they don't jump, they move, that's technique, she has freckles on her shoulders, her hair is pulled up high above her neck, where are we now, the letter C, the concrete, see how nicely the concrete flies past beneath my feet, got to look down at my feet, avoid missteps, so I don't twist an ankle from this stupidity, civilization is insanity, Caesar gets killed, this city sprawls, the whole time we'll be running on concrete past houses and trees, only at the end one last circuit through the park, if I don't die before the end, die, die, die. But I won't, despite, despite what, that I'm a night owl, that I'm a bookworm, that I had a bit to drink last night, that I said I wouldn't, that these runners on their way back are foaming like horses, that by the letter D there shouldn't be any problems yet, although I can discern, very distinctly discern that it isn't easy, that I'm already soaked in sweat, but she doesn't show a thing, no sweat, not a thing, fresh as a virgin spring, light as a cricket, just wait, just wait, you'll be sweaty too, you'll be gasping too, it'll get to you yet, by the time we reach the zoo, you may be smiling now—encouragement for me, or maybe a sneer. A sneer for the poet, praise be to the perspiring. But wait, we're not at P, what's the letter now? Come on, come on, does the brain stop working when you run, come on, draw regular breaths, two steps, draw breath, sigh, I started with three, three steps, draw breath, three steps, exhale, now I'm down to two, two steps to every breath, I'm breathing faster, when I'm down to one breath I'll be in bad shape, breath—step, breath—step, breath—step, breath—breath, breath—breath, breathe right, breathe healthy, don't lose the rhythm, live right, run in the morning, report in the evening, tell her at least once. Even just once tell her, Erevan, try to remember a Radio Erevan joke, do you run well? In general yes, ever, Epsom, entropy, my brain is failing, don't think of the fatigue that's coming, coming, coming in enormous quantities, one smile, right now I'm going to smile at her, in an ordinary voice I'll say: Shall we run back, too? I said it well, that was good, she doesn't answer, smiles, collects enough energy to answer, E, energy, to answer calmly. "We can, if you want," but she said it out of breath, try again, try to provoke her one more time, "to the moon for scotch on the rocks?" "I'd prefer lemonade," she says streaming sweat, this bet's as good as won, because she's sweating, when we reach F, but this is F already, this is, pardon the expression, fuck, fuck-you, as Gumbo says, fuck-off, fuck-you, fuck-off, fuck-you, fuck-off, not a bad rhythm this letter F, France, furnicular, my brains are going, just my body's working, hers is moving and that saves me, o body of a woman, why don't you sit at home, play the lute, o body, so soft, so smooth, so widely sung, must you ascend to heaven live? writes a medieval poet, this one runs in shorts, sweat trickling over all the recesses of her body, she's panting, she's already panting a little, now, now, at F I'll pass her, faster, longer strides, three to a breath, I'll wave casually to you, but I'm lying, I'm lying, it's getting dangerous, it's getting scary, it hurts, under my rib cage it hurts, cars on both sides, the two of us down the grass in the middle, down the elephant path worn bare by runners, she's catching up, I hear her breathing, her eyes are glazing over, she's passed me, I'm giving out, it's getting hellish. The letter H. The houses are bigger, back home they're smaller, outside of town they're smaller, here they're bigger, hello, someone says, hello, some runner says, oh my god, it's Fred, Fred B., I can't think, here on the left, here comes the first canal, they call them bayous, but why, the air should be cleaner, here on the sidewalk, past the gardens, past the pools, past the chapel, people out of church, wise people, now comes the Bu . . . I can't go on, now comes the Buddhist center, sat here in the shade, watched them, their big, shaven heads, only Bushmen run somewhere in

Africa, don't know where, they run nonstop, walking is running, for them running is walking is hiking, H, H, H, hiking, how much I'd rather hike. . . . I . . . I . . . Irregular circumstances, an irregular state . . . a state of siege . . . my legs won't carry me. Yvonne, black Yvonne on the raft across the river, but that's Y, not I, I is irresponsible, irritate, and hell, hyperbole, hypocrisy, skip J, now we're at K, karma, kyrie, definitely kyrie. Stop, my God, I'll stop, the library, air conditioners in the library, bookworms scribbling with their ballpoint pens, the air, the air conditioning, air, the weather, hot flashes in my head, heart pounding in my ears, it's over. Over . . . heart pounding in my ears, my head, nostrils, liver, what if one of my organs goes . . . My God, let me stop . . . I'll lean against a fence, expire, she's running around the corner, reaches the canal, runs across the bridge, looks back and trips and falls. She fell. She fell because she looked back . . . on her feet again, she's scraped her knee. K. K we've done, back to J, jog, jogging is a thrust, a twitch, thank you for falling, that's given me a boost, now I'm back and slowly, slowly jogging, stereophonic current in the heads of joggers, blade-runner . . . the sweep of the road beneath your feet, houses to both sides, a canal, water, thirsty . . . drink . . . Fly, flight, my knees, some tendons are giving, they're going to burst, tendons are T, but this M, I'm not immortal, how old? Thirty-five. How old? Thirty-five? Again? Never again. Never again. T, tenebrous, the lights are going out, what happened to S, silly, don't slacken. O, where is O? Over the top. But not a U-word to be found, not a thought, only this damned breathing, wheezing lungs, the drumming of my breathing, the rattle, drooling mouth, froth, she's slowed down, now we're in the park. V is victory, V is victory. Z zealous as far as the zoo. Soaplike foam at the mouth, bile billowing up in the gullet. Follow her, W, W, witch, bitch, now you know I can do it. Xerox. Xerxes. There, there is the zoo, two critters running into the zoo. One of them runs, the other one drags. Only a little farther, only a few more steps. From the beginning: A. Ars moriendi.

Avant que, which brings us to Q, qompletely. Avant que l'esprit soit hors . . .

Onward, until his soul flies out.

6

He lies in the grass, the sun spinning overhead in the sky, clouds floating past in furious haste. He catches his breath, he suffocates, he catches his soul. He may vomit, but he's reached the finish line. She keeps running lightly back and forth, bends over, exhales, run it out, you've got to run it out, not lie down in the grass right away. What was it the troubadours sang? *Le coeur qui velt crevier au corps.* A heart that could burst in the body. In the body of a poet, in the body of an athlete. Irene sits beside him, shaking her legs, relaxing the muscles; she has her legs spread apart and the flesh beneath the taut skin on her thighs swells back and forth, it undulates, all of it undulates right before his eyes.

That's not what poets are interested in, he says of the clouds.

"Clouds," she asks, "what clouds?"

Gregor takes a crumpled cigarette out of his T-shirt pocket, intentionally put there for this purpose. She stops massaging herself and looks horror-struck at him. He lights up and exhales smoke up toward the dark, heavenly travelers. Her horror transforms her expression, which had been vacant and glazed; now her eyes assume a look of horror, followed by amusement. Suddenly Irene Anderson laughs out loud, she laughs, lies on her back and looks at the clouds. When she gets up again, her eyes no longer have that glassy look, but they are troubled.

Close by they hear a howl and both of them look around. Chimpanzees with body-builder physiques go running past like madmen.

CHAPTER 13

THE LAWYER
AND THE ACCUSED

I

They sat in the restaurant of a Croat who was a well-known raiser of oysters. The Croat's name was Drago and so was the restaurant's. Drago the Croat was proud to be a Croat, and he was proud of the oyster-raising tradition of his Dalmatian ancestors, who had been the first to raise oysters in Louisiana. You can see all about it in the museum, he explained for Irene Anderson. He was pleased with the museum and with his restaurant. Drago was also pleased with Gregor Gradnik, whose picture he had seen in the *Picayune*. He was pleased because he knew where Slovenia was, something not even the reporter who wrote about Gregor's lecture had known. "They think," Drago said, "they think it's Slovakia." Gregor said that his landlord thought it was Pennslovenia. Drago burst out laughing; he was even more pleased with this witticism. So much so, that he treated them to the very freshest oysters on the house, calling into the kitchen to bring them out "for the writer from Pennslovenia." He opened them for them himself, going on at length about his fields, as he called his tracts of fenced-off ocean down in the gulf. Apparently there was some other Drago who was even more successful than he was; he didn't know where he was from, though he hoped he wasn't a Serb. The other Drago repaired shoes in New York. He started out as an ordinary shoe repairman, but now you could see his sign on every street corner:

Drago Shoe Repair. Drago was pleased and witty, but Gregor grew more despondent by the minute, because he hadn't brought Irene here to listen to success stories about people named Drago. Maybe it could have been amusing some other time, but now the world was too small for this kind of thing. And too quiet. Too quiet for the television blaring in the corner of Drago's restaurant, showing a troupe of wild wrestlers: a Russian with a red star on his chest, an American with a Mohawk, and an Iranian with the appearance of an ayatollah. Drago understood: he wasn't just pleased, but smart, too. He understood that there was nothing for him at the moment in this particular world. He sent them a bottle of Dalmatian wine.

2

Now, on Monday, the evening after their mad race, the direction was set, the world had narrowed. It had assumed its narrow center. Now it was impossible to think about anything but that. At the center was her hair, which yesterday after the race of the two lunatics had been soaked and matted like rabbit fur, like the fur of one of those wild animals in the zoo, but which was now bright and soft. The freckles on her cheeks, the slender fingers taking hold of the oysters, the mouth sucking out their slippery contents. The moist eyes, the foggy eyes of a cold-blooded animal recognizing the presence of another beast racing beside it toward some goal, into the night. An avalanche of exhausted words running across the table, indifferent to the polyphony of voices all around, exclusive, listening to and acknowledging one another in a bell jar.

3

Once they were alone, Irene began to talk about the latest case over which her wise judge had presided in court that afternoon. A convicted rapist had committed rape again after being released from prison. It was an open-and-shut case, but the defense attorney played dirty: why, then, had she gotten into his car, why had she gotten into the car in the dead of night? Irene Anderson's face flushed with an intern's righteous anger: they couldn't convict him, she said with flushed cheeks, the woman was raped and humiliated in the bargain. Juries . . . she said, juries can be downright blind sometimes. Gregor knew that the jury wasn't blind. Neither was Irene. But decent people in America, and especially not decent people, but liberal people, artistic people in the American South never speak about it. The jury could see full well who was standing before it: a black man. Irene was a liberal and so were her artist friends. Whenever she spoke about cases in court, she never mentioned an offender's or a criminal's skin color. There were no black people in her circle of artist friends, except maybe a jazz musician around carnival time, but nothing disparaging was ever said about blacks. In fact, nothing was said at all about that unfortunate skin color— this was something rednecks did. Nor did the jury speak about it. But what was unspeakable was evident—the rapist was a black man. If, in the dead of night, the woman had gotten into a car with a black man, a slightly drunk one, and, what was now obvious, a slightly dangerous one just released from prison, then she must have known what could happen to her. The jury wasn't blind; it was strict. What kind of woman would get into a car in the middle of the night with a man who was so obviously like that. The jury made its judgment on the basis of its unspoken moral instinct.

4

They will never admit that what happened that Monday night was actually a rape. Human relations are so immeasurably complex that even the closest people can never tell each other everything, to the last detail. Never! With an exclamation mark, dear Fred. Even when they would like to tell each other everything, something is left unsaid. Of course, you can do away with modesty, you can elevate banality into joy and pleasure, and you can drive out the moral and civilizing aspects, but there will always be a hidden thought that can't be told. Even Gumbo the art photographer, the inventor, the philosopher of real life, knows this: even the actors in porno-graphic productions don't give everything they've got, and possibly less than anyone else. The hidden, blurry thought that is triggered in an instant and bends the will, the body, entire value systems: everything—that thought becomes clear only later, once it is safe and unspeakable again. The thought that is never spoken, only realized.

Gregor Gradnik will never admit that everything in his being decided on that direction, on the direction that led to Irene Anderson, at the moment when his esteemed colleague Fred Blaumann said: supposedly she isn't entirely loyal to him. To Peter, the bicycling writer. Fred added nothing to that, and Gregor never pursued it with him. After all, this was a thor-oughly decent group of people. Even though they led an artis-tic life, even though they lost their heads around the time of the magical holiday called Mardi Gras—which is to say that they led an even more intensely artistic life—what happened to Gregor Gradnik then could never happen to them. They were carefully insulated against falls of that nature. They would never frequent a bar like Rigby's, although no one, of course, would have anything against it. The artistic scene is nothing if not democratic. Sunday-morning evangelists were the same sort of nonsense as pornography. You might smoke some grass at a party, but drug addiction was associated with violence and every conceivable social ill. A person's marginal impulses were always hedged with *supposedly* or *quite.* Once, when they drove past a Catholic college as uniformed girls poured out of it, Fred managed a comment about moral brakes that supposedly produced *overwhelming reactions,* but he went that far and no farther—the comment was left hang-ing in midair. Among the artistic crowd in which she moved because of Peter Diamond's artistic calling, Irene lived quite freely within carefully defined, invisible boundaries. Some newcomer from Eastern Europe had transgressed that boundary. If before he had only approached, now he had transgressed it in a way that wasn't quite decent. On the same day that Peter Diamond left for New York, he came to visit her in the evening and borrowed the famous bicycle. They had sat in the twilight, drinking Diamond's favorite whiskey. The scent of transgression had been in the air. It wasn't just unfair in the sense that no one from the artistic crowd would have done it. It was indecent and it was transgressive. It was cunning, in the way a wolf stalks a lone animal lagging from the herd, letting it know from the start that it's here and waiting for a moment of weakness. That evening in the apartment of the bicycling writer, who had minutes before called from New York, there was the scent of violation, of the convergence of human physical force which Irene Anderson knew so well from court.

5

And when someone at last turns off the idiot box, when the shouting stops, and the slapping of blows, the shouting of the crowd, and the howling of the announcer, and when the only sound in the half-empty restaurant is the clanking of utensils from the kitchen, in the sudden, empty silence the world grows even narrower and tenser. Gregor knows that he must say something absolutely trivial in order to defuse the heavy things bearing down on them like the sediments of Dalmatian red wine.

"Oysters," he says. "Oristide hit Odette on account of oysters."

Is it trivial enough? It is: Irene looks at him with interest. Insignificant things interest women when the significant ones start to get as heavy as Dalmatian wine.

"Because she was crying," he says, "that's why he hit her. And when she started to cry even more, he felt sorry for her. He tried to find a way to get her to laugh. And he came upon the excellent idea of founding a school of creative laughter."

Irene liked this. This was almost as good as discreet garlic. It was American. And it was almost artistic.

Then a bass clarinet floated by from somewhere and started a jazz theme, and instruments one after the other picked it up and wove it into a blurry, polyphonic whole.

"This music," she said, "is like some car driving down a totally empty road toward Barataria Bay."

That's where the bayous are, that was where they had driven. It occurred to Gregor that no one at home would ever say it like that. Ana might possibly say that it was *like birds darting over the swamp reeds*. Or maybe she wouldn't; maybe only he would say that, if he was with her. Ana is in Ljubljana, sleeping in front of the droning television. He wondered if Irene had thought of Peter. Peter was in New York, writing a new bicyclist's book.

"Shall we go now?"

"Where?"

"18 St. Philip Street."

"Let's drink another glass of wine."

She said this during a pause in a slow jazz fugue, the kind they play in Storyville at three in the morning. The sentence was clear, or at least probable. Credible, she might say as a lawyer. Probable, he thought, it was in fact a highly probable supposition that they weren't completely just animals running to the zoo, hooked up to stereo headsets. It's probable that this slow, black music gets under our skin, too, and gets at the heart, the runner's pump. Maybe sometimes we're also like birds darting over a swamp. Even though that's not the issue now. The issue now, put bluntly, is that the goal is fixed and the world has narrowed to the point where it can't go any farther, and it has to be split apart.

CHAPTER 14

THE LETTER Ž

I

"What letter is that?"

"Ž," he said, "that's the letter Ž."

She sat at the desk and inspected the typewriter with exaggerated interest. She struck the key for the letter Ž, as though expecting some special sound from it, a special tone that she'd never heard, probably something muted. Then she picked the letter Č.

"Č," he said, "Gregorčič."

"Gregorčič," she repeated.

She tried the letter Č with the middle finger of her left hand. The letter Č churred out into the heavy air. Both of them were tipsy. Why do we say tipsy, ah? he thought. Why don't we say drunk? We say that, too, but we also say tipsy. When we're soused. Soused, then tipsy. Ah, aren't we something special, he thought with satisfaction, as though he were the owner of Drago's Restaurant. We've got the letter Č, we've got words like *obronek* and *tolmun*—hillside, pool—which nobody else has, we say: the two of us are soused. This part he said out loud in Slovene. She repeated it. There was room here for words like that: *tolmun*, he said. And she repeated. There wasn't space here for jazz fugues. That clarinet had called out for a huge, lost space, for a car on an empty road, for birds over the bayous of the great river's backwaters. Or for an empty auditorium at three in the morning, when someone strikes a piano key or suddenly speaks up and sings. Here there was room for the letter Č, for a *tolmun* (a pool) it could go plop into. The small room was filled with physicality, with one body touching itself, the other, breathing itself, the other.

"And why has it got that hook at the top?"

"Because it's the letter Č."

"That's the only reason?"

"That's the only reason."

A copy of Peter's bicycling book lay on the shelf. His picture was on the dust jacket. Next to the famous bicycle, in a dark suit and wearing a bow tie. This, everyone said, this had been brilliantly provocative. Gradnik had never understood why it should be provocative. He covered the book with a newspaper. He went into the kitchen and uncorked a bottle of wine. Gregor Samsa was strolling across the table and took his time hiding in his hole. When he returned, Irene was still busy with letters with hooks on them.

"What are you going to call the book you're writing?"

"I don't know, I'm not writing anything."

"Writers always write. Even when they're eating oysters."

That was true. After all, she knew, or should know. She lived with a writer: his typewriter was sitting just a few blocks from here, and here was his book, covered with today's *Picayune*.

She cracked her knuckles like a pianist before a concert, bent over the typewriter, thought for a moment, then raised her head—that chin!—closed her eyes and typed with professional speed:

Now is the time to write the great American novel. First sentence: Č Č Č Č Č Č. Now is the time for all good men and women to come to the aid of their Ž Ž Ž Ž Ž Ž. And furthermore: Š Š Š Š Š Š.

He found this mysterious message in his typewriter the

next morning, and he put it in a folder. Maybe one day, in some far-off country, it would find a place in some literary museum.

And furthermore:

2

They aren't penetrating eyes, and they aren't probing eyes—this is simply the confused look of light blue, almost gray eyes, a look both confused and persistent, a look that remains fixed, doesn't flee, a look containing the leaden weight of confusion. A look that asks what, in fact, is happening, at the same time as it happens. In a creative-writing program they'd call it a foggy look; a moist look, as Fred B. might describe it. Its supple lead, the lead of warm fatigue and ever more forceful heartbeats. A flush of blood originating in spleen. Here are the trembling, damp hands, the hands really damp, here is a sudden, revealing flush in the cheeks. Here is the release of warmth on this hot March night, under the huge, birdlike wings of the ceiling fan; the release of pure human lust, made incandescent by this fixed gaze. The growth and softening of bodily tissues resulting from the trigger power of that gaze, of the hidden, internal triggers just above the stomach, and of spleen. Here is the touch of bodies before they've even touched, followed by the sticky touch of damp hands, the adhesive, damp warmth that surges over dry lips, then moist lips. Here is that melancholy matter that hovers in space and in bodies, like an invisible, organic substance. Here are its melancholic vapors that cause both weakness and acuity at once. Here is the pressure in the stomach, the convulsive pressure in the chest, and in the next instant its relaxation. Here is the heart, its soft, emotional plasma, at the same time its beating, the drumming of drums in the night, blows against the taut skin of the heart-drum.

Here is where they stand facing each other, where they lie down without breaking their gaze for an instant. Here comes that state where melancholy matter, rising from the spleen, fills space and soul and body. Where, at the first touch, at full contact, the heart and with it the body trembles and doesn't stop trembling even as damp hands in the humid night slide across skin, across an entire, sweaty body, where lips adhere to neck, where with quick, tremulous movements hands remove delicate fabrics.

But that confused gaze, wandering over the unfamiliar territory of his eyes, that lost gaze is suddenly frightened, some terror suddenly inhabits it, she has discovered something in back of his eyes, some dangerous place, and her gaze breaks free from its bondage. What is this, she says, what are you doing, she says and draws away. His greedy hands can't stop, they reach for her, and what's even worse, he clasps them together, as though pleading with her. I'm afraid, she says. Now, he says, now. You've got to. You've got to. I'm afraid of you, she says, the way you look at me. Why do you look at me that way? You've got to, he says, we've got to now. You're forcing me, she says. But I'm not forcing you, I'm not. I'm not forcing you, he says, we've gone too far. His panting is audible, he tries to breathe normally, but the panting resounds in her ear. We can't go back, he says. What is this, she says. What is all of this suddenly? She tries to get up, but he pulls her back. He looks at her, and now their eyes are locked together again. He can feel that he's started to chain her again. The fear doesn't vanish, but it gives way to her former confusion. Her pupils dart around, still looking for an escape, but their bodies are together, unrestrainably together, plunged into unrestraint, into amorphous matter.

3

Fade out. Screenwriters write *fade out* in places like this, which means that the camera wanders over the skin, across the *epidermis* for a few more seconds, takes in the moving bodies, a fragment, pauses on the face and the eyes staring off someplace. Fade out. Memory loss. And then he hears running water from the bathroom, and a crack of light falls diagonally onto the bed. He starts up and opens the door. Irene is standing under the shower, her soaked hair falling in hanks over her forehead. She throws her hair back and looks at him. I'm going, she says. You're not going now. I am, she says. She looks at him for a moment and then continues dousing herself: I've got to. You can't. What time is it? It doesn't matter, come back to bed.

Then she comes back with a cool, clean body and wet hair.

"What have you done?" she says into space. "What have you done to me?"

"We. What have we done."

All the rest is just the letter Ž: unutterable.

4

Ž, he said, *želja:* desire.

She tried it, like a tongue twister: *žel-ja.*

Želenje. Poželenje. Desire, yearning.

The Slovene words had a strange effect. They were conspiratorial, fascinating.

Djal, he said, looking for some crude word. *Dol te bom djal.* I'm gonna lay you. At least I suspect I will.

What are you saying?

It seemed brazen, but also suddenly dangerous, in this place. And inescapable.

5

There are thousands of minute apertures through which a penetrating gaze can reach the human soul. She resisted. She was genuinely afraid of something. There were elements of rape in this *prima nox.* Of violence and submission. Suddenly the world was more complicated. In court a decision has to be made. Rape either occurred or it didn't. Often, however, the truth lies somewhere in between. The mere existence of that possibility made Irene Anderson, court apprentice, nearly apoplectic. How many times did she and her gray-haired judge exchange despairing glances when it became apparent that an obvious rapist would have to be let free? The defense attorneys knew all the weak spots in detail. *A hint, unspoken consent;* they were adept at building a whole system around some insignificant mistake the woman made in her stammering testimony. And the desperate victims, who virtually had to be dragged into court, where they would have to submit to still further humiliation in cross-examination, often tried in vain to prove that *that* wasn't what they had meant, but that they had meant what they had said . . . *coffee at my place, a night drive.* Ultimately, Irene had once said, if you go by any aggressive lawyer's reasoning, every woman in this town is the very soul of a New Orleans slave, calling the master's might down on herself. These people, she shouted, think that a woman wants nothing in life so much as a nice, painless rape. The conviction of some male chauvinist pigs, as one left-leaning magazine wrote, that women enjoy rape at least a little bit was so widespread that it wasn't worth the trouble to talk about.

The acid test that her beloved judge used was clear, and this was indeed the question that he always asked: did it happen against her will? And was it just Irene Anderson, and no one else, who couldn't say whether it had happened with her consent or without it? Hadn't she stopped to think for an instant: what am I doing? Hadn't she thought of Peter's book, which Gregor had clumsily covered with a newspaper? Even if she thought just that and said *no,* even if she had just said *no* on account of Peter's book lying on the table, then it had been against her will. She didn't dare to think beyond that. Past that point were the dark regions. The man she had slept with was a stranger, in fact. Who knows where he came from? There was something in his eyes, something dangerous, something violent. Who did he keep company with over there? Maybe he had even been in prison; in eastern countries people often get sent to prison. Didn't he keep company here with people capable of any crime? Didn't he spend time with the kind of people that appear daily in court and whose body language, words, and looks ineluctably betrayed their own violent tempers? Did she think he would hit her? There was that possibility in his eyes. She had said something, she had spoken his name, matter-of-factly, although that night had been anything but matter-of-fact for her. But the time to resist, if she meant to resist, had come much earlier, long before that. Of course she knew that his visit, that evening when Peter left, to pick up Peter's bicycle was a brazen, transgressive act. That was clearly in the air, though it remained unspoken. And then, like any of those bewildered women who tell the court that they didn't know, that they hadn't thought how it might end—like *any one of them,* and no differently, she went to his apartment. But what happened later? Why did she later, when everything in her resisted, when she thought of Peter's book and his picture lying on the table, why did she then get out of the shower at his simple command and lie down beside him again? There wasn't a judge in the world who would believe that her rapist had forced her into bed by a simple command and that she was forced to submit to him a third time, in broad daylight. That she had been late for work and had walked around all day in a daze. Had she perhaps wondered sometimes during court cases how a woman might really feel in that situation? What had she wanted to find out? Why had it happened? What was all this, anyway? She was in love with Peter. Peter was in New York. She'd go join him. Irene Anderson was at a complete loss. A complete loss. She felt abject, ridiculous, inadequate to her profession or to living with an artist like Peter Diamond.

This was why she didn't answer the phone the next evening while it rang mercilessly. She didn't want to talk to anyone. Not to Peter, and not to that person who hung around Professor Blaumann one day, some idiot housemate another, and some *dubious characters* the next. Not to anyone.

This is what Gregor Gradnik thought as he dialed her phone number in vain. From home. From a pay phone outside. From Rigby's Bar, where he sat with Martin the next night, dropping coins in the jukebox and tossing ice cubes to Martin's dog. What she was thinking he would never learn. What she knew was precisely what was unspeakable. He sat beside the wide-open door, from where he could see the open window across the street. The fleshy man with tattoos on his shoulder was embracing the blond woman. She dug her elbows into his chest and kept thrusting her head back, so that hanks of her hair flopped around her head. Then Stella leaned her head against his shoulder, drew back her elbows, and hit him on the back with her fist several times. Kowalski opened his mouth to laugh, but he couldn't be heard. He still had all his teeth, although he had put on some weight and his hair was thinner.

■ □ ■ □ ■

CHAPTER 15

A VERY SPECIAL POWDER

I

He could tell that Gumbo was still alive in his lair from the fact that the milk bottles disappeared from outside his door. Also, his mailbox was practically full to bursting with advertising circulars and handbooks in shiny wrappers. It was obvious that he was working on some new business after the failure of his School of Creative Laughter.

For some time only Louisa's laughter had been missing. One morning he saw her as she carried a bag full of empty bottles out of the apartment. She was in tears, her eyes were sad again, and the black mascara was smeared around them and over her cheeks. She smiled at him sadly.

The creative-writing class was nearing its end. The young writers had become self-confident. The science of exclamation marks no longer interested them. Fred Blaumann knew this phase: now he had to let them go. Let them speak. They dissected each other's texts mercilessly. Souls crammed full of words flowed from their pens. Stylistic turns, analyses, the blank challenge of paper crying to be written on. Have it read aloud. Talk about it, all night if necessary. Gregor Gradnik watched and listened to them. For a moment he was seized with envy, a gnawing memory—just for an instant—of the time when he was like that himself. Now he wasn't like that anymore. Now he sat in the library, listlessly turning pages.

Copying out verses that troubadours once hammered out beneath balconies:

O God, how enraptured I was . . .
when the wind struck her window
and she recognized me, perhaps.
Good night, she said.
And only God knows how lordly I was that night.

He copied them, put them in an envelope, and, together with some Valentine's kitsch, tossed them up onto the Spanish veranda. The same place where Professor Popescu had delivered his historic peroration and disgorgement. Occasionally he stole snippets of modern poetry . . . about loathing at midnight . . . let us go then, you and I . . . through certain half-deserted streets . . . and sawdust restaurants. . . .

Around nine in the morning the phone finally rang.

"Thanks for the morning greetings."

"Those were night greetings."

"Did you copy that, too?"

"As ever."

"Still, thanks. I really do appreciate it."

"Not enough. Not enough."

"I'm terribly busy. Sorry."

She was very busy. She stopped. New York was getting closer, and Peter was closer all the time. Her gray-haired judge wanted to have her around constantly.

2

Now that there were no more preparations and the creative thing at the university was running on its own steam: soul—pen—word, now he could spend whole mornings on the waterfront, watching the steamships with tourists and the heavy tankers that fed the fat continent's innards.

Something is bothering me, he wrote to Ana, *something haunts me.* Maybe it's you, he meant to add, maybe it's the total absence of your voice, your hair, your body. Maybe I'm confusing it with some other voice. After all these months everything had become insubstantial. He wanted to add something essential about *her,* not himself. *I can't write. The library has turned into a loathsome place for me, a prison cell. The letters are like ants. I'm tempted to kick the computer, tear down the bookshelf, throw a trayful of food on the floor, something like that.* But this still wasn't about her. Slowly he ripped up the postcard, shoveled the pieces with his hand into a heap, and threw them into the brown water.

Some pipes blew from a clumsy river steamer, probably a pipe organ run on steam. A steam organ, who ever heard of such a thing? It reminded him of some folk instrument, of hollow reeds bound together. Who do you suppose had ever heard of a reed pipe? What do you say, America? Reed pipe! The sounds of the organ floated, hurdy-gurdylike, over the roofs of the Quarter, luring morning loafers from their streets. In the Café du Monde a telescope had been set up, around which customers crowded and cheered. He had never looked through it. Sunspots, volcanic eruptions of energy on the sun, blisters on its surface, that from here looked like spots. And that influenced the tides. People, too. The earth's magnetic poles, the swirling of magnetism at the northern and southern poles. Dear God, how full of himself man is, see what all he knows and what sorts of things interest him. Poles that attract and repel at the same time. Which can cause the wavering of a car's speedometer. That can make a magnetic needle flicker weirdly, and then a person doesn't even know what really happened on a given night. And what does it all mean, anyway?

3

"With cream? Café au lait?"

Gumbo hadn't just taught her how to laugh. A bright smile from his School of Creative Laughter. He also taught her French. Louisa is back working at the Café du Monde.

And she's laughing again. Sometimes she also cries. Sometimes shouts come from their room. Her tears and laughter alternate like showers and sun in New Orleans. White slippers, white stockings barely up over the ankles, tiny calves, round and slightly red kneecaps, thighs covered halfway by a red skirt, a cord belt, small white breasts beneath her white T-shirt, thin, smiling lips and eyes and freckles—Irene's freckles, Louisa's freckles—visible without a telescope on both sides of her upturned nose, Slavic, as they say.

"Not going to the library today?"

"No. It's nicer here."

"Black or with cream?"

"Black, black."

"Libraries are for cockroaches."

"That's right. For bookworms."

Louisa doesn't know that libraries don't have cockroaches, they have bookworms.

"Do you know what bookworms are called?"

"Oristide knows."

"Oh, for sure. They're called *Periplaneta Americana*."

"Americana? Is that Spanish?"

Louisa laughs again. That's funny, that's like *cucaracha*, which is a cockroach. Latin is Spanish, Gumbo is Oristide, all night long he makes her cry, all night long he makes her laugh, tears are laughter, cockroaches are worms, libraries are coffeeshops, sunspots are freckles. The steam organ intones, the *Natchez* wheezes and slowly puts out to sea. In the middle of the river the huge wheel starts to turn faster, the boat slowly sets about, the current pulls at its bow, and it quickly sets off downstream.

4

That night cats yowled.

Half-asleep, he heard something that at first sounded like a child whimpering. The music from the bar across the street had stopped, and now something outside was sobbing and moaning. At first it was subdued and gasping, then it grew in volume, turning into long, drawn-out howls. He went to the window and turned off the noisy air conditioner. She was quietly perched on the roof of a car, while he paced up and down the sidewalk. He jumped up on the hood and an instant later landed next to her with feline lissomeness. A moment of silence as he approached her, followed by more howls. A wild midnight courtship. The pain of desire amid the Vieux Carré, the home of desire. Someone opened a window and said something in a raspy voice. The animals didn't even move. Finally the insomniac lost his temper and hurled a bottle of milk at them, which hit the street and burst. Only now did the black seducer and his siren companion jump off the car and go running side by side into the night.

He turned on the light in the kitchen and caught a glimpse of Gregor Samsa. He was scurrying away with his flat thorax, stopping for a moment, then vanishing into a narrow crack beneath the cupboard. Humidity invisibly permeated the room. His limbs felt heavy and the black tar in his blood was coagulating. He turned the air conditioner back on. Then came a commotion from the hallway, followed by a knock at the door.

"Gumbo, ya-ya," it said.

He opened the door.

"Did you hear the cats?" Gumbo said. He was dressed in pajama bottoms, drops of sweat glistening on his forehead. He looked tired, sleepless. His eyelids were swollen from insomnia. But his eyes! His eyes shone with feverish excitement. He didn't wait for an answer.

"That was fantastic," he enthused. "They're in heat."

He had to come with him, right now. It stank in his tiny living room. But not of neglect or sloth, and not of alcohol.

"I've sent Louisa to her friend's house," he explained in passing. "When I'm creating, I can't stand any interruptions."

The stench was from chemicals, and it was infernally hot.

The room was full of bottles, test tubes, and distilling equipment. Something bubbled and steamed in the kitchen, and the traces of various fluids led into the bathroom. Alchemy. A real *Theatrum Chemicum.*

5

Gumbo, what an infantile fantast.

He picked up a rag and nervously wiped his forehead and hands. Then, rag in hand, he gestured triumphantly at the room and said, "Poudre de Perlainpainpain."

It was obvious to Gregor that some new school or night courses were going to be held here.

"Powder of what?"

"Perlainpainpain."

When Gumbo has a pocketful of dollars, then Gregor would understand. Then he would invite him and Martin and *tante* Onesia and all the rest to Storyville. When the Dirty Dozen would play through the night for him and all the rest—about a hundred guests, when they would eat gumbo and jambalaya, rice and beans and oysters, then he would understand. And that's when Gomez would understand, too, because this was the end of all that business with penetrations and distributing photographs.

"This powder," he said and took a pinch of the brownish-white substance from a plate, "this powder is going to change life in this city. Maybe all over America."

There wasn't going to be any school, and there wouldn't be any lessons, either. And this time he didn't have Europe in his sights, at least not for now. Gumbo looked at him, his eyes feverish and his mouth open.

"You don't understand. I didn't think you would." He carefully shook the powder back onto the plate. "Did you hear the cats wailing? Why do they wail?"

"They're mating."

"That's right, they're mating. But when two of them are mating there shouldn't be any need to howl so loud, should there? They're howling because she won't let him. The she-cat won't let him. And she won't, because she knows that once she does, she'll lose him. He'll use her and then beat it. That's how life is, my friend. She'll be left high and dry among the trash cans. And it's the same way with people, isn't it?"

"It happens sometimes, yeah."

"Not sometimes. Always. Unless she holds onto him. That's it. Unless she holds onto him; then it's a different story. If Louisa had held onto that guy, she wouldn't be crying so much. The guy was a jerk. He used her, a waitress, poor Slavic soul."

Gregor knew this. It seemed wise to keep quiet. Apparently Louisa also thought it wisest.

"How long do you suppose she waited for that jerk? At the Lafitte she'd cry at the bar night after night. And when a woman cries it just tears my heart to pieces. That's when I get my ideas. When my sister cried, I got an idea. When Louisa cried on account of that louse, I got another one. That's Gumbo for you. I said, Louisa, listen to me, if you'd had the powder that *tante* Onesia had, you could have kept that louse; and not only that, he'd be running after you. Then, of course, she wouldn't know me from Adam anymore. What kind of powder, Louisa said. Perlainpainpain, I said. I saw with my own eyes how *tante* Onesia suffered. *Jamais!* she shouted like a person possessed. *Jamais I see him again!* She was about to throw herself to the alligators on account of the jerk who's her husband now. And she would have done it. If it hadn't been for *poudre de Perlainpainpain.*"

Gumbo wiped his sweaty forehead with the rag. He turned on the faucet and put his head under the cold running water.

"A woman who wants to hold onto a man takes *poudre de Perlainpainpain* and rubs it into his clothes."

The plan clearly wasn't such a bad one. In the Vieux Carré there were at least several thousand women who cried at bars or wanted to throw themselves to the alligators. If each of them bought just one package of the powder—and it was entirely probable that they would buy more—and if each package cost just a dollar, then . . . Then Oristide wouldn't have any trouble hiring Storyville and the Dirty Dozen and inviting Aunt Onesia and sister Odette and all the rest.

There would be some problems with production, Gumbo complained. Poudre de Perlainpainpain was made from the blossoms of a floating thistle that was found in the swamps of Bayou Country. Seventeen seeds had to be plucked from it in windy weather. The lower part was removed, and the upper part had to be cut with beeswax, covered with clover leaves, and then carefully mixed with three grains of a bean that had been buried under salt for three days. Then you had to add three dashes of salt from a black thimble, mix the whole thing, and use it. And it worked. *Tante* Onesia was proof. He had stopped being *infidèle*.

Beneath their swollen lids Gumbo's clear eyes glanced from the powder to him. Now that he had doused himself, the sweat ran down his temples even faster, streaming through the hair on his chest and over his great belly.

"Gumbo, you can't possibly believe that."

"Does it matter if I believe? *Tante* Onesia believes. And she's the most distrustful woman there is down there. And if she believes, then who wouldn't? Maybe they'll think to themselves *this is stupid,* but they'll try it even so.

Gregor wetted his finger and tried the powder.

"It's kind of salty . . . And floury."

Gumbo was insulted.

"Perlainpainpain isn't for eating. It isn't some spice. And besides, it's made syn-the-tic-ally. Where do you expect me to get so many thistle blossoms?"

"Then it's a fake, Gumbo. It isn't going to work."

"Are photos fakes?" he shouted. "They're the original and a counterfeit all at once. Only the negative is original. And it isn't, really, because it's a *negative.* The first one is just as effective as the thirtieth. Believe me, it'll work."

Gregor admitted that photographs were also made in laboratories. The same as Gumbo would be manufacturing his love powder *initially* from the right ingredients, but after that synthetically.

Then the two of them went to Rigby's to put together the text of an advertisement. They came home in the morning. When he got up, Gregor saw Louisa on the other side of the street tearing off scotch tape with her teeth and taping a poster to the door of the bar:

> *Unhappy? Has love left you?*
> *Poudre de Perlainpainpain*
> *Can help.*
> *Also instructions for Use! Free!*
> *GUMBO & LOUISE*
> *18 St. Philip St.*

A good-looking young blond man walked gracefully out of the bar. He stood in front of the poster for a long time. He looked around and then quickly wrote something down.

O Gumbo, o sorceror Oristide! Alchemist in search of melancholy matter. *Homo faber, artifex maximus,* for whom the world is one huge *Theatrum Chemicum.* A world of limitless, magical possibilities.

CHAPTER 16

SNUG HARBOUR

I

In those days the very best jazz was in a bar on Frenchmen Street called Snug Harbour. The blond student in his creative-writing class had discovered her inspiration here. One day she brought to class a whole collection of poetry with that title. These were poems of refuge, of a safe, unending embrace, no one was unhappy and no one stood beneath balconies. They were antitroubadour poems, happy poems, poems of a warm nest. Every Sunday evening at Snug Harbour featured Ellis Marsalis, a tall, black piano virtuoso, and Lady BJ sang.

At Snug Harbour something happened to Irene Anderson. Or maybe it had happened before. Suddenly she made up her mind. Suddenly, that evening she was no longer *hopelessly busy.* I've got loads and loads of time, she said. And she would like to hear Marsalis. With you, she said. Something had happened with her, because suddenly she was completely changed. They listened to Marsalis and Lady BJ. They drank Beaujolais. Not the real kind, but from California. The place was full of bodies moving in time with the rhythm, and hands clapping with the rhythm. When she left to powder her nose, he shook some *poudre de Perlainpainpain* into her glass. Maybe that's what did it. Maybe it was the way Marsalis kept shoving his glasses as they slid down his nose, the way he droned as he played, or the crazy, totally crazy way he played. She put a metal object in his hands. It was a lighter. The kind for lighting cigarettes. For blowing smoke up in the air after jogging. This happened while Lady BJ was singing like a prima donna at the Salzburg Festival. Look at what it says, she said. He looked at what it said. A word, a single word, was engraved on the lighter. It read: AGAIN.

She was leaning in a dark corner of the balcony and looking into his eyes, motionlessly. Her blue irises were foggy, but they glistened. For the first time he wondered whether she wore contact lenses. He asked whether she wore them, and it turned out that she did. But they didn't hurt her eyes at all. Cigarette smoke didn't bother her; her lungs seemed to take everything in: his gaze, the music, the wine, the smoke. Someone improvised on the piano, then a throaty voice sang:

> *I love you once,*
> *I love you twice,*
> *I love you next to beans and rice.*

He tried to remember. Before he'd left on this trip, someone had told him about rice and beans. That had been somewhere else, long ago and far away. He was no longer an observer. Now he was here, unmistakably here. Only now.

2

What's wrong with you, Gumbo asked. It's the powder, Gregor answered. Perlainpainpain. It's working.

Give me some more of it, I'm going to put some more in her glass.

The wet stuff that the wind brought up the river spread out into every street and dwelling. A warm, grainy rain poured out and then vanished after a few minutes. It left behind thick, humid air, making bodies lazy and thought processes slow. A hot steam descended on the city. They lay in bed in his apartment, all wet. After that evening at Snug Harbour all of her inhibitions had suddenly given way. Something crazy was coursing out of her. Again. She would come to visit him in midmorning, leave her car on the sidewalk, get into bed, and within an hour or two go back to court. And again. One evening they sat at the Two Sisters and watched the delight-fully tasteless commingling of rainbow colors in the fountain. And then to bed again. They never went to her apartment. That meant that this sudden insanity would just as suddenly stop. Gregor could sense this clearly, the temporariness of it all. As though that ridiculous powder of Gumbo's was really working. The effect of which was about to wear off.

But for now she was here. She talked about her sister, who had married when she was eighteen and had been rotting in comfort up in Indiana for ten years now. At the bend of some river. Every day she watched the barges on it. Steamships were long gone. Nowadays people traveled by plane, or by train at the least. It was only here the steamships still carried tourists. If the *Natchez* were to steam past up there, there would be nothing that could stop her sister. She called her every week to tell her she was going to drop everything and come join her. But she would never do it. At the most, she—Irene—would some day return to the quiet town where she belonged. But only when she was an old woman. Before then she would go to New York. Soon.

Gregor would return somewhere, too. One day he would disappear from this boundless continent. The movable dot down here on its soft geographic underbelly would be nowhere to be found. And no one would know it had ever been here. Suddenly he would be back home, where he belonged, among people that were his own kind. Living in some valley of suicides that would disappear someday, too. And the whole nation with it. Had she ever heard of the Lan-gobards? They were extinct, only the name remained. Like some animal that's born and wanders off somewhere, every trace of it gets lost and no one realizes it had ever lived. That's how it was with him. That's how it was with her. But now they were together. Unmistakably for the time being, for this instant together.

<h3 style="text-align:center">3</h3>

Lovers, but also those who only think they're in love, tell each other their business. Stories from their families, stories about their friends, stories about cities. This isn't just an effort at building trust, an attempt at generosity, it's also a somewhat narcissistic effort: at leaving a mark on one's surroundings. At creating a broader picture of oneself, at duplicating one's narrow world. Creating a group portrait with a background. The narrator, of course, stands out markedly in the picture. And the picture acquires a new dimension—depth.

They had to be careful in choosing subjects. Peter, whom they had both deceived, wasn't a good one. The conversation always got stuck here. Even his bicycle, which Gregor used to explore the city outskirts every day, invoked a bad conscience for both of them. Ana was far off, but her letters were always lying around someplace, her voice entered the room by telephone and hovered in the air. Their stories from Indiana and Slovenia were fictions. The only real world was here. A world reduced, depopulated, islandlike, and temporary. Part of the real world that till now had filled their lives was irreparably missing for each of them. The living, existing part of the world that was in New York and over there on the other side of the ocean.

One night he woke up to find her sitting on the edge of the bed. Her shoulders were heaving. It's no good, she said. It's no good. She can't stand feeling shut out. This is almost criminal. It won't do, it just won't do.

An awareness of the provisional nature of it all constantly came between them. This is why she talked about her sister and her town in Indiana. This is why he talked about his suicidal tribe. These were the most intimate things that each of them could rip out of their living images of the world and

Preface or Introduction. *Subsect.* 1.

Love's definition, Pedigree, Object, Fair, Amiable, Gracious and Pleasant, from which comes Beauty, Grace, which all desire and love, parts affected.

Division or kinds, *Subs.* 2. — *or*

Natural, in things without life, as love and hatred of elements; and with life, as vegetal, vine and elm, sympathy, antipathy, &c.

Sensible, as of Beasts, for pleasure, preservation of kind, mutual agreement, custom, bringing up together, &c.

Rational —

Simple, which hath three objects, as *Memb.* 1. — *or*

Profitable, *Subs.* 1. { Health, wealth, honour, we love our benefactors: nothing so amiable as profit, or that which hath a shew of commodity.

Pleasant, *Subs.* 2. { Things without life, made by art, pictures, sports, games, sensible objects, as hawks, hounds, horses. Or men themselves for similitude of manners, natural affections, as to friends, children, kinsmen, &c., for glory, such as commend us.

Of women, as { Before marriage, as *Heroical Mel. Sect.* 2. *vide* ♈. / Or after marriage, as *Jealousy, Sect.* 3. *vide* ♉

Honest, *Subs.* 3. { Fucate in shew, by some error or hypocrisy; some seem and are not; or truly for virtue, honesty, good parts, learning, eloquence, &c.

Mixed of all three, which extends to *Memb.* 3.

Common good, our neighbour, country, friends, which is charity; the defect of which is cause of much discontent and Melancholy.

or { God, *Sect.* 4. { In excess, *vide* Π. / In defect, *vide* ℥.

Memb. 1.

His pedigree, power, extent to vegetals and sensible creatures as well as men, to spirits, devils, &c.

His name, definition, object, part affected, tyranny.

Causes, *Memb.* 2.

Stars, temperature, full diet, place, country, clime, condition, idleness. *Subs.* 1.

Natural allurements, and causes of love, as beauty, its praise, how it allureth.

Comeliness, grace, resulting from the whole, or some parts, as face, eyes, hair, hands, &c. *Subs.* 2.

Artificial allurements, and provocations of lust and love, gestures, apparel, dowry, money, &c.

Quest. Whether beauty owe more to Art or Nature? *Subs.* 3.

Opportunity of time and place, conference, discourse, musick, singing, dancing, amorous tales, lascivious objects, familiarity, gifts, promises, &c. *Subs.* 4.

Bawds and Philters. *Subs.* 5.

Symptoms or signs, *Memb.* 3.

Of Body { Dryness, paleness, leanness, waking, sighing, &c. / Quest. *An detur pulsus amatorius?*

or

Of Mind. { Bad, as { Fear, sorrow, suspicion, anxiety, &c. / An hell, torment, fire, blindness, &c. / Dotage, slavery, neglect of business. / or Good, as { Spruceness, neatness, courage, aptness to learn musick, singing, dancing, poetry, &c.

Prognosticks; Despair, Madness, Phrensy, Death. *Memb.* 4.

Cures, *Memb.* 5.

By labour, diet, Physick, abstinence. *Subs.* 1.

To withstand the beginnings, avoid occasions, fair and foul means, change of place, contrary passion, witty inventions, discommend the former, bring in another. *Subs.* 2.

By good counsel, persuasion, from future miseries, inconveniences, &c. *Subs.* 3.

By Philters, magical, and poetical cures. *Subs.* 4.

To let them have their desire disputed *pro* and *con.* Impediments removed, reasons for it. *Subs.* 5.

8 Jealousy, Sect. 3.

His name, definition, extent, power, tyranny. *Memb.* 1.

Division,
Æquivo-
cations,
Kinds,
Subs. 1.

   Improper
     or
   Proper

To many beasts ; as Swans, Cocks, Bulls.
To Kings and Princes, of their subjects, successors.
To friends, parents, tutors over their children, or otherwise.
Before marriage, corrivals, &c.
After, as in this place our present subject.

Causes,
Sect. 2.

In the parties themselves, or from others.

Idleness, impotency in one party, melancholy, long absence.
They have been naught themselves. Hard usage, unkindness, wantonness, inequality of years, persons, fortunes, &c.
Outward enticements and provocations of others.

Symptoms,
Memb. 2.

Fear, sorrow, suspicion, anguish of mind, strange actions, gestures, looks, speeches, locking up, outrages, severe laws, prodigious trials, &c.

Prognosticks,
Memb. 3.

Despair, madness, to make away themselves, and others.

Cures,
Memb. 4.

By avoiding occasions, always busy, never to be idle.
By good counsel, advice of friends, to contemn or dissemble it. *Subs.* 1.
By prevention before marriage. *Plato's* communion.
To marry such as are equal in years, birth, fortunes, beauty, of like conditions, &c.
Of a good family, good education. To use them well.

give to each other. The whole live world went on living its life. The two of them were just a story.

4

It stayed muggy for several days, and then the rain suddenly poured. At first it looked as though it would only be a shower. But the beneficent waters from heaven practically deluged the city. The spring rains are a time when a certain *tristitia* bathes the soul. Blaumann had registered this in the category *Romantic Melancholy.*

The monotonous drumming of the rain changed everything at once. Houses and streets and people. He lay on his bed in the dark half-asleep, sensing the open window, the freshness pouring in through it, and he listened to the rain streaming onto the sidewalk. The voices on the street had long since fallen silent, even the far-off, nightly roar of the city's amusements was no longer to be heard. Tourists stayed in their hotels, and residents of the Quarter crawled into their holes. They lay on their beds or possibly leaned against windows, absorbed in themselves and submerged in the gurgling of rivulets and the trembling of rain on the roofs. A gentle tempest from the heavens, transporting the mind to a state of primitive wonder, of safety, back to the hearth, to the cave, to a state of childlike understanding, the safety of a swallow's nest, of a fox's lair.

That morning in the library he could distinctly sense it was getting dark, although the neon light in the reading room continued to hum. Then he could hear a rumbling, though the library was soundproofed. But when he stepped out into the vestibule he found smiling, drenched students coming in from the campus. They shook their manes like young animals. Drops of rain bounced off the hot asphalt in front of the building. The whole broad expanse was draped in a curtain of rain. Clearly a storm was moving through the city and the sun would return any minute. He drove with Fred along Lake Pontchartrain, where they saw the rain splashing onto the water's brown surface, the wooden houses along the piers swathed in rainy fog, the lonely masts of sailboats at anchor. When it rains like this, Fred said, I feel like . . . I'm at home. Then they were silent. Fred never talked about his home. But it had been said as though the home he had here with Mary and the children suddenly wasn't his home. Or perhaps his home was just his childhood somewhere in Boston . . . But Gregor's *home* was immeasurably farther away than his, something that didn't even occur to Fred. Everyone is from somewhere, everyone has a home someplace, and then everyone finds himself someplace else. The first few weeks everyone treated him like some exotic animal that was experiencing the famous *culture shock,* and it struck him that for them this must be like some kind of electroshock, something he ought to shake off or slay just as soon as the plane landed. Now Fred mentioned only his own home; everyone had a right to think about home and mention it as he saw fit. His business. He dropped him off at Rigby's and remembered how it had poured that day he arrived. How he and Meg ran under the same umbrella. Because *suddenly* he was thinking of home and *suddenly* this home was no longer that.

The rain wouldn't stop. By afternoon whole rivers were rushing down the streets. People kept watch in the doorways of bars and shops, glancing up at the sky. Like cockroaches they thrust their feelers out of their murky shelters. Finally they retreated indoors entirely and took refuge in their apartments. Water rampaged through the streets as though the Mississippi levee had burst, sending the river's brownish-yellow waters flooding through the Quarter and foaming over its sidewalks. Perhaps the ancient memory of the floodwaters that had once rampaged there kept the city in quiet suspense. The word *home* bored its way into Gregor's brain. A stream of water pouring down onto the sidewalk suddenly became the plash of water escaping from the broken gutter of a mountain cabin. Somewhere amid pastures in the Pohorje mountains. A nighttime pastorale with its cool freshness, with resonant channels running from that splash to the clear, silver murmur of a brook, the splashing of a lake, the dark silence of a fountain.

He lay still. Names, gestures, phrases from the library, from printed and written sheets of paper, pastel colors, the peaceful breathing of familiar bodies: all of this came to him now in an indistinguishable mass and retreated, but in such a way that he could sense the details and make out their sharp contours amid the soft presence of it all. Personal memories and learned memories, experience and knowledge of what was, what was just now beginning and what was yet to be, all of that was here. This is now, now, the one and only now. His motionlessness on the bed was in contrast to the movement of the waters all around, the confluence of waters, rain and river, earth and sky. Water was in touch with everything, the river levee was high, but now he had the sense that it was insignificant, it separated nothing, he was both under the water's surface and above it. That which was washing off of roofs and down streets was in contact with the river, the ocean, the continent on the other side of the ocean, with his own rivers and lakes. It no longer mattered at all whether he was here or at home, ten thousand kilometers east or west, north or south, yesterday or today. The Gulf of Mexico and the Adriatic were linked, the mouth of the Mississippi was somewhere near Savudrija, the Soca emptied into the gulf near Biloxi. He was lying here, a fifteenth-century monk lying in his cell, listening to the divine presence, understanding its fragments, and sensing its unity. The painter of the Dance of Death in Hrastovlje huddles under the eaves of the church while the warm rain of the littoral pours onto Istria. He huddles there and can sense the Mediterranean over there somewhere on the other side of the Alps; exhausted from painting all day, with the iridescent figures and colors before his eyes. No matter who, no matter where, no matter when, he'll sense the unity of yesterday, today, and tomorrow, of this or some other space. Similarly the reality of this city, where his life observed other lives, was now spread out over time and space. It evaporated in the drumming of the rain and its cycle of heaven and earth. And the human destinies that were interwoven here, or interwoven there: Ana, Irene, Fred, Meg, Gumbo, himself, everyone else, came and went with the cycles of the rain. And in the end all of them together with their worries would be washed away. The water of being, the water of impermanence.

From the bed he could see an aged Stella pressing her face to the windowpane. Her nose was flattened like a child's, and streams of rain ran past her glassy image, trapped in a prism.

Do nothing. Just lie still. Listen to the drumming of the rain, to the stream of water pouring onto the sidewalk.

■ □ ■ □ ■

CHAPTER 17

VOICES IN THE NIGHT

I

The voice that woke him seemed familiar.

At four in the morning he heard the sound of people talking in the street. A man's voice in clipped sentences, and a woman's voice answering. It got quiet and he tried to go back to sleep, but the man's voice started talking again. Now it was speaking mutedly, in waves, like a somewhat muffled siren. The voice seemed familiar. He tried once more to escape from this nocturnal nuisance back into sleep. But the voices wouldn't stop. The man spoke in long, muffled monologues, while the woman's voice was short interruptions of his flow of speech. He got up and went over to the window. They stood facing each other in the dark space below.

I didn't, she said, I didn't.

Her voice struck him as familiar, too.

He pronounced a name. He said that he'd seen him. I saw him. You didn't, she said, nothing happened, nothing at all. He was here, he said, that jerk. Her ex-boyfriend was a jerk. He wasn't here, she said, nobody's been here. Go inside, he said. She shook her head. He pulled her by the sleeve. She didn't want to go inside. He let go of her. He raised his hands, as though in prayer, and begged her. Then his arms fell to his sides, and for a few moments they stood silently facing each other. The female shadow bowed its head. Instantly, his right hand rose and struck her cheek with a lightning-swift, short twitch. There was a smacking sound, and her hair fell over her forehead. He immediately struck her again. This time she staggered. Both blows followed in such quick succession that at first Gregor didn't understand what was happening. She staggered and grabbed onto a streetlight. Her hair lay like a curtain over her face. The man stepped close to her. Gregor could see his stocky back as he approached. His arms, dangerously calm, hung at his sides. She raised her hands over her head. He stood, waiting for her to drop them. The instant she did, he struck her again. Now the streetlamp illuminated her face. Gregor experienced a flash of unease.

It was Louisa.

She was bent over trying to pick up her bag. It looked like he might kick her in this position.

With his fist he hit her from below, causing her head to fly up and blood to run from her nose. She fell down and picked herself up again. She looked around, as though trying to decide whether to run or call for help. When he hit her, she just moaned softly. Now she was quiet and looking at him. She brushed her hair off her forehead. She may not even have known that her nose was bleeding.

Now he raised a hand to his face. He clasped it to his forehead and groaned, and his shoulders started shaking. Gregor recognized that groan.

It was Gumbo. He was beating Louisa in the middle of the street.

He wanted to open the window and get involved. He was shaking all over. He wanted to run out on the street and stop him. He wanted to grab him by the undershirt and shake him, like he'd done once before. But Gumbo was groaning and his shoulders were shaking. There was a stubble on his face. Gregor pulled his trousers on with shaking hands. Of course, the trousers were just a coward's excuse: he didn't have to take action *immediately.*

Louisa stepped over to the round shadow. Slowly, she raised her hand to his face and stroked him. Gumbo turned around abruptly and stepped quickly inside. Gregor could hear the outside door being unlocked. Slowly, she followed him. He could hear her sliding down the hall. Across the street someone closed a window. Somebody else had been silently watching the nighttime spectacle.

Poor Louisa. Now the good angel had really abandoned her.

2

The good angel of laughter, as every good angel, is invisibly submerged in two, in the dual. It can also be in one, he can also be with a single one, just with Louisa and no one else. He's never a third. The world is for two and for the good angel with them; three is a crowd. The good angel never goes with the plural. The plural is the ill-bringing third. The plural is not good; the dual is good. Still worse than the plural are the multitudes. Multitudes, thy name is Satan. Slovene is the most beautiful language, because it has the dual. The dual is beautiful, the dual is cozy, the dual is Snug Harbour. In English and every other language you have to specify the dual, in Slovene it comes of its own accord: we-two slept, we-two had breakfast. The dual excludes third parties; in the dual Louisa's boyfriend, the jerk, and the landlord, also a jerk, are nowhere to be found. *My back ached when we-two fell asleep on the grass,* Ana writes. Because two-together fall asleep on the grass, the two fall asleep as one, both fall asleep and both of their backs hurt, whenever they-both remember that nap. It's impossible to say: *our backs ached when we fell asleep on the grass,* it's just not possible to say. The dual has shared favorite places and shared things. Whatever derives from the dual isn't excluded: a child is an organic part of the dual. Memory, a lake, a foggy morning, everything derives from one or two, but never the plural. The plural can't think, can't feel, can't hurt. A third is the beginning of misfortune. On account of a third Gumbo beat Louisa in the dead of night. On account of a third the good angel retreats. Stretching from a third to infinity is terra incognita with dangerous, jagged peaks and a vague sense of the dangerous, dark, uncertain world. But the dual sleeps in the grass, rides boats, climbs up on balconies and feels just fine in a hotel room next to the elevator, despite the rumble all night long and the shouts of multitudinous drunks.

3

He took Ana's letter out of his jacket The dual comes by night, when voices outside awaken Gregor Gradnik. When he steps back over to the window and the street is surprisingly quiet. The crowd of gays has moved someplace else for the night. When a boat whistles from the river. That boat isn't the *Natchez;* the *Natchez* rasps. But this one whistles, as though it had steamed in from Vladivostok. Or Koper. It's a spring evening there now. Here, a humid, quiet night. *For no reason I keep remembering Bohinj,* Ana writes, *the green water, green grass, green mountains,* the mountains were gray and white, the water isn't green, *the green tree trunks and crowns, the green toadstools, the beefy, green cows. My back ached when the two of us fell asleep in the grass, I can remember it exactly. Good lord, how good it all was. Now everything aches: the damned waiting, the damned telephone calls, the damned mailmen who never bring letters when I need them most.* And suddenly she was writing about balconies. Suddenly she was on the trail of some third person who was turning the dual into a triple, a quadruple. *I look at those strange balconies on your picture post-cards and I have to tell you they upset me somehow. Do you remember how I climbed through your window one night to be with you? On a ladder that had been left lying on the ground. I hope you remember what came next. Not a world within sight except ours, except for the two of us. And now, with such a beautiful night outside I can't go to sleep. I'd rather climb up onto your balcony. I'd knock on the window and say, Come, love . . . Actually, I wouldn't say anything, I'd just climb in.* Where did you get that balcony, here the site of balcony parties, where they sip drinks, chew ice, sweat, fan themselves, whisper and sometimes shout. Popescu vomits onto the street from a balcony. Last night he'd walked a *third person* home. Wait, she'd said, and a minute later she was on the balcony, leaning against the railing. Do you know any songs? she said. So that a lonely girl can fall asleep, she said. You'd sleep poorly, he said, if I sang to you from down here. Doesn't matter, she said, next time, then, she said. Good night. Night. Sleep well. You too. Me too. You too.

He doesn't sleep well. He doesn't sleep at all. Suddenly this night has become too quiet. Suddenly he can hear Ana's voice through this night all too clearly. Suddenly she is pacing over several dozen square feet of apartment. When are you coming, she says, when are you coming? Suddenly Irene isn't far from here, her body perspiring in her sweats, Irene, looking at the ceiling and hearing Peter's voice from far-off New York, her white and soft and fragrant body covered only with a sheet, only with a sheet on hers and Peter's bed, on Peter's and hers, on their wide bed, suddenly he can see Louisa through the wall stroking Gumbo's big head, his powerful body heaving as he sobs noiselessly.

And from all sides voices, night voices, a murmuring multitude, voices in his sleep, the sounds of Jesus's harmonica as he plays it in the bar's doorway, the throaty voice of Lady Lilly, words, moans, muffled moaning into a pillow, at two, at three a quiet rumbling in the night.

He goes out into the quiet street. Kowalski throws a cigarette out the window and closes it. The bars are closed. Only at Rigby's a faint light falls through the open door onto the sidewalk. Martin's dog lies in the doorway, gently snoring.

CHAPTER 18

FRAGMENTS OF BUGGED
CONVERSATIONS

1

Fred Blaumann in his creative-writing class: I want you to write a dialogue, an everyday conversation. We all know that three-fourths of the time we say meaningless things, but underlying it all is an invisible current of intensive contact. Engage your memory, record those conversations, let a tape run through your mind recording everything. Record it, write it down. Then give it shape. Repetitions, interruptions of patterns, Hemingway, be laconic, precise. Never begin with "Hi," and never end with an exclamation mark. Never!

A tape, Fred Blaumann says. Record this for me. Listen to the way the empty room echoes off the tape. Two people talking in an apartment, and you're bugging them. Bare-bones dialogue: what the policeman listens to. The echo of a voice in the bedroom, an exchange with the car engine idling, a tête-à-tête accompanied by the chatter of people in a restaurant. Listen to yourselves without thinking about it too much, eavesdroppers.

2

G.: The landlord said he wasn't giving me the deposit back.

I.: How much is it?

G.: Four hundred.

I.: Four hundred?

G.: Right.

I.: That old miser's got a nerve. He has to give it back.

G.: He's not going to. The firemen forced their way in and broke everything—the door, everything. I'm at fault because I left the gas on.

I.: You said it was leaking.

G.: It was.

I.: Then he has to give it back.

G.: He doesn't want to.

I.: He has to.

G.: He said he knows my kind and he'll fix me.

Laughter.

I.: Then you fix him. In court.

G.: Are you crazy?

I.: You paid the bill for the door. He didn't replace the safety valves on the gas line. Sue him.

G.: Are you crazy?

I.: What's his name?

G.: The landlord. What else do you call a landlord?

I.: And that other guy, are you still spending time with him?

G.: What other guy?

I.: The fat one that rolls around.

G.: Gumbo.

I.: What's his business now, what's he doing?

G.: At the moment he's making love powder to sell.

I.: No good.

G.: Love powder?

I.: Him. He's no good. I've seen him in court.

G.: You can see him everywhere. Even at the cemetery.

I.: Stay away from him.

G.: What are you saying?

I.: All I said was, stay away from him.

G.: Well, you can see you in court, too.

I.: And you can stay away from me, too.

Silence.

G.: What's going on?

I.: Go home now. I'm tired.

G.: No, it's something else.

I.: Of course it's something else. Peter's going to call soon.

G.: I get it.

I.: You get nothing. Get going now.

Well, Fred, how's that? Or should it be done differently. That's what memory's tape records, no more, no less.

3

She started speaking in exclamation marks. Smiling ironically the whole time, but with exclamation marks. Fred wouldn't have been pleased. It wrecks a sentence; an exclamation mark destroys the rhythm. Each exclamation mark was introduced by a question mark:

Aren't you running anymore?

I ride the bike instead.

It's not the same!

Suddenly nothing was the same anymore. The hour of her departure was nearing, she was constantly busy by day, and in the evenings she was waiting for Peter to call. Peter was getting an apartment ready in New York. Her apprenticeship was drawing to a close, and the apartment had already been done up in new wallpaper.

4

Your picture of America!

Whose?

Yours! You come across some interesting thing and then you start making all kinds of generalizations. Wrestling! Televangelists! Harlem!

You're my very special generalization.

What are we talking about now?

About you. About me.

We're not talking about anything. This is nothing, what we're talking about.

They should have been talking about something else. About something that was inexorably approaching. About something that began the instant they came closest to one another. Leave-taking always begins just as the circle of intimacy closes. At that point the *fortunae rota* rolls away, the angels roll it away, the wheels turn, feet bear down on the pedals on a hot May evening. Resisting good-byes. Not a word about that. Words about other things.

5

About bicycles. About running.

Gregor didn't run anymore, ever. He dug his way through piles of anatomical melancholy matter, drilling holes through it, a toiler in Fred Blaumann's mine. In the evenings he rode the famous bicycle. Her bicycle; theirs. He was the *third party* when it came to the bike. He didn't use Peter Diamond's book anymore. His portrait on it bothered him. And every time he tried to follow his complicated itineraries, with their urbanistic, historical, and ethnographic commentaries, he got lost. The two of them never talked about the bicycle. The bicycle was sacred and beloved. And he drove it mercilessly, with pleasure. On hot May evenings, through black neighborhoods redolent of cooking, into paved cemeteries, amid streams of cars, past the white fences of colonial mansions on residential streets, over the delicate, sprouting grass that edged the canals. He lay beside it and gazed at alien stars, at the stars of the southern sky, as he listened to the sounds of the big river.

6

Of odors. The first time.

Drago, the oysterfield owner, arrived in America with one pair of shoes on his feet and one pair in a box. He put the first stack of dollars he ever earned into that box. He was afraid to take them to the bank.

Don't you people take your dollars to the bank?

We put them in socks, under our mattresses. In a shoe box, in socks, money stinks.

7

Of odors. The second time.

Things are denser where you're from, in Europe.

How do you mean, denser?

Denser. The houses are closer together. The streets are narrower. I saw it in Greece. The air smells of food, of garlic and meat. The garlic stinks.

8

Of the river.

Where you're from a person can be an instant success effortlessly. Today you're in prison, tomorrow you're president of a corporation. Like that Walesa.

He's not the president of a corporation. He won the Nobel Peace Prize.

Even worse. Even more successful and even less effort. Here you have to know what you want. Everyone knows what he wants. Except for my sister in Indiana. She sits looking at the river bend, watching her life trickle away.

9

Of black people and various prejudices.

He took her to the bar where Jesus played. It was a tiny, ramshackle hole-in-the-wall near the train station. There were people there, and the musicians collected their meager earnings from them. It smelled of grass and unwashed bodies. Jesus was ugly, but he played divinely.

"He is ugly," he said as they were driving home, "but he plays well. The uglier they are, the better they play."

She grabbed onto the steering wheel more tightly.

The black man whose drink Gregor had bought was named Jesus. He played the harmonica mostly, but also some guitar. Jesus's face was pockmarked. Jesus played divinely.

"He's pockmarked, and he smells bad because he drinks too much, but can that black man play . . . "

The car lurched to a stop. Gregor almost hit his head against the windshield.

"Never say that again," she said, "never say anything like that in America again."

"Where am I supposed to say it? In Madagascar?"

"For all I care, say it in Madagascar, but not in America, and not in Louisiana."

"But it's a free country. You mean I can't say that there's a guy named Jesus, a black man whom I happen to like, that he's pockmarked and doesn't smell great."

"That's how rednecks talk."

"Redneck is what you call a person who does manual work."

"That's not the point."

"They have red necks because the sun shines on their necks."

"That's not the point."

Silence.

"Should I apologize?"

"Shouldn't you?"

"What am I supposed to do after this cultural clash?"

"Nothing. Bring me the bicycle. I'll put it on the train."

"Will we see each other tomorrow?

"No, I've got work to do."

"With your gray-haired gentleman?"

"That's right."

10

O, Gradnik!

The hour of her departure was approaching and their meetings had become less frequent. Life had been broken into fragments. Poudre de Perlainpainpain no longer had the desired effect. Just as unexpectedly as Gumbo's powder had started to have an effect, it now suddenly stopped working. Fickle powder. One evening they sat at O'Brian's drinking some fluorescent cocktail. He was going to walk her home, but she refused him while they were still at the table. As a matter of fact, she gently pushed him away. At O'Brian's. O, Gradnik, you understood nothing.

A gray-haired gentleman, the judge with lofty moral views, who was courteous to women and never said anything about blacks, was sitting in a car near her house. Gregor, who had ridden the bike there, stopped at the corner. The man of high principles yawned and looked at a cluster of squealing black girls roller-skating down the middle of the street. Irene came out of the house with a big paper bag in her arms and got in next to the judge. The two of them laughed. He could hear Fred's wife's mousy voice. They say she isn't entirely loyal. Fred had added: *supposedly, completely*. This woman was walking out of his life, and he didn't understand a thing.

Even though things were just as simple as they always are in these forever identical stories.

CHAPTER 19

A CRITICAL PUNCTURE

I

The accident happened on a warm evening in May, when he was riding the bike home through some side streets. If what happened can be called an accident. It was a sacrilege, and it was the finger of fate clearly pointing downward: from here on things are going downhill.

In the afternoon he had tried to reach the river. He was riding past an industrial harbor downstream from the city center. In the sweltering heat he had an image of a grassy waterfront, perhaps with willow trees bending over the river. Not one of the ten routes described in Diamond's book showed an outlet or a stop like that. But he was convinced that the bicycling author hadn't exhausted all of the possibilities. Once he had passed the long boat docks laden with rusty iron, rows of warehouses cropped up. Sweat ran down his temples and oozed through every pore of his body. He pedaled wildly through the heavy, humid, odorous air. He strayed far from the river and tried to gain his bearings from atop an overpass. The desert of the industrial harbor with its mountains of containers and iron seemed to be limitless. He descended into a residential area, with black people sitting among the rough-hewn houses. To the river? They pointed him in different directions, he took off to the left and then the right, sensing the vicinity of the water all the time. He heard ships blowing their horns, but the wide Mississippi was farther off than ever. In a crosswalk, gritting his teeth as huge trucks blew their exhaust in his face, he finally gave up. There wouldn't be any grassy waterfront, no weeping willows. Evening was approaching. Trucks roared their engines and sent clouds of hot, vile air in his face. As though mocking him for not believing Diamond's book and its bike routes. He returned past the gigantic warehouses, and amid heaps of discarded metal and disassembled crates he once again found himself in an impenetrable labyrinth. He was tired, thirsty, and confused amid a monstrous industrial landscape. In his breast anger mounted against Diamond, against himself, against the twentieth century that had refused him access to the river. Against the bicycle that had brought him here. He threw it on a heap of rusty iron. He sat down on an empty box and immersed himself in a map of bicycle routes, trying to find a way out of the labyrinth.

When he lifted the bicycle up off the iron heap he heard a snakelike hiss. It hissed and spat. With a malicious rustling sound, the air was slowly but surely escaping from the back tire. He got onto it anyway and started pedaling. But once he was on the street in the suburb outside, he noticed that he was riding on the rim. The famous bicycle that was the very origin of the famous book *Cycling New Orleans* had now been punctured, and there was nothing he could do about it.

Like a crippled nag, he dragged it over the warehouse yards, down lonely streets, and through a black neighborhood where he had to endure taunts from the doorsteps. And a bunch of squealing black brats running after this pathetic sight.

He dragged himself into the house, totally beaten, around eleven o'clock. He hurled the bicycle down in the entryway, and when he switched the light on he shuddered.

Two men were standing outside of Gumbo's door. One of them put a finger to his lips, and the other motioned to him nervously to get lost.

He did. He pitched into bed and fell asleep instantly, anyway. It seemed as though he heard voices during the night: the two black men in the dark inhabiting a dream of his. Then he dreamed about a deep pit full of rusting iron and hissing snakes.

2

The bicycle wasn't just famous, it was holy. It was the origin of the book. Peter and Irene had talked about it lovingly of an evening. It was an old, chrome bike, the kind no longer made these days. The author stood beside it in the photograph, wearing tennis shoes and a bow tie. In the extremely felicitous photo. The bicycle on the title page of a book that was sitting on the shelves of bookstores. In the photograph for a promotional poster of a best-selling book. The bicycle that had brought the writer good fortune. The bicycle that was going to travel to New York. The bicycle that would one day stand in the author's museum. The bicycle that Peter had patted like a horse. The bicycle that Irene referred to as "him."

Gregor remembered that Sunday afternoon in the park. Peter had given him a copy of the book, autographed. Their friends had applauded. Everyone was photographed with the bicycle.

In the morning he noticed to his horror that not only had he blown the inner tube—the tire itself was shredded. And the tire rim was twisted, because he had ridden on it for a while. He tried to remember if it had been intentional, with malice, that is to say, premeditated, or due to neglect, in other words, due to extenuating circumstances, as a lawyer might say. Apparently Gumbo had stumbled into it with his full weight drunk last night. Or the two strangers standing in front of his door may have trampled on it. The chain was stretched across the floor.

3

In any case, it was worse than he expected. After one look at the broken bicycle Irene went as pale as if he were showing her a beloved horse with a broken leg. He wanted to tell her that he would do everything necessary to restore it to its former state. He wanted to say that he'd look for a repairman. He wanted to say that he knew how to fix bicycles, himself, after all. He wasn't a mechanical idiot, even if he wasn't a mechanical genius. When he was small he knew how to install a chain. His father had praised him.

There was nothing he could say. The sight of the crippled creature was too grim. A faint flush colored her pale cheeks.

Ah, need one add that it wasn't just the tire that had been punctured, although that was part of the problem. Everything had been punctured.

And, on top of everything, this:

"And a neighbor called Peter long distance to tell him that someone is standing beneath my balcony every night."

And then:

"And at the top of that ridiculous poem that flew up onto the veranda you wrote: For Ana. Were you drunk?"

And then:

"And do you really not have a single damned thing to do at the university but copy poems and stand under balconies?

"And wreck bicycles."

This was incredible. The hissing of an inner tube. The hissing of a bicycle inner tube. This wasn't anger. It was something completely incomprehensible. It was totally incredible. This was some other person. An inner tube hissing, losing its air.

"As a matter of fact I do have something—to do," he said.

"Then go do it."

The flush of her cheeks, like the flush produced by a short jog, gave way to pallor. The pallor of a deflated tire.

So this was the end. He didn't want to think about it. All endings are banal. Simple: endings have to be banal and simple. It's my bad luck, he said, to be in love with two women.

That isn't bad luck, Martin said, that's just a generous heart. The only question remaining was how he could confuse the two names. And which one did he love if something like that could happen? Both of them, Martin decided as the two of them tried to solve this riddle over bourbon the next evening. Both of them. Everyone knows that's possible. And besides, Martin said, if you have two, then when it's over you've always got one left. There's something to be said for that. Because if you've only got one . . .

All night he lay in bed and stared at the ceiling fan whirring over his head. The air had become too hot and too humid. It was impossible to think. There was something he couldn't understand. His head felt heavy, as if it were Gumbo's head. It seemed as if a huge, exhausted, bored Oblomovian head was lying on his pillow. Then it slowly changed into the head of a big, lazy dog that was too hot and bored with everything. Slow, black music was escaping from a bar. The words something about rice and beans.

■ □ ■ □ ■

CHAPTER 20

RICE AND BEANS, OR
JAZZ WITH BREAKFAST

I

At some point he sensed a body behind his back. He was sitting on a bar stool and he sensed that someone was standing behind him. But he thought—if he was thinking this evening at all—that someone was just standing behind him, the way people here tended to sit or stand around when they weren't lurking in their lairs, without really knowing why they were standing in a particular place. Somebody's looking for you, Debbie said and gave a broad wink.

This was the first time she'd come here. Anytime before this and it would have surprised him. She never went to this bar—to bars like *this*. Out of which many a character ventured forth to face her gray eminence. The one she had sat next to in the front seat, with a paper bag in her lap. A bag full of *what?*

"I've come to say good-bye," she said.

"You're leaving?"

"I'm leaving."

He ordered drinks for both of them and she joined him. Martin made room for her. Debbie and Liana exchanged a long glance full of feminine intuition.

"So you're leaving."

"Yes."

Martin scratched his dog behind the ears. A drunk black Jesus stirred, raised his pockmarked face, and took a swig from a bottle. Debbie leaned back and started drumming her fingers. Liana's ears twitched. At the poker table in the next room there was a sudden ruckus, which instantly died down. From the corner of his eye he could see her lawyerly left eye looking at the glass in front of her. Her eye understood where she was. But she was calm, determined to do this thing. This didn't surprise him, either. Ultimately, she was a person of liberal views. And her fiancé, after all, was an artist. A long time ago he had made him a gift of his book. He accepted the book, and then took her. And their bicycle.

"I'm leaving tomorrow morning."

"Flying?"

"Yes."

"And the bike?"

She didn't answer. The bottle fell out of Jesus's hands. Martin's dog barked briefly.

"The bike went by train."

She picked some ice out of her glass with her fingers and chewed on it.

"Look," he said, "that's the dog I told you about."

He threw him an ice cube; the dog snapped it up and started crunching it.

"Martin's dog. And this is Martin sitting next to me."

Martin grumbled a greeting. Irene asked whether she could throw the dog some ice, too. Martin nodded. The dog chomped on it. Everyone waited for her to laugh. She laughed. Everybody laughed.

"In a month or so," Gregor said, "in a month or so I'll be in New York, too."

"On my way home," he added. "I'll be there a good while.

"I could call you," he said.

He emptied his glass. She asked for water. Debbie banged the glass down in front of her.

"I don't want you to call me."

"No?"

"No."

This unconditionality was very lawyerly. It didn't belong here. In this place unconditional sentences didn't sound right. In this place unconditional sentences produced laughter and endless wisecracks.

"Fine," he said. "I won't call."

2

From the very beginning things were probably headed for this, he thought, from the very beginning, though that was so far removed, though from the beginning it was probably just a coincidence that she—who supposedly wasn't entirely loyal— had been left alone as she finished out her court apprentice- ship, which then turned into a life apprenticeship for . . . for what? . . . for life with a bicycling author in New York, she was alone when suddenly they found themselves thrown together, full of misunderstandings . . . from the biggest misunder- standing, from the *prima nox,* which each of them had under- stood so differently, at first with her consent, then in the next instant without her consent, from the unexpected impetus of Peter's book on the table, from Ana's letter on the table, from a sense of decency, of gray-haired principle, of rape, and possi- bly rape three times in one night . . . so that the whole time she felt something was happening against her will, because *here everybody knows where he's going,* oh come on, oh come on . . . then why this tension, all these brief encounters, impa- tience, impossible to subdue . . . and for him a sudden erup- tion of melancholy matter, spleen, from the soul into his body, from his body into the soul, a sudden malady of everything that Blaumann's computer knew about melancholy matter . . . the details are insignificant, and all of it not worth a . . . not worth a . . . discreet garlic, even though some biologist had explained to her that no substance like that could still be what it had been before . . . garlic sizzles, smells, reeks, lives its life, for God's sake: don't change it. Leave the poor garlic alone. Mardi Gras, on the other hand, had been a bad scene. Beauti- ful and bad. And the shellfish? The oysters? And the mid-morning visits from work? And the trip down there, when the needle spun and the world began to vibrate. What about all of that? What about that now?

These were rambling, drunk thoughts. The slow and ponderous black music that had played all last night. He ought to tell her all of this, and yet something else, too. Maybe: still, it was nice. Even if I never see or hear from you again. Even if you never raise your head again like you did now. If you're serious about not getting a double chin. Instead of the words that ought to have been pronounced now, from unknown depths there came something that wanted to contradict the unconditional voice, the irrevocable word.

3

"Fine," he said. "I won't call."

He was silent for a moment.

"How could I even dare to call you? How could I face my friend Peter, who gave me a copy of his book? I punctured his bicycle . . . And his fiancée."

She didn't bat an eye. Only her fingers, clasping her glass, played over its surface. When she stood up she didn't lift her eyes. Behind their contact lenses they flashed vacantly. Those fingers, though, still holding onto the bar, were trembling.

Liana sent Debbie a long, significant glance. Debbie nodded almost imperceptibly. Martin's dog had lain down in the doorway. Jesus picked up the bottle that was still slowly dripping.

4

He caught up with her outside of a display window where a huge television screen was flickering.

"Not one more word," she said.

"I'm sorry," he said.

"That was so pitiful," she said, "that was so pathetic that it makes me sick."

"I'm sorry," he said. "It was spleen made me do it."

"Back off," she said.

He backed off.

Behind her head the television screen flickered. A middle-aged American woman with a nice hairstyle, but cookie-cuttered otherwise, performing in a soap opera. She talks, he paces in front of the fireplace with a glass in hand.

"Just one more thing," Irene said. "Just this."

The well-coifed woman behind her back was saying something, too. There was no sound.

"I came here to tell you something. And I'm going to do that. And that's because you and I aren't going to see or hear from each other again. Ever. Period."

The huge picture in the display window got bigger as the camera focused on the woman's face. Her eyes flashed, perhaps from tears. Gregor knew what came next. How many times have we already seen this famous scene in contemporary iconography. Calmly, quietly she'll say: I'm pregnant. Slowly, shyly she'll smile. In a Slovenian or Hungarian film she'd burst into tears and then go stumbling down the rainy street. In an American film she'd smile. She smiled.

"I'm getting married," Irene said. "It doesn't matter now."

The man on the screen, who an instant before had been angrily pacing back and forth, looked at her and the corners of his mouth twitched. The camera focused in on his face. In a Slovenian film he would bury his head in his hands. But this man, his hair flawlessly moussed and combed, smiled, and then started to laugh. He lifted her up in the air—he was a powerful man—and danced with her before the fireplace. The camera cut to the fireplace and focused on the cheerily flickering flame. Cut to commercials.

"It doesn't matter," Irene said. "Now I can tell you. I'm getting married on account of you."

He could feel the corners of his mouth twitch. She looked at him for a space: was he capable of understanding?

"What sort of . . . " he said.

"Be quiet," she said. "This spring I fell in love. All at once. I'm marrying Peter, now, because I was in love with you."

"Till now I thought women divorced over things like that," he said.

"This shouldn't have happened to me," she said almost noiselessly, her hands shaking again as she reached pointlessly for her hair. "It was against my will . . . and then. . . . You're going to leave and there won't have been any point to the whole thing."

O, Gradnik! O, Gregor! Do you understand now?

"What I mean is that this could happen to me again anytime if I don't stop. Now. Immediately. And totally."

Now and totally she delivered the sentences as though she were pronouncing a verdict.

"And that's the only way. It's that simple."

Verdict. Period. No higher court. No chance for appeal.

"As strange as it may be, and if I understood you at all," he said slowly as the television flickered from scene to scene in his face, "if you're marrying somebody else, and on account of me at that, although you're also doing it on your own account, then I can ask you to the Lafitte to say good-bye. Lady Lilly sings there. With a heavy Slavic accent."

He could. And this was how she had pictured their leave-taking. Even though farewells usually run like the one they had just had at Rigby's. With an abrupt departure, a spill out on the sidewalk, and Liana's loud laughter ringing in your ears.

5

There was no television there, no wrestling, no soap opera. The bar was empty. It was another late Sunday evening; the tourists had disappeared and the cockroaches were asleep. Lady Lilly sang, and here once again was the car ride down to Barataria Bay, the solitary birds darting over the bayous, the voice in an empty auditorium, an hour for remembering, an hour for silence.

Something abruptly shook him. Louisa Dmitrievna Kordachova was sitting at the bar. The scene was so familiar, so totally familiar, that he thought it must be his alcoholic stupor. With tears streaming over her freckles, the little waitress was sitting there again telling the bartender something.

When she saw that he'd noticed her, she grew agitated. She tried to make some signs to him, there was something she wanted to communicate. But he couldn't get up, he couldn't listen to her complaint. Here one of the fateful events of his life was unfolding. It was happening to him and Irene. He was drunk and indifferent to whatever was happening to this girl, whom the good angel was constantly abandoning.

Irene said that the Dirty Dozen were playing in Storyville. She wanted to hear them, those harbor musicians, one more time. When they walked out past the bar, Louisa said to him in a strange, deep, and aged voice:

"Terrible things are happening."

He broke a cold sweat at that strange voice, not because of the word *terrible*, but because of the terror and horror that her transformed voice contained. This wasn't a voice that could talk about a boyfriend who was a jerk, and not even a voice that would tell him about the collapse of the Perlainpainpain company. This was a threatened voice. For a moment he could see the two men standing outside Gumbo's door, and a dark foreboding told him that whatever was terrible had to do with them. He couldn't, he simply couldn't think about that. He couldn't handle any of it. First soap operas and now cops and robbers. It just didn't work. It wasn't his business. His business was Irene and the road to Storyville. The Dirty Dozen. He blocked out her voice, he blocked out his foreboding. The two of them walked to Storyville. Outside they held hands. The air of the hot May night shimmered.

6

In Storyville things were winding down. People were walking from the terrace into the auditorium, into the auditorium and out of it. Only a few tables were still occupied. The twelve-member band was playing its last piece for winds. In the empty theater it had a shrill effect, entering your raw chest like a blade.

It was three o'clock, and Irene said that they ought to have breakfast. In case you still don't know, she said, this is called a jazz breakfast. I'm going to have rice and beans. They always have it. They put lots of garlic in it. In New York I'll make it myself.

He didn't care what she was going to make herself; what he cared about was whether the food went with whiskey. Oh, sure, it goes with everything. Before I get on the plane, she said, and that's soon, I want to have coffee at the French Market, in the morning, hot, with hot milk. She wanted everything, absolutely everything on this last night, every last thing.

The Dirties were putting their instruments away. A black man from the audience sat down at the piano and let his fingers dance over the keys. It sent a hollow echo through the large auditorium.

She called a waiter and asked for two glasses of water. From the tap. No one in New Orleans drinks tap water. Tap water is from the Mississippi. That's what she wanted.

Are you sure it's tap water?

Don't worry, the black man said. You can wash your feet in it, baby. And his white teeth showed in a broad smile.

They say that anyone who drinks river water will come back, she said. In other places they throw coins in fountains. Here they drink Mississippi River water. That brownish-yellow water that used to bring yellow fever.

Exuberantly she lifted the glass toward the light.

This, she said, this is Mississippi water.

They each drank their glasses in one draft.

Her shoulders heaved and she suddenly began to cry. My eyes sting, she said, and I've lost a contact lens. They looked for the lens, and she picked it up off the dirty tablecloth with the tip of one finger.

I'm drunk, she said. Jesus, am I ever drunk.

They ate black bean gravy and rice. It was redolent of garlic, of perfume, of whiskey, of the early morning hour.

What is it about that early hour that it seems made for a writer?

The black man at the piano moved the microphone to his mouth.

Over there, he said, his voice booming through the auditorium. Over there in the second row there are two people eating rice and beans. This here is for them.

And he played and sang those strange blues that Gregor would never hear again:

I love you once,
I love you twice,
I love you next to beans and rice.

7

They didn't go for coffee. They didn't go to his place. They went to her apartment. For the first time. And the last. They smoked out on the balcony, leaned against the railing, looked out over the street. Dawn was showing just behind the river levee. Some early birds were waking the morning with their warbling. From the corner somebody was washing the street down with a hose, causing the sidewalks to glisten in the feeble yellow twilight. Then they went back into the empty, totally empty apartment. They lay down on the floor in the living room, next to the packed suitcases and parcels.

They waited there till morning and the arrival of the taxi, which honked protractedly on the street below.

CHAPTER 21

THE HEMORRHOIDS OF
SAINT FIACRE

I

Notes for Blaumann:

Particular symtoms to the three distinct species			
	Head melancholy	In body	Headache after drunkenness, red eyes, buzzing in the ears
		or In mind	Fear, sorrow, suspicion, discontent, loneliness, anger
	Hypochondriacal or windy melancholy	In body	Cold sweats, heart problems, pain in left side, ringing in the ears, burning sensation
		or In mind	Lasciviousness, desire, windy soul, impatience, mournfulness
	Over all the body	In body	Dilation or constriction of the veins, thick, gross blood, hemorrhoids, constipation
		or In mind	Fearful, sad, solitary, fearful dreams, averse from company, etc.

Gumbo vanished, as he had so many times before. The magazines kept stacking up in his mailbox, and outside his door there was a crate full of milk bottles. But Louisa had vanished, too. He looked for her at the Café du Monde, where she worked before she started helping with Gumbo's new business. He asked about her at Rigby's. The old woman's voice that came out of her that night; the two men standing in the dark . . . Terrible things are happening . . . But in the Quarter something terrible was always happening . . . He consoled himself with the thought that some things defied understanding, especially when they had to do with Gumbo. Maybe the two of them were down in the bayous somewhere, among all his brothers and sisters with names starting with O. Maybe there were mountains of crayfish shells around their bed. In any case, he felt uneasy, and her strange voice kept pursuing him.

Fred Blaumann held a farewell party for the students in his creative-writing course. He handed out diplomas. He thanked his visiting colleague, Gregor Gradnik, for his assistance. Number 9 was pronounced the most successful of the newly created writers. He had published a few things in the student magazine. Then they stood in one of the university's concrete courtyards, unwrapping hamburgers, munching potato chips, and sipping beer. It was scorchingly hot, but no one retreated out of the sun. The course was over. They had survived the long months together. The most talented had found the least talented. Number 9 and the blond art gallery cashier were glowing, beaming from an inner glow that had welded them together. Number 9 was in the big leagues now, and the art gallery cashier no longer had a need for any courses. She had found what she was looking for. Gregor hadn't found anyone. His life in this city unfolded elsewhere. He had established no rapport with these young people. They were a distant planet that he didn't understand. In fact, he hadn't even tried to get to know it. They had tried at first; they had been curious and open, and then they gave up. A strange guy from some foreign country. Lots of them visit American universities. Momentarily parallel, separate paths through the same time and space. In the sweltering heat Meg was drinking can after can of beer. Fred Blaumann watched her with concern.

"Meg," he said, "you'll be sick."

She responded with something very abrupt, because his expression became serious and an instant later turned into the suffering mask of the misunderstood man. Since Mardi Gras Professor Blaumann had become serious. The fall he took on the street as he was running after his student had been a sign that he wasn't going to ignore. He assumed an armorlike dignity and threw himself into his gigantic melancholy project. But whenever Meg was in the vicinity he followed her around like a sheepdog. This was the extent of it. Nothing else happened with the young creative people. In fact, as far as Gregor Gradnik was concerned, nothing at all.

4

The photograph showed a Japanese man in a white lab coat. He was holding a huge head of garlic out in front of him. The garlic in his outstretched hand was as big as a pumpkin, while in the background his head with slanting eyes was positively minuscule. Over the picture there was this banner headline:

JAPANESE GARLIC DOESN'T SMELL

and beneath it this article:

TOKYO, 28.—Garlic is exceptionally healthful and an essential ingredient in many dishes, but it has the disadvantage of leaving an unpleasant odor. Japanese specialists have devised a method of cultivating a "discreet" garlic that retains its characteristic flavor, but not the unpleasant smell. Dr. Kotaro Saki, who patented the new variety of garlic, has signed a contract with the American Garlic & Onion Corporation. In the opinion of experts the project has enormous potential.

He cut the article out and wrote in: *Kotaro Saki beat you to it. A pity. But how did he discover your idea. Personally, there are other secrets* . . . He took his typewriter to pepper the letter with some Č's and Ž's and . . . and . . . nothing. He left it at that.

5

After a week there was still no sign of Gumbo and Louise. The milkman stopped leaving milk at their door, due to protests from the neighbors. They had started tripping over the bottles at night. Gumbo caused problems even when he wasn't around.

There was a letter from home. It was spring. It was May. Was he ever coming back? His mother was sick, write to her.

Ellis Marsalis was still playing every Sunday at Snug Harbour, and Lady BJ sang. He went there once with Meg and Fred.

To Storyville he went alone. In the wee hours, when they were putting their instruments away. A drunk Jesus approached him for money. He gave him enough for a drink. They had fought over him once.

He walked along the Mississippi and the algae weighed down on his lungs.

He kicked a newspaper vending machine. In broad daylight he kicked a defenseless box. It hadn't opened immediately when he dropped four nickels into the slot. Instead of kicking the computer, that shameless, puffed-up Gargantua full of knowledge, a metal cretin on the street corner paid for it.

He sat in Jackson Square in the early morning hours when

it was still chilly. Homesickness, suddenly homesickness again, something he had left over there that was starting to pull at him now. Ana's letters were few and torn to pieces. He wrote little. Their conversations were rare. A sudden twinge of pain, and out came a kick at a vending machine. Home was still a long way off.

6

He wasn't going home. Not even for a vacation. Without a moment's hesitation he accepted Fred's offer to extend his stay and assist with his research into melancholy matter. In August he would leave for New York. He would stay with a college classmate of Fred's. Things were running a course of their own. The world happened to him, and he was all for observing it. I'm an observer, he would say.

Yet another annotation:

Albrecht Dürer, Melancholia I. *The picture simultaneously portrays sorrow and great hope.* Tristitia et Spes. *The sun, a woman's face looking into the sun. Her eyes look forward, into the future. The world of ideas and knowledge at her feet, the magic square, the scales, astrology, astronomy, mathematics (sorrow of the spirit). The face resting on a hand (typical of melancholic drawings). The melancholic as a figure of profundity. Dreamy and sorrowful. Not true. Melancholics laugh in company. Loudly and often.*

It was June and the temperature in New Orleans was approaching a hundred and five. The air conditioners in the library labored noiselessly. The computer hummed lightly. The world hummed. Back home was sunny Ljubljana, the green hills of Pohorje. His mother was ill. Ana had stopped writing. Irene was gone. Gumbo and Louisa had vanished.

7

Fred Blaumann was blue with melancholy. Meg Holick was unquestionably moving to New York. Fred Blaumann was a decent professor. He never talked about desire, except when he was dealing with it as an academic question. Which is to say, as a question of melancholy matter. He never gave any sign of the grim forces that bound him to Meg, except once, when he fell on the street. Just once and never again. His desire was transformed into a blue, perpetually postcoital melancholy. You could tell this by the fact that he was blue and his glasses were constantly misting over.

Fred Blaumann hit one of the keys on his computer. A message appeared on the screen:

Lonely?

The computer liked these little pranks. He turned the machine off. With a coffee stain on his trousers, he leaned back and started wobbling dangerously on the back two legs of his chair. It was obvious he was dangerously shaken.

"Just think," he said and wiped his misty glasses. "I moved from New York to this place, where you can find nothing but cockroaches. While my students move from here to New York."

"It looks like everyone's moving there this year," Gregor said.

"True enough," Fred said and looked at him attentively. "The artistic couple have moved, too. That leaves just you and me, friend.

"And our melancholy," he said a moment later.

"And the cockroaches," he added. "Wait till you see how many of them there are in July."

He put his glasses back on and scrolled through the text. Where did we leave off? Oh yes, melancholy diseases. Gangrene was St. Anthony's fire. And hemorrhoids were St. Fiacre's disease, weren't they?

CHAPTER 22

LAST STOP

I

Finally, Louisa appeared in the most unexpected of places: a used bookstore, among the bookshelves.

That day he discovered in a big, disorderly stack a book by his countryman, the once famous and now forgotten American writer Louis Adamič: *The Native's Return.* The discovery excited him; the presence of another Slovene fate buried under a stack of dusty books in a used bookstore on Decator Street in New Orleans moved him in a strange way. Fifty years later, when the author and his sudden fame were gone, all gone. His trembling fingers leafed through the yellowed pages of a bygone life, distant and foreign, yet so near.

He heard a woman's voice insistently asking for some book. Through a gap between books on the shelf he could see her legs, dressed in white stockings, and heard a voice that he didn't recognize immediately. We don't have that, the bookseller answered politely, we're a used bookstore. But the husky voice wouldn't relent: But you do sell books, don't you? You've got to have them. The white stockings seemed on the verge of stamping. The stockings were youngish, though the voice was aged, tired, nervous. It was Louisa. Suddenly he recognized her voice as Lady Lilly's.

But not just her voice had changed. A sunken and utterly drained face looked at him. The eyes—her lively eyes—were empty.

"Louisa!" he exclaimed. "What's happened?"

She looked at him, her face showing no sign of emotion.

"Tell this gentleman," she said, "that I need some simple little books. About Shakespeare, and Tennessee."

"I don't understand what she wants," the bookseller said.

"You can kiss my ass," she said.

And she walked out the jingling door. The bookseller shrugged and filled his pipe.

2

They sat in the Café du Monde, where Louisa obviously no longer worked. She let herself be waited on and didn't exchange a word with the waitresses. Even her eyes were like the old Russian pianist's eyes. They looked someplace else.

"What an old fart that was," she said, referring to the bookseller. "He doesn't know anything about life."

It wasn't clear what the connection was between knowledge about life and little books about Shakespeare and Tennesee. Gregor didn't want to be an old fart who didn't understand.

"Where've you been?" he asked. "I've been looking for you."

She drank all of her hot coffee and looked off somewhere across the river.

"In jail."

A strange tension seized onto his stomach. She turned to look at him.

"Why are you staring at me? I've been in jail. Awaiting trial."

With trembling fingers she unzipped her canvas bag and shoved a folded piece of newspaper in front of him.

"Haven't you read it? Everybody's read it. Why do you think those girls are looking at me like this?"

He turned to look at the bar, where a bunch of her coworkers were standing, craning their necks to watch them. Their necks retracted and the heads sank back between their shoulders.

He hadn't read it. The last few weeks he hadn't read anything. He'd been putting holes in bicycles. Ate rice and beans. Described Dürer's *Melancholia*. He didn't know if some new war had broken out or if the Russians were walking on the moon.

He spread out the folded newspaper page. There was a photo of Oristide Lagniappe and Tonio Gomez, in handcuffs.

DRUGS FOR CERTAIN. PORNOGRAPHY TOO?

In the midday heat he broke into a cold sweat.

"Where's Gumbo?"

"He's still there. Inside."

"Inside?

"Yeah, inside."

She calmly leafed through Louis Adamič. *The Native's Return.*

He quickly scanned the contents of the short article. The two dealers had fallen into a trap set for them. The had sold a large quantity of heroin to two detectives who presented themselves as pushers. Gomez's conduit for the heroin started in Panama, where it was processed. Oristide Lagniappe was part of the network of dealers. Huge amounts of pornographic material had also been discovered. A small part of the criminal underworld exposed in our city. Still other individuals are under investigation, but an official announcement will follow once the inquiries are completed.

Gregor Gradnik wiped the cold sweat from his forehead and with a nervous gesture spilled his glass of water.

"You don't have to be afraid," she said. She raised her eyes from the book and was looking across the river again.

How had she known he was afraid? That was it exactly: in that fraction of a second his first thoughts were of himself. They would investigate him next as a friend of Gumbo. And Louisa. He shuddered at the thought of having to answer questions at a police station or in court. At the same time he could feel himself blushing. This young girl who had changed so much in an instant, whose face was suddenly sunken and whose voice was like an old woman's, this girl had just experienced grim things. Gumbo was still experiencing them now. And here he was suddenly shaking, with nothing threatening him at all. You don't have to be afraid, she had said, but she left the last part of the sentence unsaid: for your ass.

"You didn't have anything to do with it."

He lit a cigarette. The hollow tension at the top of his stomach was subsiding. Not because he didn't, in fact, have anything to do with it, but because things were the way they were. He followed her gaze across the river. Women never look off into the distance; they always see things close up. Louisa was looking at some undetermined spot far on the other side of the river. Lojzka—Louisa. Louisa—Lady Lilly. She was gazing into space, into limitless, free space. The kind of gaze that comes from time in jail—however short, however investigatory.

"Was it bad?"

She didn't take her eyes off the unknown point in the limitless expanse across the river. Only her shoulders suddenly started to quiver. When he touched her hand to calm her, she gasped as though she were short of breath. Then her eyes flooded with tears, as they had once long ago at the bar in the Lafitte, where Lady Lilly sang and the world was piggish, but still bearable.

3

Heroin was first synthesized from morphine in 1874. The Bayer Company first began producing it for medical purposes as a pain reliever. Pure heroin is a powder with a sour taste. The kind that reaches the market varies in color from white to dark brown, depending on the method of processing, impurities, and additives such as sugar, pudding, or powdered milk. Effects: euphoria, drowsiness, weakness, contraction of the pupils, and respiratory depression. Consumption of too great a quantity leads to death. Drug users claim that when they take a 50% solution they experience a "mental and physical orgasm." It is distributed in the form of a white powder for inhaling (sniffing or flexing), or used as a solution to be injected intravenously.

Was the miracle powder, the Poudre de Perlainpainpain, really heroin?

Louisa: No. Those were two separate powders.

Apparently the whole business with the powdered aphrodisiac had been a good cover for distributing the *real* stuff. In New Orleans there were also shops maintaining the rich tradition of voodoo, which sold various tinctures and powders. This is why Gumbo's Poudre de Perlainpainpain wasn't all that unusual. Yet something remained unclear for Gregor: Why had he invested so much energy and imagination into convincing even him that he believed in the aphrodisiac himself? Was it an endless game of concealment? No, the world couldn't be that simple. The truth had to be elsewhere. After all, the aphrodisiac had shown results. Was he selling it, too?

Louisa: Yes. It was a hot item. Gumbo was trying to move into just Perlainpainpain.

You're saying that he was using the latter powder to escape from the former. And from Gomez. The latter powder was the real one, the love powder; the former, heroin, was a temporary commitment to earn a living until his real business got going. But first and foremost, the main thing in life for Gumbo was inventiveness. Life as an ongoing invention. He couldn't reconcile himself even with *art* photography. Life was there every instant to be filled with new designs. Otherwise, why would he have gathered so much material for his School of Creative Laughter? And Perlainpainpain worked— Gregor knew this. Better than most modern products touted by the colossal commercial advertising system. Did he believe in both businesses?

Louisa: Absolutely. So did I.

But, given his nature, how did he manage not to confuse the two powders and deliver Perlainpainpain to a heroin customer, or vice versa?

Louisa: First, there was the difference in price.

And second?

Louisa: Second, it did happen. Only it was the other way around.

How do you mean, the other way around? The investigation had found that instead of 50-percent heroin he had sold one customer a brownish-white powder of indeterminate substance. The customer went wild. Started looking for him. When he couldn't find him, he informed on him anonymously. Then two characters appeared, wanting to buy a large quantity. Those two were undercover narcotics agents. That was the end. The next day the *Picayune* printed the story in its Metro section.

Louisa: I believe everything he says. He taught me how to laugh.

Gregor (after a thoughtful pause): I believe him, too.

4

It was another week before Louisa moved back into Gumbo's apartment. Where she was in the meantime, he didn't ask. Ultimately, it wasn't his business. He was an observer. He didn't like getting overly involved. And when it came to this business, he was also a coward. The policeman who sometimes stood on the corner dangling his nightstick looked twice as wide as before. He spread out over the entire sidewalk, and when Gregor Gradnik walked around him in a wide arc, he felt his eyes following him as he chewed his gum. At night somebody stood under his window. He anxiously watched a man in an undershirt walk in circles around a streetlight. Then a young blond kid joined him. He took him by the hand; with the other hand the man seized onto the pole of the streetlight, and the two of them started spinning around it as if in some children's game. He wanted to acquaint Fred Blaumann with the whole story. But the words he would have to use were such that he preferred having someone else say them. Fred was intoxicated with his research and preoccupied with his student, Meg Holick, and her departure for New York. He was blue with melancholy. During his runs his scholarly and writerly thoughts drifted across Audubon Park, through the profound and lofty material of his research, over the text flickering across his computer screen. Fred had only one life, and there wasn't enough room in it for anything that happened on St. Philip Street.

On Sunday evening he and Louisa were sitting at the Lafitte, listening to Lady Lilly. She didn't smile, didn't cry, her eyes were strangely absent. For a second he thought she might want to pick up where they had left off one night long ago. But that was just a dim memory. She couldn't squeeze out a tear or a laugh. Dmitrievna Kordachova was gone, the Slavic soul drained out of her, leaving something shell-like. When they were alone for an instant, she put a pinch of powder on her palm with two fingers and with short, snuffling sounds inhaled it. It wasn't Poudre de Perlainpainpain.

5

Ovide, Oristes, Olive, Onesia, Otheo, Odalia, Octave, and Olite each contributed their one-eighth share to make bail. And one morning Gregor's door shook from a familiar kick. There was no sign that jail had damaged Gumbo. Gomez was still inside, he said. Which meant that his chances weren't bad. At worst he'd get a year. What's a year? he said. In a year's time he could write a book. Though there was still the probability that he would get a suspended sentence. In that case he wouldn't write a book; he'd try something else. He winked mysteriously. At Rigby's, where the regulars hadn't particularly grieved, they celebrated his return. They were better at celebrating than grieving—there was nothing wrong with that. Gumbo stood drinks for the whole bar. Even for the tourists who happened to be there, who toasted him enthusiastically.

"I'll bet," he said, "that they always ask what really happened in that streetcar."

Why was it called *Desire?* The streetcar named Desire. Had the driver and one of his riders made love at the last stop? On the seats? What happened during the run and how did it come to that? This was the question his book would answer, if he went to jail for a year. The driver's name would be Kowalski and the rider's name would be Stella. The night would be hot. The title of the book would be *Streetcar, Last Stop.*

Louisa would be dressed like Stella from the movie and would sell the book in front of the streetcar.

"Ah," he sighed after a short while, when he saw that his latest inspiration hadn't made a strong impression on Gregor Gradnik.

"I'm running short of ideas. That's bad," he said, "very bad."

6

They drove to Biloxi. Waves of hot air washed in through the open windows. Jesus didn't want to play. He was sober and short of breath. Louisa sat shrinking into a corner of the back seat. G. and G. debated the odds that Oristide Lagniappe would get a suspended sentence. Gumbo suggested that Gregor call the blond that used to come visit him. Mostly at night, but sometimes in the middle of the day. Sometimes she would jog over in her running gear. Gumbo sees all, Gumbo knows all. Gregor lit a cigarette and looked out over the fleeting coastal countryside. He thought of the trip down to the delta shortly after his arrival. All three of them had sat in the front seat in Peter's Buick. Discreet garlic. Gumbo said that he'd seen her in court. Clutching a file under her arm. Maybe even his. Surely, she could help. Shut up, Louisa said. What did I say? Gumbo said. Jesus moaned. It was hot and his thirst was getting to him. Gumbo didn't want to stop. The three of them bickered all the way to Biloxi.

There they sat on the beach among bronzed bodies. Jesus had brought two cartons of beer from a wholesale store. And as evening drew on and the bathers began to disappear, they still sat there. Now Jesus started to play. Suddenly he pulled a harmonica from his pocket and drew it across his lips. Suddenly he was by himself, uninterested in any musical requests from the group. He played for himself. And perhaps for the ocean as it lapped the beach in its endless motion. The sand was hot and a breeze was coming in from the water. Gregor lay on his back and watched the limitless sky slowly darkening. Louisa suddenly stood up and waded into the surf. She kept going farther and farther, and then they saw her waving her arms and losing her balance. G. and G. raced into the water and carried her up onto the beach. Gumbo's face had darkened completely. There you went again, he shouted, there you went again. He landed her a swift, heavy slap to the face. She hung her head, her wet hair draped over her face. Jesus kept playing.

During the ride back Gumbo tried to lighten the mood. As if life wasn't screwed up enough to begin with, he said, we have to go screw it up even worse. He turned the radio up and sang along loudly. Jesus had a paper bag now, and a bottle inside it. He was talking about the musician he played with. There's no one worse than me, he said, when I play sober. But when they were both high, they only had to take one look at each other and they knew. Jesus played the low notes, and he never crossed over. Sometimes with the dirty notes he'd cross over, but then he'd get a look and he'd go back down. He plays the blue notes himself, he won't let anybody else get near them. Jazz musicians are the last bohemians in America, Gumbo said. The writers are all tromping around the universities, teaching kids how to use commas. Exclamation marks, Gregor Gradnik thought, exclamation marks. And they study melancholy. The painters are painting portraits in Jackson Square. There are no Tennessees anymore. Making things smell of perfume, of whiskey, of urine and blood. Only Jesus was still an artist. He didn't give a damn about universities. Jesus agreed: he didn't give a damn.

They drove across Lake Pontchartrain, over the low-slung, infinitely long bridge on wooden piers. Endlessly dark water on both sides. It was night. Louisa was asleep, Gumbo was finally quiet. And Jesus played.

7

But when they crossed the viaduct into the city, things worsened again. Gumbo explained that he and his brothers and sisters were going to open a restaurant where they would serve gumbo, jambalaya, shellfish, and things like that. Louisa spoiled Gumbo's most promising plan to date when she suddenly awoke. She wasn't going to cook that sludge. Or serve it. What sludge? Gumbo asked. That stuff that smells like stinky fish. Gumbo shouted at her. Louisa shrieked. Jesus threw his empty bottle out the window. Gumbo stopped the car. Do you want the police to arrest me? he shouted. Black bastard, he shouted. Jesus opened the door and got out in the middle of the honking, speeding traffic. He approached the driver's door. Never again, Gumbo, he said, never again. Gumbo stepped on the gas and drove away. Then he thought better of it and tried to drive back in reverse. Brakes squealed, a siren howled, and a police car approached.

"Damn," Gumbo said. "I really am going to have to write that book."

8

That night with painful clarity he felt the presence of another body next to him. He heard breathing, gentle words, a familiar voice. Someone was sitting on his bed and saying something to him. It was a woman, an old woman, a creature radiating something that reached into his breast and locked around his heart, something that was warm and good and yet painful and unclear. He ought to do something—this he understood. He ought to do something. I'm going now, said the woman sitting on his bed. He shivered at the simultaneous presence of something near yet foreign, familiar yet unknown, good yet painful. His body dissolved into fragments that floated away into space, body, and soul at once. He bolted up and the woman vanished. Only her voice remained. Even now he could hear it clearly. It was his mother's voice.

It was four o'clock in the morning.

With effort he sank back into a troubled sleep. At six the phone rang. Ana's voice was on the other end. I'm afraid I can't come, she said. We just took mother to the hospital.

When?

Two hours ago.

Gregor.

Yes.

Are you still there?

Yes. Do you believe that . . . ?

What?

Nothing.

CHAPTER 23

THE CUPOLA

I

The white-hot cupola of the sky envelops the city. Summer has come to a halt, the wind has come to a halt, and the damp heat flickers. The cupola is saturated with humidity, with steam that creeps through the skin's pores and malodorously trickles back out of them. Gregor Gradnik, head propped against the wet wall, lies on his bed watching the huge paddles droning monotonously around overhead. The air conditioner sputters, sending streams of tepid, moist air into the room. The street is empty. A young black man sits on steps opposite, blowing his slow, muddled story into some instrument. Across the street Stella is moving through a prism of yellow light. Wearing just a slip, the woman is opening and closing the window; he can see her mouth opening but can't hear her voice. The man in the undershirt with a tattooed emblem gets up, angrily opens the window, and drinks down a can of beer. His undershirt sticks to his body from the sweat. Both of them are sweat-drenched. Gregor Samsa's antennae poke out and wiggle from the crack under the kitchen door and then slowly disappear. Gregor Gradnik ought to disappear from this place, too, once and for all, and retreat to the shore of some cool, Alpine lake. But he can't. He doesn't feel like getting up. He watches a rivulet of sweat creep across his stomach and drop onto the crumpled papers with their blurry jottings. The sky's white-hot cupola envelops the city. The humid air flickers. The heat weighs down. Summer has come to a halt, and so has the story.

There isn't a trace of wind anywhere. The bell jar is motionless. Its invisible weight presses down on the landscape like a lid. Tourists wipe their sweaty faces. There isn't a cloud to be seen. Cloying air drifts in from the bayous. The river flows slowly.

Sometime around mid-morning Bob walks past the windows. Tyranosaurus rex is moderately stuffed. Wobbly legs carry his powerful body; with sleeves rolled up high, almost to the shoulder, and pressing into the skin, his arms jerkily dance around him. In the evening Martin's dog lies in the doorway of the bar and snores. His snoring blends with a plethora of other sounds into a musical theme. Somewhere a jazz fugue goes scampering.

2

He got a picture postcard from Gumbo:
We're cooking jambalaya. Come join us.
Come where? It was hot, and he didn't want to see him.

Fred and his family had left for some cool forest. That was fine, too. Meg found an apartment in New York without Fred's help. Irene was in New York, possibly riding a bike. Love Conquers All. All Conquers Love. Ana was standing next to a hospital bed. He was here. Now.

Now he was alone amid the slow, hot slouch of summer, as he had been alone in the middle of winter when he suddenly appeared here, a forlorn dot in the midst of the huge continent. Fred had left behind a mountain of papers and diskettes in the library. This business with the anatomy of melancholy was turning into a maze of data that would never produce a book. Gumbo would write his *Streetcar, Last Stop* before Fred Blaumann ever wrote his *Centuries of Melancholy*. He burrowed into the work, thoughtlessly copying out sentences that he later realized he had copied out long before. He would strike the wrong computer keys, and medieval scenes of melancholy sensual delusion flashed before his eyes. The lightly clad librarian sat weary-limbed at her desk and waited to be rescued. He caught himself standing outside a bar where nude women danced on the tables, thinking of going in. He saw himself take a seat among a row of men looking up at the dancing legs. He saw himself ordering a drink, joining the others in banging on the table and howling at the naked flesh that moved through a swath of light within arm's reach.

Debbie told him she had caught his scent.

3

You can tell a lonely man by his scent, she said. A lonely male smells very distinctive. And lonely women don't? Don't females give out some special scent? It's possible, Debbie said, but we specialize in lonely males. And what is the scent of a lonely male? Like gas from a stove. Invisible and indistinct, but unmistakable. If you don't believe me, she said, ask the girls. He didn't ask the girls, because he knew why she was telling him this. It was because she had caught his scent. Bob—Tyranosaurus rex—had caught his scent, too. Bob was always on the prowl. Such was his prowling, cockroach life. One hot evening, as he sat listlessly next to Martin, he sent his feelers out toward him. He brought him a tall, young, fragile, and slender creature with amazingly long, lianalike hands. She was in some difficulty, Bob's beginner. Would he like to meet her?

Why not? Sure.

The creature ordered a glass of champagne and then said she was having some problems.

He said he would really like to help her out, but he didn't know if he could.

He could, he probably could. She needed fifty dollars.

The offer was swift and unambiguous. In a single interval between two sentences he first had to deal with himself: would he pay money to sleep with a woman? He would never have thought temptation would come in the form of a fragile, lianalike creature whose voice and long hands shook. But his thoughts were thickset and heavy, as the evening was hot and heavy. Warm, pungent, animal interchange between the sexes, slow, undulating tension. She smiled. She knew that his palms were wet from her nearness, from the hot night and her nearness.

He said something else, something irreparably different from what he had wanted to say on this hot night.

"What do you need the fifty dollars for?" he said naively and stupidly, albeit—ah—with quivering viscera.

This is what people say who are perplexed when they discover they've taken an umbrella out on a sunny day. This is what academics say when they're fearful every step of their life that they might be shut out of the elite club. If he took this girl with him, his sluggish thoughts told him, he would leave nothing but derision behind. In the eyes of the Rigby's club he would forever be no better than some pathetic tourist from Texas, some lecher. A fool, a customer, food for cockroaches. He would never be a full-fledged member of this illustrious group, this exchange of human wisdom, and Martin would never show him his brilliant invention. He would be a passerby, to whom a little bit was given, but from whom as much as possible should be taken. The kind that, when drunk, can be kicked and robbed, because they're not worth anything. His fear of becoming the absentminded professor who carries an umbrella around on a sunny day—a terrible, conformist fear—was stronger.

"What do you need the fifty dollars for?" he said naively and stupidly, albeit—ah—with quivering viscera.

The smile faded. She cautiously looked toward the head cockroach. Rex raised an eyebrow and the creature pulled a picture of a beautiful, small child out of her handbag. The child didn't bear the slightest resemblance to her. And he realized to his horror that he was only now being expelled from the club for good. They were treating him like a plainclothes cop trying to sniff out illegal prostitution. He gave her ten dollars. For the kid. Martin gave an almost imperceptible nod. Debbie rolled her eyes. Rex growled. Gregor Gradnik said good-bye and left abruptly, wrapped in the cloud of his treacherous scent.

4

He opens a can of Campbell's soup. The can opener gets stuck and won't go forward. He sips some of the thick, sweetish liquid out of the opening. He spits it out into the sink. Why does everything in this country have to be so damned sweet? And hot. And humid. He tries to read. He grazes through the television channels. He tries to go to sleep. Her inclined head, her slender neck under the black hair, her attentiveness. Studied, experienced, ready for anything. She was still sitting there. He could still change his mind. Pay the difference. He tosses in bed. There won't be any sleep. Is this his imagination, or a body? Her body, formless but present. In detail. The neck. The corners of the mouth. The hands. Surely she has some contagious disease. This thought makes it easier, but girls like that stock condoms in their handbags. Hermit, preacher, moralist Gradnik amid the sin of this quarter with an umbrella in the noonday sun. In every room around him at night there was touching, contact, human contact, breathing, gentle moans. Across the street were Stella and Kowalski. Getting on in years, but still desirous. All around there was a current of desire, pliant human slipperiness. Only here Gregor Gradnik was lying in bed, writing a book about melancholy in his head. About loneliness. About desire. At the thought of her getting up from the bar stool, draping her arm over his shoulder and squeezing it conspiratorially, of her hips brushing against him, of the two of them leaving together: at this thought the blood, the vapors, the melancholy matter (is that it, Blaumann, is that it?) course unrestrainably through his system and threaten to burst out his nostrils and eyes if he doesn't escape. The inflamed spleen's bile rushes from mind to body, from body to soul. He unfastens her buttons, wordlessly: no. No, he offers her good advice while hitching up her skirt. No, women like that take their clothes right off and probably shower, too.

Pull yourself together, you've got to pull yourself together in this crazy, hot, summer, cockroach-infested, nightmarish night in a foreign country, where there are no thoughts that can stop its slow, sinister surge.

5

From Blaumann's computer:

How to defend against assaults of melancholy caused by the devil's temptation of body and soul? Scorn the world. Contemptus mundi, 1775.

First: In bed at night assume the position of a corpse.

For how long, it doesn't say. How to avoid thinking sinful thoughts, it doesn't say.

Second: At every meal eat a piece of bread to feed the worms that will consume one's body.

That one is good. That one is really frightening. It could feed the cockroaches, too. His cockroach is crazy about bread crumbs.

Third: View illness as death's helpmate.

Fourth: Keep a skull in one's room and meditate on what it once was and what it is now. Think similar thoughts of oneself.

Fifth: Have one's burial site prepared and a tombstone erected and kiss it every day.

Scorn the world. Kiss one's grave. Sleep. Tonight, at least.

Wild laughter from outside shatters the midnight silence. That's the devil roaring at his human distress, tied up in an embryonic knot on his bed: a sweaty mass of male tissue desperate to escape desire. The tempter laughs when a person cries. So does God.

■ □ ■ □ ■

CHAPTER 24

SUMMER AMONG
THE COCKROACHES

I

The neon's first gleaming.

Shadowy figures on the sidewalk outside the gay bar
waver, run here and there, enter a sheaf of light and then run
back out of it. Cockroaches. He knows them from Rigby's, he
knows their life. Rigby's is a safe cockroach den, a swarming
nest. Every morning they squint into the sunlight and run
back. Or into their lairs, which are scattered around the
Quarter or the suburbs. In humid wooden houses. In old
rooms around the city, where the wallpaper rots and peels.
American biologists have discovered seventeen species of
cockroach in the genus *Blatidae* and *Blataria*. The New
Orleans cockroach hasn't been given a name yet, though it
certainly deserves one. Gumbo was for *Blatidae Louisiana.*
There were the cockroaches from Rigby's: Debbie, a soft, fat
Blataria; Liana, a flat, quick-moving creature that seeks out
the floodlights out there on Bourbon Street somewhere,
undresses quickly, and jerkily dances around right under the
eyes and hands of all the drunk cockroaches, then runs back
into the dark, preferably to Rigby's, where it rejoins its cohort
of cockroaches gathered around a table; Martin, a wise, old
cockroach that never moves, lurks in its corner, watching the
world, and hardly even wiggles its feelers—he's learned his
lessons from cockroach life; Bob, a brutal, muscular cockroach stuffed with power, the undisputed ruler of the lair and

the surroundings—a cockroach Tyranosaurus rex; Jesus, an ugly, rumpled, black cockroach that mutters to itself, tanked until it starts to play . . . and when it plays, all the other cockroaches love and admire it.

And all the others that go swarming back and forth around the Quarter, in and out, their ceaselessly wiggling feelers trying to scrounge a dollar, a scrap of life.

They flee from daylight. By day they lurk in their holes, or at most they hang out at Rigby's and similar nests. Occasionally one of them will squint out onto St. Philip Street, shield its eyes from the harsh sunlight and dart back inside. By day you can see them lying on the banks of the Mississippi. They lie in the grass or sit on the benches; but those aren't local cockroaches, they're newcomers, arriving in the warm, dank city from all over the country.

French Quarter cockroaches really only come to life at night. They can tolerate the glare of streetlights, and so they wait to go out until the neon's first glow spills onto the sidewalks. And how they come to life! How their pallid faces brighten, and their black, feelerlike arms start flickering in all directions. Every night, at the neon's first gleaming, the swarming of the cockroaches begins; when night falls, when it becomes possible to catch some food, drink, or tourist droppings; every night when the feelers start to wiggle, when the legs eager for prey tremble in anticipation, when the arms shake, when the mandibles quiver; every night at the opening of a new season, a season of a single, long night, of prolonged cockroach prowling after the drunk, the stupid, the rich, the ones that have lagged from the herd, and in an instant the cockroaches swarm over them. The female cockroaches reach for the trousers and into the pockets, while the males take their share, crawling, swarming into pockets, under skirts, into collars. In order to devour the soft substances, the sperm, to shoot sperm into the warm pubic regions of aging tourists.

When night falls, the flat-thoraxed orthoptera that shun the light and feed on garbage begin to swarm. In order to bite off a piece of money, flesh, earlobe, dream, life. That piece of everything that by the natural order of things belongs to them.

2

Martin's dog and dreams.

Beneath the vault of the great, hot cupola Martin's dog has it best. He lies in the doorway, chomps on ice, snores, and sometimes snarls contentedly in his sleep. Martin explains that this is because he's dreaming that he's sailing down the Mississippi with his master. Martin used to be an actor in Hollywood, something everyone knows. He never talks about it, although Gregor occasionally tries to prod him into that subject. Martin likes to talk about the gadget he invented. Before he became an actor he was an engineer. Since he stopped being an actor, he's become an engineer again. He invented a device for cleaning mud out of the boats that navigate the Mississippi. He likes to talk about that device. His invention is patented, and he always carries the certificate from the patent office around in his pocket. Whenever there's a mechanical engineer in the vicinity he goes running to fetch his complicated schematics. But this doesn't happen that often. For the most part Gregor Gradnik has been his company this summer.

"I'll have a bourbon," he says. "When I go to bed totally sober I fall out of airplanes all night."

"Every night?" Martin asks in disbelief.

"Every sober night."

"Now my dog dreams that the two of us are sailing on a boat. Actually, that's my dream. But I'm sure it's his, too. That's well known."

"When I fall, it's always just outside of Kennedy. There's an infernal fire and heat up above, and down below are cool, heavenly expanses."

"I'd say it's the other way around."

"No."

"Well, maybe not."

"Definitely not."

"If somebody told you that the Mississippi flowed up over some tavern, would you believe him?"

"No."

"Well, see. You're sitting in that tavern now."

"Lucifer falls and the angel takes his soul away. The angel doesn't have any individuated will."

"How about the dog, does he have a soul?"

"Martin! Falling in your sleep is a recollection of the fallen angel."

"My dog's got a soul. Otherwise he wouldn't be sailing the Mississippi with me. We sail, and my machine washes the mud out, washes it out and cleans the boat so it gleams."

"It's the fall, Martin, the fall!"

Debbie: Be careful one of you doesn't fall off his bar stool. You're pretty high up.

Martin: Hell is empty. All the devils are here.

Martin knows Ariel's lines from one of his auditions.

Their words are garbled and stop making sense. They snarl and drawl like the thick, humid air.

3

Liana and Jesus.

On one side is Jesus, about to pass out.

On the other side is Liana, dancing on a round table and shouting: I'm gonna screw that black man, I'm gonna screw that black man. Her sailor of the night tries to get her off the table. He laughs at her. He's very kind.

Jesus plays for money, and sometimes he improvises with his friends at Fritz's. Fritz has German helmets and medals decorating his walls. This doesn't bother Jesus; all he cares about is the music. He sees his partner's expression as they play together, he feels his rhythm.

Jesus always carries a bottle around with him. In a paper bag. Debbie doesn't like him. She doesn't like him because he carries the bottle around. She doesn't like him because his head drops onto the bar and the bottle breaks. But Jesus is such a good musician that he can do what he wants. Jesus is the only black person you'll see at Rigby's. Jesus can also lie drunk in the middle of the lobby at the St. Charles Hotel. They never throw him out. They always remove him, carefully and politely. Jesus has numerous privileges. As a result, Debbie is afraid of him and never throws him out the way she might single-handedly throw out a bum or some rich tourist with too many ideas. Only after Jesus passes out does Debbie allow herself to take a few potshots at him.

This evening his head dropped early. The night before he played all night. Tonight he's earned his rest. There are still a lot of people in the bar, and it's only two in the morning. Jesus's head lies on the bar; the bottle in the paper bag is empty. Debbie lifts his heavy head. "He's loaded," she says.

"Leave the artist alone," Martin says.

"Some artist," says Debbie.

The sailor keeps pulling Liana off the table. Liana shoves him away.

"I want Jesus," Liana says.

Debbie says she's going to vomit. The sailor laughs and tries to entice her.

"Come on down," he says. "Come on down, I'm your Jesus. You'll see."

"No, you're not," Liana says, "my Jesus is black."

"Your Jesus is loaded," Debbie says.

4

Cockroaches, close up.

All month long he wanders around New Orleans. Amid the tourists, amid the musicians, amid the cockroaches. The coins that he caught during Mardi Gras gather dust on a shelf. The Rex parade. When was that now?

Samsa picks up a crumb of bread and runs with it. His

feelers poke out of a crevice. Happy cucaracha, one day somebody's going to squash him against the floor or a wall.

News from home. Where is that now? Mama is doing better. I'm still not coming, Ana. Who is that now? From the computer: *Melancholy has the characteristics of death.* What is that now? Melancholy . . . death . . . a sinful person is a wolf in its own vomit.

Look: a time of long, lazy motion, a time of summer among exhausted people. A time when the long summer's dough stretches around them. A time when you miss no one. A time when no one misses you. A time of living with those closest to you, with Stella and Kowalski, as their sweaty bodies move lazily upon the bed. A time of cockroaches. A time when heavy, fat food is eaten, acrid fat grilled on top of iron screens.

Listen: to the hot, slow expiration of time. Listen to the voices singing, to the heavy, monotonous rhythm. To the music that slips through walls into the room. Listen to the rushing of the shower water as it rinses the body, listen to the beating of the organism as it tries to find the slow, hot rhythm, but can't find itself, can't find itself in the rhythm, can't keep up.

5

The madwoman.

The old, flaxen-haired woman that used to be queen in these parts but now doesn't even have her own apartment shakes her head strangely and combs her flaxen hair. Her hair is long and still beautiful, her face is furrowed, and a thin scar stretches along one side of her nose. Tonight there are three sailors here, joking with her. She spends all her days and nights here—she has no apartment, no home, no friends. She does have her hair, which everyone used to admire.

She is the European, because she spent time in Europe. She worked in Germany, on an army base. Some officer committed suicide on her account. He was from Louisville, Kentucky. They raise horses there, and he was a horse breeder. He had a wife and her. He drank too much. He shot himself in the PX.

Everyone likes her. She's crazy. She was queen of these parts when she returned from Europe. She combs her hair and sings.

Just like some other old woman combed her hair! Just like she sang! His mother.

6

The dreams of Debbie the waitress.

She dreams. Debbie dreams. Just as soon as she finishes working in the bar, just as soon as her last hour is up, she starts to dream. Martin says that when Debbie dreams she becomes a steel magnolia, like those women in the movie about yellow fever in the South.

In the early morning Debbie sits on *the other side* of the bar. With her head down amid glasses full of the very best drinks. Liana offers her coffee.

"Debbie," she says, "don't sleep in the bar."

Debbie raises her head.

"Who's sleeping in the bar?" she says.

"You're sleeping in the bar where you work," Liana says.

"I'm not sleeping in the bar, I'm sleeping at the bar."

She drops her head back down among the glasses. Debbie is loaded.

"You worked all night," Liana says, "and now you're going to throw it all away."

Debbie raises her head and directs the young waiter, "Pour that witch a martini, on me. And tell her to keep quiet."

"Debbie, go home."

"Quiet, I said. Otherwise I can't sleep."

For a while everyone is quiet. They don't, in fact, have much to say to each other at this hour of the morning. The night has been long and sleepless. The silence disturbs Debbie. Suddenly she gets up.

"If it's going to be quiet," she says, "I won't even be able to sleep. Let me tell you something," she says. "Something you've never heard before. You think that Debbie on the other side of the bar is a big ear for all your bullshit."

"Now she's going to be wounded," Martin says to Gregor.

"I'm a wounded woman," Debbie says. "I'm Deborah."

Deborah reaches behind the bar and pulls out a book. "This," she says, "this is the book." And she bangs it on the bartop. The book bears a big, red title: *The Wounded Woman.* "And I don't give a damn about any of you. I've got a car, I've got Bob, I've got a painter in love with me. I don't give a damn about any of you. I don't give a damn about New Orleans. This is one shitty town. One of these days I'm gonna leave here, with my painter. We'll do something that will make you gape in awe."

"Here comes the real estate business," Martin says.

"What did you say?" Debbie says.

"Nothing, nothing," Martin says.

"You just take care of your dog," Debbie says. "But I'm going to buy up real estate down in Bayou Country."

"It's not worth anything," Martin says. "It's nothing but swampland."

"I'll drain it. You hear?"

Everyone heard.

"And do you know what I'm gonna build there?"

No one says anything, because everyone knows. She points her finger at Gregor.

"You! Do you know what I'm gonna build?"

Gregor shakes his head.

"I'm gonna build a new New Orleans. A real one."

"You'll do no such thing," Martin says. "This city's already been built, and it's the real one."

"Like hell it is," Debbie says. "This city is shit. Just crap, wherever I look. Bourbon Street's the biggest pile of shit, with tourists from Kentucky in their white pants coming down here to find something to screw. The river's screwed up, the

Superdome's an obscenity. Who?" she says, banging *Wound-ed Woman* against the counter, "who built that obscenity?"

"The painter told her that," Martin says to Gregor. "He's a big influence on her."

Then Debbie falls to dreaming again. She looks toward the door, through which rays of the morning sun are falling. From various glasses she sips her expensive drinks. She speaks softly and everyone listens:

"My New New Orleans is going to be completely different. It's going to be a small city. Right in the middle it's going to have a cemetery with those stone crypts and flowers, St. Louis Cemetery. It'll be quiet there. Around that will be the Vieux Carré, without Bourbon Street, and tourists won't be allowed in. All the balconies will be there, and the little cathedral, and Preservation Hall will be close by. There won't be any Canal Street, there won't be any business, or police, or soccer, or Jackson Monument. There will be little Cajun houses, an old Creole villa, and a plantation barrack. Inside the barrack they'll play drums at night, practice voodoo, and talk about the old days. There'll be lots of Dixieland, blues too."

"Where will Rigby's British Pub be?" Liana asks.

"This lousy pit? Nowhere."

"Then you'll be jobless," Liana says, and everyone laughs.

"You'll be jobless, because there won't be any lousy Bourbon Street."

And they laugh even harder.

"Come to think of it . . . ," Martin says. And silence falls. Whenever Martin thinks, silence falls.

"Martin will be there," Debbie adds quietly, "and his dog, too. No libraries, though," she says to Gregor. "You can borrow books from me: *Wounded Woman* and stuff like that. There'll be a gallery for my painter. There'll be all kinds of things."

It gets quiet again. Everyone thinks along with Martin. About the city that Debbie is going to build down in the river delta, where there are swamps now and where they show the tourists alligators. An entire old city tucked away safe and sound. All the good people and all her friends will be safe there in Debbie the waitress's dreams, in her warm belly.

"Come to think of it," Martin says, because now he's had time to think it over, "it's not a bad idea at all."

Martin's dog growls contentedly in the doorway. His ponderous, Oblomovian head rests on his front paws. In his dreams, he and Martin are sailing down the wide river. Martin's invention flushes the mud out of the boat. It's quiet and peaceful: the morning sun shines onto the boat and shines into Rigby's as it sails with all its passengers toward the delta where the new city is growing. The city for Deborah and her painter, where there will be room for all the others, too. The old woman combs her hair. Slowly she pulls the comb through her long, flaxen hair, and Gregor wonders why she doesn't have any gray, like that other old woman does, his mother. This one has flaxen hair, like Louisa, who sits wordlessly by the window, gazing at some indeterminate point across the street. The air is warm, and soon it will be hot. The young waiter, afraid to say anything, cautiously turns on the fan. The paddles start slowly moving, then they start to whir, and a wind sets up from above, causing the boat to sail all the faster.

Everyone looks toward the door as Bob appears there. Tyranosaurus rex. He steps inside and sits down next to Debbie. He looks straight ahead.

"Dreaming again?" he says.

Jesus raises his head and feels around for a bottle, then gets up.

"I'm going to sleep," he says.

"Where's your painter?" Bob says. "Isn't your painter here?"

Her painter is in Jackson Square. Gregor knows him. A little guy, every morning he's the first to set up his easel, and till evening he paints people in ten-gallon hats and girls with blond hair.

"Leave my painter alone," Debbie says.

"You drank all this?" Bob says and sweeps the glasses off the bar with his arm.

"Show's over," he says.

"No, it's not," Debbie says, and she grabs a bottle and smashes it against the floor.

The customers get up. The show really is over. Some of them keep dreaming once they're outside—lovely, cockroach dreams.

7

Unseen hours, abominations.

Shave and wash the night's abominations away.

In the morning he wanted to shave. He looked at his bloated face in the mirror. The bags under his eyes. Shave, every morning lather up and shave away the night's abominations. And listen to the babbling fountain on the patio, out in the yard. He looked at his eyes: there was something missing from them. Memory. The memory had been erased from them, as if from Fred's computer. All that remained was the present, the dull presence of the body, melancholy matter. The substance of memory dissolves in the organism and escapes like gas through pores in the skin. With the smell of a leaking gas line.

That had been in the morning, and now it was evening. The day's hours had gotten scrambled. He couldn't shave—that had been in the morning—because the landlord had disconnected him from civilization. The landlord had shut off his electricity. Again he had forgotten to write him a check for the rent. That was in the morning. The man that had welcomed him as the Pennslovenian Dostoevsky was determined to fix him: "*I'll fix you.*" Now it was evening. There was no light, the flickering screen was dark, the air conditioner had stopped rattling, and the fan's paddles stood still beneath the ceiling. So this is how these slow summer cockroaches used to live here, Gregor thought slowly. He opened a bottle and drank from it thoughtlessly and immoderately. He lay on his bed and watched the woman across the street in her slip as she walked into and out of the room, all the time saying *the women come and go, speaking of Michelangelo.* The bald man, beer in hand, gestured and tried to explain something to her. At Rigby's they were playing poker. Now, in the evening, they were playing poker. He lay on top of his bed and drank. Streetcar, last stop.

It struck him that Samsa was cautiously observing him from somewhere. And many other eyes, a multitude of them.

He went to watch them play poker. Mitch was bloated from lack of a night's sleep. Pablo twisted a cigar between his teeth. Laughter was coming from somewhere—streams of crystalline, hysterical laughter. That was Blanche. She was laughing from some glass cage.

Then he dropped some coins into a video game and mindlessly pressed its buttons. Things lit up, clanged, and boomed. Omnivorous chickens ran through a labyrinth devouring each other. Before his eyes their gaping beaks turned into huge jaws that chattered and devoured. The chickens flickered like cockroaches and went racing through labyrinths of walls, cupboards, streets, storm sewers, the whole city.

Past tense, present tense. Same day tense. Invisible hours.

A group of homeless people gathers outside his window. They rifle through the bags of garbage. They trample the aluminum cans to get as many of them as possible into a bag, each of them worth five cents. They swarm around buildings that are the daytime gathering points of businessmen, and they collect the leftovers. They rummage, this cockroach demimonde, this parallel world, the underground of American civilization.

8

Suddenly in some other story.

Suddenly in some other story. Suddenly in some other, horribly different, horribly dreamlike story. That had to come in ten days' time. Suddenly in the dream of some cockroach.

How do you say ambulance? How do you say doctor? Suddenly he only knew the Slovene words. I don't feel well, he said, I feel bad. Somebody laughed. Loaded, Debbie said. I'll get him home, Martin said. He could hear their words, but they couldn't hear his. He had drunk this evening, he had drunk all evening, and inhaled some horribly strong stuff that Bob brought. He mixed it with booze, Bob said. He shouldn't have done that, Debbie said. *Ambulance, that's* what he was trying to shout, but he couldn't produce a voice. He's not used to it, said Martin, it isn't for everybody. But his voice had vanished, all that remained was a weakness that hollowed out the walls of his body, shoving at them in immense waves. Amid the wall-lessness of his soul the sound, ringing, and fall of a glass resonated as though within inches. Myriad stars, myriad things in the vault of heaven, and then a prolonged fall through the crowds of Mardi Gras, teeming, excitable crowds. He heard Liana call to Jesus, heard Jesus playing: all of it was close up and distinct, only he was falling, and crowds carrying sharp instruments waited below. Then he lay on his bed: devils, he screamed, get away, damned devils! The window receded, growing smaller and smaller. A huge bird kept flying in starts at the ceiling, with huge fanlike wings propelling streams of thick, warm air at him through its rear and beak, through both orifices. A fingernail jutted out of a female sex organ, out of a cuntlike furrow very close by his face. The broad fingernail of a broad hand. I feel sick, he said. Help me, he said, dear Jesus, help me. He kept falling. The abyss was bottomless.

9

He lies on his bed in the dark. His face is illuminated by neon light. He can feel something slowly crawling across his face. The darkness, in the darkness he's brave. Samsa, Gregor Samsa is crawling across his face. He has recognized Gregor Gradnik as his own, and now he's crawling over his swollen, cockroachlike face. He gets up slowly and the cockroach runs. He can see him flickering on the floor next to his bed. The cockroach flees. His hand swoops down. Down by the floor there is a crunch: he's squashed. A squashed spot on the floor.

Now he gets up. He staggers into the bathroom and shoves his head under a stream of water. A jingling, jangling streetcar. Some woman's hysterical laughter—Blanche.

A quiet scraping sound came from the kitchen. When he opened the door something crunched and splattered underfoot again. For an instant he went leaden with fear and awful disgust, both at the same time. A horde of cockroaches was swarming over the floor, crawling out of all the cracks, over the walls, up the table legs. The vile mass started swelling through the doorway and fleeing in its muddled commotion. He clapped his hands and the swarming horde snapped and darted to all sides. But a second later it had spread back over the floor like a black carpet.

He opened the windows. Outside there was dazzling sunlight. The fountain burbled on the patio, and the green leaves of the trees rustled.

When he turned around, the cockroaches had vanished. Where was I, he thought, in whose dreams?

That was the end. From then on there was no other road. Only the one leading home. But he had been moving in that direction all along, from the moment he set out on his journey.

CHAPTER 25

THE WEST WIND

I

It was August, the last days of the month. A dry west wind from the continent attacked the hot and humid cupola over the city. All at once the leaves started rustling and the trees stirred. Summer lightning from the river's many curled peaks worked its way across the river's surface. The light became transparent and saturated the bright facades of buildings, suddenly green, their subtle, limelike shades. It was time to go.

Fred had come back. He wasn't pleased with what had been accomplished. But he was pleased with himself. Mary and I are getting along well, he said, this is my home. Meg is in New York. It looks as though she'll stay there. Every evening he ran to Audubon Park. Irene is in New York, too. Every evening she runs to Central Park.

2

Gumbo was gone. It was impossible to raise him by phone. A black-haired Palestinian woman from Arizona had occupied his apartment. She parked her handsome, new bicycle in the hallway. She wore white stockings. She was enrolled at the College of Liberal Arts. Every morning she caused a ruckus outside his door as she unchained her bike. He made her a present of his copy of *Cycling New Orleans*.

Gregor and the landlord came to a friendly understanding

about the electricity. The landlord apologized. You looked pretty bad, he said, but that's artists for you. He didn't return the deposit. Because of the damage that the firemen had caused to his property.

3

Before he left he saw Louisa on Canal Street. She was sitting on the sidewalk, on a sleeping bag, in front of the department store. She was selling little pamphlets. The wind kept raising her flaxen, Slavic hair, which otherwise hung in hanks over her forehead. He watched her for a while. No one stopped. Then he approached her. She looked at him vacantly. I'm selling plays, she said. Plays? She had copied out dialogues from Tennessee into the little pamphlets. They're one-act plays, she said. Now and then somebody buys one. A person can enrich himself with them, intellectually. *Enrichissez-vous . . .* she said. *Enrichissez-vous.* Had Gumbo told her to do this? She shrugged. The skin on her face and hands was cracked. From the wind. She probably slept in the sleeping bag somewhere down by the river. Where's Gumbo? Gumbo's in jail. He got three years. Gumbo's in jail . . . the thought of him there, a rotund man of movement and freedom . . . in those angular rooms . . . with hard edges.

A stocky man with a sparse red beard walked by. He was carrying a sleeping bag over his shoulder. I'm with him now, she said. I can't wait for three years. She gave him one of the little pamphlets, which contained a dialogue between Stella and Kowalski transcribed in an attractive hand. What about the powder? Gregor asked. Perlainpainpain? She smiled.

I'm going now, she said. He watched the two of them walk off through a crowd of midday shoppers, with all their worldly belongings on their backs. The man picked up an empty aluminum can, smashed it with his heel, and threw it in a bag. Louisa turned around again. Gumbo said you should come visit him, she called out. He needs your help with what he's writing, the Last Stop.

Finally, Ana announced her visit. She would be arriving in

201

New York at the beginning of September. Fred helped him find an apartment. He would be living in some building called Whitby; Fred's college roommate had left town and the apartment would be available for two months.

There was nothing left for him to do here.

He had no one to say good-bye to. All of that had been taken care of long ago. One morning in Storyville, when he had rice and beans for breakfast. Even that had been a long time ago.

CHAPTER 26

HOFFMAN SCRATCHING

I

It had been winter in New York when he arrived. There had been slush on the streets. Now summer was coming to a close, the leaves were turning yellow, and the skyscrapers were donning yellow and brown.

His apartment was on the ground floor of an old but well-preserved building on West 45th Street. Not far from there, almost a year ago, he had experienced what's commonly referred to as culture shock. What's meant by this is probably something like finding yourself in a movie. All at once you're walking across a stage familiar to moviegoers in every small town theater of the global village. The silhouettes of skyscrapers and bridges, black faces and yellow cabs, the Empire State Building and Macy's, a river of lights and the floodlit sky: all of this is just a set in some studio where they manufacture images for you and where you suddenly happen to be. Before he had stayed at the Edison Hotel on 52nd Street. Before, when he landed, an icy seascape had ushered his plane to a hard landing, and the windows frosted over. Culture shock was the slush on Times Square bathed in light, the pulsation of light and bodies. Culture shock was the homeless people who warmed themselves in the steam coursing out of manholes, and the black limousines that docked like ships alongside theaters. It was cold, and the streets were full of slush. Life was open to a new story.

Now it was almost autumn. In the evenings the wind coming in from the Atlantic thinned the warm air that hovered over the streets. The floodlit sky quavered above the lights of the big city.

2

The doorman who gave him his keys moved lazily around his cabin with its barred window. He spent a long time looking suspiciously at his documents.

"The Whitby," he said and snapped his fingers, "the Whitby isn't just any building."

Just any and the snap of his fingers meant what Gregor already knew: it wasn't just any building, it was one for artists. In an arch over the door the bronze plate bearing its name was tarnished. The building's facade was tarnished, too, and the stucco was falling off in places. Elderly people sat inside the entrance, around the doorman's station. At one time they had been famous. An old man with black glasses and a cane was Wally Radeau, the famous vaudeville star. Nuncio Mondello wore a tiny hat and had false teeth. At one time he had played with Benny Goodman. The Whitby was a building with an old reputation. The Whitby was a building for has-been artists. Or for ruined ones. The old ones had been famous, and the younger ones lived in the Whitby because they couldn't afford anyplace else. They ran from one audition to the next and collected assistance. One old musician who gave him a friendly welcome was named Willy. There was a dog lying at his feet. Willy was blind.

The Whitby was an unusual and lively if elderly place. It's still standing there today if they haven't torn it down.

3

In any case, Fred Blaumann didn't trust this world, the world of the Whitby. It was too greedy. It never delved very deeply into things. Like his college roommate, who was almost as gifted as Meg, but then suddenly decided to go into acting. In New York, Fred said, there are about ten thousand actors waiting for a break. At least half of them are doomed to failure—auditions, waiting for parts, scraping together a living, slow decline. On the table in his college roommate's apartment there were some unwashed glasses and a bottle with one finger of wine left in it. Mold was growing on its red surface. Somebody had lived here. Somebody had waited here at night for a cab. This strange apartment was also artistic: there was moldy, undrunk wine on the table, an upright piano in the corner, and the artist's photographs on the walls. This actor, who could have become a Ph.D. and had instead become one of thousands waiting, didn't look doomed in his photographs. You couldn't tell that he had to run from one audition to the next and stand in line for a welfare check. A broadly smiling, blond young man in a baseball uniform, his arms around the shoulders of his classmates, Fred among them. Reclining, with outstretched arms, on a chair, a woman in a hat sitting across from him—a scene from some play. A group of actors in a restaurant, amid glasses and the leftovers from dinner, after a premiere. Here he is with still blond but thinning hair, and dark circles under his eyes, sitting at the piano in this very room. The entire wall was papered in photographs. Right in the middle was an enlarged group portrait, also taken in some bar, with a broad signature stretching across it. The aging blond actor was standing in the back row, pipe in hand. Among the crowd at the table was a face that Gregor Gradnik knew well: Dustin Hoffman. In the corner was the date and a few illegible scratchings, probably a dedication. Dustin Hoffman was smiling. He was scratching his head and saying: What are you doing here, Gregor Gradnik?

4

It was the apartment of a single male in late middle age. The rooms were stuffy and hadn't been aired out in quite a while. It smelled of deteriorating organic matter—urine,

Gregor guessed. He opened the window in the kitchen alcove. It opened onto the courtyard, onto the trash bin that stood next to the wall. He went into the bedroom, where the window looked out onto the street. Iron bars were fastened to it from the outside. He could see passersby, from the knee roughly up to the neck, depending on how tall they were. But it was impossible to see the head and legs, unless a dwarf happened to be walking past. Iron bars were fastened to it from the outside.

Affixed to the refrigerator door was a big sheet of paper with heavily underlined instructions. All of them began with "please" and ended with big exclamation marks. Please don't open the windows. Ever!! On one side is the trash bin! Cockroaches!!! On the other side is the street! Break-ins!!! The windows are shatterproof and soundproof!!! And airproof, Gregor thought. The cats should never leave the apartment! Ever!!!

What cats, for God's sake?

For now they're in apartment no. 23, first floor, at his friend Marilyn's. She's also an actress. She'd like you to pick them up. He picked up the the telephone to call Fred. Why hadn't he told him that there were cats living here, too? He had never taken care of a single cat, let alone two. And . . . His head spun at the thought of running from one landlord to another landlady in the big city. He put the phone down. In despair he turned and looked at the blond cat lover on the wall standing behind Dustin Hoffman. Yeah, Gradnik, Hoffman was saying, what do you have against cats?

He went to pick them up.

5

He learned that one was called Sam and the other Sally. The black one was Sally and the calico was Sam. Sam's fur was falling out, so he had to be given special cat food. Sally was touchy, but she only understood when you spoke nicely to her. She was pesky. Sam was stubborn. He had been neutered and you had to scratch him under his chin—he liked that.

When he dropped them on the floor, one of them hissed and showed its fangs. The other jumped onto the bed in the bedroom and curled up in a ball. Never scold them. They don't like it and will take revenge. Never!!! He asked Marilyn whether she would mind, these three months . . . no, she said, she had her own cats. And a dog. In fact, when she had rehearsals, would he mind . . . No, because he wouldn't be home much. He had work to do at the library and meetings of various kinds.

6

He didn't have work to do at the library and he didn't have meetings of any kind. Or rather: he could have had both, if he'd wanted, and if he'd overcome his own frame of mind. Fred had put together a list of books for him to look for at Columbia University library. Suggestions. A list of work contacts. A list of social contacts. Of restaurants where he could eat well and cheaply. You had to be everywhere. Every contact was valuable. Every instant you had to be in motion. Write down every phone number. Work at your business. Work on yourself. With a finger he etched canals through the spilled milk on the table. He tossed pieces of salami at the cats standing at a cautious distance in the bedroom doorway, even though that was strictly forbidden. Item 37: *Never feed them salami!* But Sam and Sally thought differently. They were excited about the salami. Eat, he said, because it wasn't explicitly forbidden, eat. If you don't eat, I'll skin the both of you alive, then throw you to the cockroaches and those little ants. First I'll skin the one while the other watches, then I'll skin the other while the first one watches. The cats greedily gobbled up the greasy food. Because it didn't stink the way their healthy cat food stank. Which, according to experts, not only had to contain all the right vitamins and minerals, but also had to stink.

I'm feeding the cats, he said, I'm feeding the cats. I'm turning the pages of the phone book. He turned the pages of the phone book and checked the numbers that Fred Blaumann had given him to take along. They were for various offices, various research institutes where Gregor Gradnik was supposed to check in, various foundations where he should at least introduce himself, various *contact persons* . . . he stopped at this phrase: contact person. You have to say this over and over: contact person, contact person. Everywhere there were contact persons, influential persons, very important persons, special persons, personal persons. But nowhere a single human being he could go drink beer with. Except for Willy the musician in the lobby next to the doorman's station. And he could barely make it that far. He was a person on the way out. He crumbled some bread and was amazed at his sudden spitefulness. It came thoughtlessly, out of the ether. He crumbled some bread into the canals drawn through the milk spilled on the table, and for a long time he glared at the weather forecast. Along the Eastern seaboard, beginning in Florida—*your mother is dying,* a voice said to him—a minor tropical storm front was moving north. It was unexpected and entirely unpredictable this time of year. The announcer grew unpredictably excited. In thirty years, he shouted, we haven't experienced anything like this in August, at the end of August. Like what? Rains lasting several days. *What are you doing here?* a voice in the studio, behind the announcer, said to Gregor Gradnik. Hoffman wasn't saying anything anymore.

7

On some sheet of paper was written the word: call. He would call Irene.

All you have to do is dial a number and the world steps into your room. The telephone, making the world smaller and closer; a dark object perched motionlessly on the shelf: a lonely person knows there is life hidden in its motionlessness and silence. That there is a whole, living world inside it, within arm's reach, so to speak. But often, before the arm does reach for it, more time passes than it would take to walk there. He hadn't called home, hadn't called Ana, hadn't called a single contact person. He found his name in the phone book. He picked up the telephone and slowly dialed the number.

"Yes?" a deep, female voice said on the other end.

"I beg your pardon," he said, "I just want to tell you that my name's the same as yours."

"I don't understand," came the voice from the depths.

"Your ancestors may have come from my country. Gone through the crack of Ellis Island."

"Just what is it you want?" it said.

"My name is Gradnik," he said.

There was a brief silence.

"You must be insane," the deep, female voice said, followed by a click in the receiver.

People from his part of the world weren't friendly. He knew this already. Sometimes they were downright rude.

He dialed again. A relative of his with the same last name owned a mortuary in this city. He had lost his address. He didn't find it listed under mortuaries.

"I'm calling the police," she said. "They'll find you quick."

He shoved the phone back among the bread crumbs and milk spilled on the table. He shoved the cat, which was licking the gelatinous stuff, aside. What the heck. He would call his contacts. And Irene.

CHAPTER 27

STATE OF EMERGENCY, CASUAL CONVERSATION

I

The streets were filled with trash. East River Park looked like a craggy, abandoned wasteland. Groups of homeless men were wandering through the piles of trash, shoving anything still usable into bags. If he squinted, it looked like ruins, like Dresden after the fire bombing. From the subway stop he pushed forward to Sixth Street and picked his way through a labyrinth of trash bins to the great water: the East River. He jumped over fallen trash cans and plastic bags showing their riven guts. He steered clear of heaps that in some places reached as high as second-story windows. It all reminded him of a harsh winter from his childhood. Then they had shoveled passageways through the snowdrifts. The area around Greenwich Village was thick with rubbish. The sanitation workers had been on strike for a week now.

It was humid, with heavy clouds lying low over Manhattan. It looked like it was going to rain. A child's furious shriek pierced his eardrums. The tall, ragged building that he was looking for was buried in trash, too. Here there were also heaps of plastic bags lying around, with trash leading all the way to the entrance. An older gentleman was shoveling it away and cursing audibly. With every thrust of his shovel he cursed and looked at Gregor Gradnik, as though he bore part of the responsibility for this state of emergency. He spent a long time searching through the long list of names and only now, as he rang the bell, did his heart start beating faster.

"There isn't any elevator," she said. "It'll take me a minute to come downstairs."

During that minute he watched the man as he rhythmically shoveled the garbage and rhythmically cursed. He pitched it on top of a tall heap that was slowly crumbling and sending bits of trash rolling down its sides. He suddenly seemed to notice a familiar object on the slope of the mountain of garbage. The handle of a bicycle was jutting out like the hand of a drowning person. Beneath it was a bicycle light, like the drowning person's eye.

2

He heard soft slippers running down a metal stairway. Then she was standing in the doorway, holding the door open with her leg. Her leg was tanned, with fine golden down on late-summer skin. Farther up was the edge of her light running shorts.

"*Trashy,*" she said. Feelsy, trashy, nicely. That was her. "Won't you come in?"

Following her, he climbed up the steps as they went past countless doors, leading to the top of the tower, somewhere at the edge of heaven. Before long he was panting.

"It's a long way up. Are you going to make it?"

"No problem."

"Are you still smoking?"

3

"It's a state of emergency," Peter says. Behind him the screen shows trash being blown down Fifth Street by the wind. The apartment is smaller, even the windows are smaller, and there's no Spanish balcony. Irene sits on the floor, crosses her legs, and throws a fistful of something to munch in her mouth.

"They're going to cram us all into our buildings," Irene says.

"I'm already sitting in the dark," Gregor says. "I'm on the ground floor."

Irene catches his eye and pulls a cover over her crossed legs.

"I remember when there was a huge amount of snow . . . ," Gregor says.

"This isn't snow," Peter says. "Snow doesn't stink."

"Of course," Gregor says, "what I meant to say . . . "

Peter pours them wine in silence.

"I didn't get the job," Irene suddenly says.

"That's New York," Peter says.

The picture on the screen pans across heaps of garbage in front of City Hall.

"That's not far from here," Irene says.

"If things don't work out," Peter says, "we'll pack it in and head back south."

"We will not," Irene says.

"Did you read the book *The Slaves of New York?*" Peter says.

"No," Gregor says.

"You've got to read it," Irene says, "everybody's reading it."

They sip their wine and listen to the announcer's agitated voice. The camera tracks a rat as it investigates a trash can and then crawls up a wall.

"My God," Irene says.

"That's disgusting," Peter says.

"I'll write that down," Gregor says. "*The Slaves of New York?*"

"That's right," Peter says. "Slaves."

"Once you're a slave, it's too late," Irene says.

Peter presses his lips tightly together. Wine comes dribbling out of his mouth. All at once he explodes in laughter, producing a shower of wine.

"I'm sorry," he says. "Are you still into jogging?"

Irene is busy watching the TV screen.

"No," Gregor says. "But I do smoke. And drink."

"Irene told me how you tried to prove yourself," Pedro says, and the wine comes spewing out again. "I'm sorry," he says, "but it really is funny."

"Of course," Gregor says, "of course it's funny."

Irene watches the TV screen.

"And you?" Gregor says. "Are you writing a new book?"

"Of course," Peter says.

"*Cycling New York?*" Gregor says.

"Something like that," Peter says. "Tandem, actually."

Her head significantly raised, the taut chin, and glinting eyes behind contact lenses.

"And you?" Peter says. "Have you finished your book?"

"No," Gregor says. "I'm still writing it."

"How far have you gotten?" Peter says.

"I'm working on the last few pages," Gregor says.

The TV screen shows sanitation workers getting into trucks.

"Something's happening," Irene says.

"Nothing's happening," Peter says.

"It is happening," Irene says. "They're getting into their trucks."

All three of them watch the sanitation workers as they jump onto their trucks.

"What's become of the famous bicycle?" Gregor says.

Peter and Irene exchange glances.

"There wasn't enough room," Irene says. "We had to throw it out."

"And we've been looking at it for a week now," Peter says, "because of the strike."

He steps over to the window and looks down. Irene looks at Gregor, then quickly shifts her glistening eyes to the TV screen.

"You can't see it anymore," she says.

Peter fetches a bicycle bell down from a shelf.

"This is all that's left," he says.

He sits back down and finishes the last of his wine.

"You did puncture it for me, you know," he says.

Gregor looks at Irene. Her eyes are glistening even more, and the soft skin under her eyes starts to twitch ever so slightly.

"It was an accident," Gregor says.

"Of course," Peter says, looking at Irene. "It was an accident."

Irene stuffs a fistful of peanuts into her mouth.

"No problem," Peter says, still looking at Irene.

The garbage trucks drive out of a parking lot and form a column.

"Now we're riding a tandem," Peter says.

"A tandem?" Gregor says.

"That's right," Peter says. "*New York by Tandem*."

"That's original," Gregor says.

"It is," Peter says. "There's just one psychological problem: who gets to steer? Because the one in the back only pedals."

"And who does steer?" Gregor says.

"It varies," Peter says.

The announcer agitatedly describes something. The sanitation workers are driving down Broadway, with people waving to them.

"It's time," Gregor says. "As we say back home, time to raise anchor."

"Are you in such a rush?" Irene says.

"Yes," Gregor says, "I've got a meeting at Columbia."

"At Columbia?" Peter says. "That sounds impressive."

"Can't you stay?" Irene says. "Finish your wine?"

Peter looks at her, then focuses on the column of trash trucks. For a long time he says nothing.

"Something's happening," he says.

4

They can hear shouts coming from the street. Many voices excitedly cheering. Irene jumps up and runs to the window.

On tiptoes, she stretches her head and torso far out over the edge of the window. When she stretches, her T-shirt hitches up, revealing the smooth, freckled skin on her back. The shouts get louder and louder. They can hear the rumble of a fleet of trucks. Peter and Gregor go to the window, too. People are standing on balconies and at front doors. All three of them stretch their heads out the window. Garbage trucks are driving down Sixth Street. The ground shakes from the rumble; the glasses on the table chatter. Gregor's side and arm touch Irene. She flinches. Both of them flinch. The needle comes to life, wavering in the charged field between two poles. The trucks stop in front of some buildings and load on trash. Children wave at them.

"They've started," Peter says, "they're taking it away."

"My God," Irene says, "at last."

They step back from the window. All of them sigh in relief.

Gregor walks over to the table and drinks down the last of his wine. He scoops up a fistful of peanuts.

"I'll be able to get through now," Gregor says.

"I'll see you out," Irene says.

"No, I will," Peter Diamond says.

"Stay in touch," Irene Anderson-Diamond says.

"I will," Gregor says.

"Send us a postcard," she says.

"I will," he says. "You don't have to see me out," he says. "I'll find the way."

5

There was a hellish racket down below. The whole street was filled with garbage trucks. In front of the building, iron jaws jutting out from one of the trucks reached into a pile of trash, snatched a mawful and bore it away to the yawning abyss up above. A few steps later he turned around and looked up. The window was open and empty. An empty eye in the face of the gray building. Down below the jaws had chomped onto the somewhat rusty, chrome bicycle and lifted it and a pile of trash into the air. For a while it hung there, under the vault of the clouds, its broken spokes jutting, its limbs broken, until it dropped into the gaping maw and vanished.

He set out through streets still carpeted with trash bags, past trucks and to the shouts of garbage men. Tompkins Square Park had already been cleared. He walked faster. He only vaguely kept his orientation; it was virtually impossible to get lost in Manhattan. He had raised anchor, the ship was sailing, the balloon was flying, the shadows of skyscrapers flickered past at his temples. Now he was running, and at once he felt lighter. He ran down First Street and turned right toward Union Square Park. He ran down the stairs of the subway stop and jumped into the open car of a waiting train. He got out at the 57th Street stop, ran up the steps, ran down the sidewalk and then along the edge of the street, leaped to avoid hitting a vegetable cart, A—B—C—Č, chunks, chips, shards, he jumped over a street person lying on the ground, the river of automobiles rumbled past, he turned into Central Park, ran down a horse path, his feet started sinking into the viscid earth, and he slipped on some horse shit. He didn't stop, running down the narrow paths until he reached a crossroads next to a pond.

He sat down on a bench next to a black man and gasped for air. The black man smacked his lips and shook his head.

"Where's the zoo?" Gregor Gradnik asked through wheezing lungs.

The black man looked at him and shook his head again.

"That's right," he said, "life is a zoo."

He laughed uproariously.

He slowly climbed a low hummock and lay down in the grass. He propped himself up on his elbows. Black youths were running along the path down below. A young woman carrying a child on her back was running. A tall man resembling Blaumann was running with his jacket over his head. Uniformed baseball players with bats under their arms were running. The mounted police were running. After the first few drops fell, the shower started in full force. There was lightning and thunder that reverberated back into the sky. In an instant he was soaked to the bone. He got up and slowly merged with the crowd that was racing off somewhere. Toward the lights on 57th Street, where the garbage trucks continued to rumble.

CHAPTER 28

THE FLAPPING
OF METAL WINGS

I

All night long he walked up and down the airport runway. He watched an airplane approaching, flying low over the icy surfaces, aiming straight for him as it hugged the narrow, icy lowlands. He could see Ana's face pressed to the windshield in the pilot's cabin. Her face distorted, with her nose and pale face pressed to the glass, she was giving him a sign: get out of the way. The plane was going to land right where he was standing, and indeed it got larger and larger, until he could hear the roar of the motor and the whistle of its huge wings.

When he opened his eyes he saw two glowing pupils. A cat was standing motionless next to his head, watching him. He had probably moaned in his sleep. In the next room the telephone was ringing insistently.

He felt his way through the room, between the light switch and the telephone, and he tripped in the dark. Sally squealed and ran. He was afraid the phone would stop ringing, since this must be Ana. It was Fred.

"Meg," he gasped into the deaf night from the continent's underbelly.

"Fred?"

"Has Meg vanished?"

"What's wrong, Fred?"

He tried to remember who Meg was. Meg was Meg Holick. She had moved to New York. Both cats paced nervously around the apartment. He saw their noiseless silhouettes barely visible in the feeble yellow light falling through the window from the street.

"I've been trying to reach her for two hours. I dreamed something horrible happened."

"Maybe she went running at night," Gregor said, "and now she's fast asleep."

"She doesn't sleep," Fred moaned, "that's exactly why I'm worried: she *never* sleeps."

"Is she sick? Does she have insomnia?"

"Listen to me for once and stop interrupting. I talk with her every night. She works at C.N.S. City that Never Sleeps, it's a night information service. She couldn't find anything else and she wouldn't let me help. She's very gifted, you know."

"I know."

"So this is why I'm asking you," he said, almost imploringly, "please, go there—do you have a pencil?—it's at St. Mark's Place, number 5, apartment 4, take a taxi, I'll pay you back, ring the bell, break the door down, I'll pay for it, find out what's happening."

"Break the door down?"

"Or have the fire department do it if you don't know how. But please, don't wait another minute."

"All right, Fred."

"Thank you."

"Don't mention it."

"No, seriously. Thank you."

"There's nothing to thank me for if I'm going to break a door down."

"Better get going. And call me right back."

"I will, Fred. What should I say if Mary answers?"

"She won't. I'm sitting next to the phone, in the dark."

He switched on the light and quickly got dressed. The cats watched him intently. Ana's arriving in five hours, he thought. In five hours I have to break a door down and take care of everything else. He called a taxi.

The night was warm. On Broadway, which stretched out like an endless serpent, lights flickered. The city that never sleeps, groups of loiterers, sleepy Vietnamese greengrocers in front of their stores, young blacks in perpetual motion with wildly wailing boom boxes on their shoulders, individuals returning late from who knows where. He was riding across town to find Meg, who never slept, either. Under a pipe with gas rushing out of it? He wasn't worried. Suddenly he was glad that he would be awake till morning. Now they were driving through virtually empty streets and squares. In the rearview mirror the driver's eyes were red from lack of sleep. Ana was arriving this morning. Tomorrow morning the two of them would buy up all of the vegetables the smiling Vietnamese had to sell, the exotic fruits, papayas, mamayas . . . and he fell asleep.

"Saint Mark's Place," the cab driver said, stretching his arms. It was three in the morning and everything was alive. On the street he suddenly found himself in a crowd of young people. They were sitting on doorsteps, behind panes of glass in brightly lit nightspots, the sidewalks were filled with loud walkers in leather clothes, draped in shiny chains. There was the smell of grilled meat and fried potatoes. In the humid autumn night colors and smells mingled in a thick, pinkish conglomeration.

At number 5 he pushed his way up the steps past young male couples sitting on the steps, embracing. He pressed long on the doorbell. No one answered. He glanced at the windows: no smoke was billowing out, no sirens were wailing in the vicinity. He slipped in behind a tenant who unlocked the door, and he climbed up the rickety wooden flights of stairs that steeply linked one narrow hallway to the next. The halls were heavy with street smells and were never aired out. Apartment 4 was on the fourth floor of the building. The door was wooden, papered over with posters, the plaster on both sides was crumbling and let the wooden joists show through. So this was the door he would have to break down. He rang the doorbell and knocked. No voice answered from inside. Then he banged several times with his fist, but not too hard. Heavy footsteps thumped through the apartment: this wasn't Meg. A young man wearing earphones opened the door. He was clad in a thin, pinkish robe, and a heavy metal chain was draped over his hairy chest.

"Excuse me," Gregor said, "I'm looking for Meg."

"Huh?" the other said, stupidly.

"Meg," he said, "M-e-g Holick."

The young man took his earphones off.

"She's not here," he said. "And who are you?"

"A friend of Fred's," Gregor said. That made no impression. "Professor Fred Blaumann . . . "

"She's not here," the man in the pink robe said and put his earphones back on. "Call tomorrow."

And he was left standing in front of a closed door. Now what was he supposed to report back to Fred, sitting with bated breath in his hallway in New Orleans, waiting for the phone to ring so that he could pick the receiver up right away, before *Tagenaria domestica* woke up. What was he supposed to tell him in his distress? They may have had a nasty fight, Meg may have become a prostitute: what if she was standing this instant on the Brooklyn Bridge, looking down into the water? He knocked again.

"You again," the acoustically equipped tenant said.

"This is urgent," Gregor said. "Fred is waiting beside the telephone . . . in his hallway . . . Meg and Fred . . . "

The man in the pink robe took off his earphones. With his middle finger he drilled in one ear.

"Sir," he said with utter seriousness. "Is it your habit to bang on the doors of peaceful American taxpayers every night?"

The tone of his voice didn't bode well. Lucky he hadn't broken the door down, as he'd been instructed.

"No," Gregor Gradnik said cautiously. "I'm not from here."

"Fine," the polite, hairy-chested man said in the same tone

of voice. "Then let me ask you, sir, never, never to do that again. Never."

"I'm sorry," Gregor Gradnik said.

"Don't mention it," the other said, put his earphones back on, and slammed the door shut so that some of the deteriorating plaster on both sides fell to the floor. He looked at his watch. Half past four. He had to get to the airport. What was he going to tell Fred? Where could he call him from? It was . . . what time was it there now? And where was Meg? Meg wasn't far away. At the front door, as he was trying to make his way past the young people sitting on the steps, somebody called to him.

Meg was sitting there, smoking, looking at him astonished with her pretty eyes that never slept. He explained fast, because he was really short of time now.

"Oh, Fred," Meg said. "What is it with that man?"

Gregor Gradnik explained what it was: he was sitting in his hallway, waiting for the phone to ring.

"Fine," she said, slowly getting up. "I'll give him a call. Are they asleep upstairs?"

"No," he said. "I think they're listening to music at this very moment. And they're not in the best of moods."

She asked him in for coffee.

"No, thanks," he said, "I've got to get to the airport."

Dawn was breaking. The street was a little less noisy and the young people had dispersed among the buildings. Except for the ones who never slept. The morning light mingled with the faint, feeble light of the bars.

He took the steps down into the subway station and waited for a train to Kennedy. He was out of patience. He ran up to the street and tried to flag down a taxi. He didn't manage to catch one of the yellow boats until just outside Union Square.

3

He leaped over suitcases and bundles, and shoved people aside on a conveyor that seemed to have no end. It was only a few minutes until the plane was supposed to touch down. He was running, melancholy fool, into Ana's embrace, into the embrace of home, aching from a sudden onslaught of melancholy matter. At last, she would say, at last, at last, she would whisper in his ear. At last, when he sprinted into the waiting room soaked, he ran into long faces. The flight was delayed. Real flights, the ones that you really need most to come, are always delayed. Suppress and disperse the taut anticipation, shove it back into the anteroom of memory. Everything that's alive and impending shove to the bottom of your heart, wall it in: the past, the person, the face, the body, the smile, the blurry field, the rustling woods, the sweet-smelling river, the quiet street, the translucent mountain: mortify all of it, put it in deep freeze. Return to a state of repose, of deadened defense, to a sense of apathy, of insensitivity, gained at so much expense during the long stay abroad. The acquired, practiced knowledge that memory, immersion in it, hurts, cuts, and severs. Sometimes the pain is incapacitating for hours. All expressions were dull and self-absorbed. Everyone waiting was wearing upbeat, American-appearing clothes and carrying flowers and gifts, and holding cigars between their trembling fingers. Restrained, monotonous, cagebound pacing.

As soon as he sat down someone offered him a cigarette. A swarthy southern type wordlessly offered him a cigarette. At this unexpected, hospitable, and unself-conscious gesture that only people from southern countries know how to make—people who expect nothing in return, for whom a shared experience of the world is compensation enough—at this unself-conscious gesture that was made the minute he started to pat his empty pockets, suddenly . . . suddenly he was sitting somewhere else. On a bench in some remote railroad station in southern Serbia. The wooden floor is black, the waiting room full of peasant women with wicker baskets. The men exhale clouds of smoke that waft toward the ceiling. Behind him is a sleepless night—two guard duty assignments of two hours each. And Ana is coming.

He walked around the guard post with a loaded rifle over his shoulder. His boots sloshed monotonously through the mud, and he could hear the distant commotion of a rollicking Gypsy wedding. It wasn't so rollicking anymore, and now, under the stars of the expiring night, the songs were becoming sorrowful, anguished, and sensual. Time moved differently here, with the wind. The Gypsies were singing Serbian songs, Oriental sensuality and Slavic sadness, ah, that Slavic soul. The wind brought the sound of trumpets and drums, then an accordion and a violin. When light washed across the sky and the stars began to fade, the revelers sang a Serbian song whose words he could distinctly recognize as the gentle breeze wafted them toward him. A young fellow was asking a girl to open the door for him. Open the door, fair Lenka, and let me see, fair Lenka, your lips so red. Her skin is white, but her lips are red, open the door so he can kiss them. And Ana's white skin and red lips were suddenly all around him everywhere—up among the fading stars, in the August morning sunlight reflecting off the windows of the barracks still asleep; and from the warm, rain-soaked field came the sweet smell of grass, redolent of that skin. Shivering, he waited for the minute his replacement would arrive. And then two more hours in the guards' bunkroom, with the sound of Gypsy music, amid his sleeping buddies, with his gaze and his cigarette jutting up at the low ceiling, with a cigarette in his mouth, with Ana in the compartment of a train that was traveling south from a far-off city eight hundred miles away, that was racing through rolling countryside that this expansive morning could surely, easily fill.

For eight months he had waited for this morning. For a month he had fought to get this leave, performing every task assigned to him with lightning speed. He had sat up all night typing orders for the commander, had raced through the mud, been the first to appear at morning roll call, until he finally won a smile from the commander, a smile with a gold

tooth, and a signature from his bejeweled hand. A grandiose
signature that guaranteed him three days of freedom. And
when they turned in their ammunition and aimed their
empty rifles skyward to pull the triggers, he still had two
hours until the train arrived. He washed and shaved with
cold water, scraping his skin. He wanted to purge himself of
everything that stank of barracks, of uniforms, of anything
remotely military. With a laugh he accepted a few lascivious
instructions from the guards on morning watch and bade
farewell, as if he were taking leave forever of these male
bunkrooms, fusty hallways, latrines that stank of shit and
Lysol, these command post offices that stank of coffee,
brandy, and cigarette smoke; mess halls—former horse sta-
bles—that stank of onions; and rifles and bayonettes that
stank of motor oil. He walked through the sunny morning of
this small, south Serbian town, past squat, rough-hewn houses,
then through the Gypsy quarter where drunk wedding revelers were dancing, and where in front of one house they were
butchering a lamb and letting its blood flow into the gutter of
the street . . . The train was late. All real trains—the ones that
should come most of all—are late. He found a seat in the
waiting room with its black floor. A swarthy fellow sitting
next to him offered him a cigarette. He smelled of morning
freshness, of fields and sheep. A ruddy Comrade Tito looked
down at him from the wall. The loving gaze of the great
leader that had followed him all his life, from childhood; his
ruddy cheeks, his long, white uniforms. Gratefully, he looked
up at the gentle face of his Supreme Commander, who
through his lieutenant had granted him three days' escape
from the barracks.

5

And then a ridiculous local train screeched to a halt outside. Ana. At last, at last, she breathed in his ear. Let's go then,
you and I, through certain half-deserted streets, with sawdust
on them. In a wonderful-smelling, empty bakery they ate a

burek, both of them short of sleep, both of them in a strange, early-morning daze. In a trance of traveling, in a trance of waiting. From there they went straight to a hotel room with a rustic wooden floor and crumbling ceiling with the cross-beams showing. The faucet dripped and the bed squeaked comically. And this was the most wonderful and the most powerfully impressive hotel room of Gregor Gradnik's life. Ana's skin wasn't white, it was tanned. From the seaside she had brought with her the smell of salt and dry wind, and from their mountainous native land a crystalline tautness of the air. Her lips were red, as in those Gypsy lyrics he had heard sung at daybreak. They made love amid pieces of his coarse uniform and silken fabrics, amid the smell of Estée Lauder perfumes and the smell of gun and leather oil, amid the sweet scent of her skin and the sharp smell of sulfuric mil-itary-issue soap, jerkily, greedily, sweetly, prolongedly, repeat-edly, and until they let blood. At one point, when she had raised herself up and bent her head down over him, her nose started to bleed. That's celibacy for you, she said, eight months of celibacy. I've slashed you, dear heart, and your red, red blood is dripping on my hands. The blood of release, of divorce, of brute force, the blood of strength steadily draining from languid limbs.

Three days of freedom. They rowed a boat down the brown river, they lay in the August grass and listened to the distant drums of the wedding that wouldn't end. They sat in a quiet church and listened to the mysterious, baritone, thou-sand-year-old chant of the bearded Orthodox priest. The smell of the basilica, of candles at Sunday mass, the evening cool of vespers. A bird flapped its wings beneath the round cupola. It kept flying into its vault, unable to find a way out of the church.

In the huge waiting room at Kennedy in New York the loudspeakers abruptly crackled. A woman's booming voice announced something incomprehensible, something that got trapped in this place and fluttered its wings under these arches like a bird, something that came from the outside world, from that place where planes flew. The indistinguishable mass of words and sounds collided with the walls and ceiling, and the message flapped its wings through the huge, enclosed space.

He stepped up to the screen. The plane was finally arriving, and the line of text that denoted it was slowly crawling toward the bottom of the screen.

6

She hadn't come. She indisputably was not there. He hadn't been prepared for this. The avine announcement of an empty—pointlessly empty—plane's arrival was still fluttering around the gate area. People were suddenly walking toward the exit, embracing. The area around the gate emptied almost immediately and then began to fill with new people to wait. Her failure to arrive was incomprehensible. He ran up to a stewardess and asked her to check the list of travelers. She wasn't on the list, she hadn't been on the plane, she wasn't at the gate, she wasn't in New York, she wasn't in America, she wasn't anywhere.

Feeling hollow from the sudden uncertainty and empty from his sleepless night, he retreated to the Whitby. The old-timers were sitting around the reception desk, heatedly arguing about the sanitation workers' strike that had just ended. In the hallway outside the apartment he could hear a cat's meow that sounded like a moan. He had forgotten to feed them. He opened a can of fresh, revolting cat food, poured out some milk, and began dialing telephone numbers. On the other side of the ocean the phone rang in a void. He wasn't hungry, and he wasn't sleepy. He looked at the cats, which were greedily gulping down big pieces of ground meat.

There was a sharp ring and he jerkily lifted the receiver, but it was silent. It was the doorbell ringing. One of the cats ran off into the vestibule and he shoved it aside with his foot, so that it went flying back squealing to its food. That was the castrated one, and it started to growl and bark.

Outside his door the doorman squinted at him.

"It's been a week since you picked up your mail," he said.

Damnation. Why hadn't they told him that you got your mail from the doorman here? He grabbed the bundle of paper out of his slow hands.

"There's a telegram for you, too," he said sleepily. "The owner and I have an agreement that I'll sign for those."

He closed the door and his trembling hands ripped the envelope apart.

Doing badly. Come back immediately.

The metallic sound from the airport echoed emptily in his ears and head. He could hear the wing strokes, the flapping of the bird trapped beneath the vaulted ceiling of the church, in the airport's huge waiting area. He opened the refrigerator and poured himself some liquor.

■ □ ■ □ ■

CHAPTER 29

WINDY MELANCHOLY

I

In his *Anatomy of Melancholy* there is a separate section where Robert Burton describes the most complex cases. These are the ones that his all-encompassing knowledge was unable to explain. A special kind of melancholy, where it was impossible to determine whether the soul or the body was afflicted, since the victim himself was unable to say what was wrong with him. At first his ears would ring, then he would break out in cold sweats. Sometimes his pulse would race, then he would have problems with his heart and pain in the area of the liver. He would feel lonely, seized with a sense of loneliness, nameless fear, and sadness. He would wander around, unable to to tell anyone why. His thoughts were disorganized and he was unable to collect them.

For Blaumann:

Windy melancholy, owing to the absence of clear symptoms also called hypochondriacal. Just as thick, black clouds conceal the sun and its beneficial, healing light, so does this melancholy cloud the mind, forcing it into every sort of absurd thought and imagining. Like smoke through a chimney, these move up from the body into the brain, leading to the most unusual notions. The victims are often convinced that they have toads or snakes inside their bodies. Male victims fall in love frequently and, in extreme cases, with almost every woman they meet.

He spent the next two weeks in a kind of airless space. Objects didn't touch him: they hovered. At night he battled the cancer cells that were attacking his mother's poor, old body. Strange, abstract ants crawled all around him, and outside the window of the Whitby he could hear the crackle of cockroach nests.

In the mornings he rode to Battery Park, at the very tip of Manhattan. There he could clearly sense that not just objects and buildings were hovering, but that the whole island hovered in vast, empty space. He stood at the edge, trying to determine the uttermost point of the island and then step onto it. For long hours he stood there, thoughtlessly watching the tourist ferries that plied between three islands, hovering chunks of land. He took one to Ellis Island and there, for an instant, he emerged from his hovering and felt a strange anxiousness in his chest. First on the boat, with happy old people taking pictures of each other, and then all at once on the island. Too great a concentration of hopes, happiness, and dread left behind in this quarantined crevice, from which people surged out across the whole, wide continent. Too harsh a compression of souls, which the Atlantic wind was unable to scatter.

Pigeons were darting back and forth across the water. Homeless people crept up to the waterfront to stare vacantly at the pigeons screeching. Clouds, water, land, land that wasn't yet a continent, not yet, that was only a long island. He stood among the pathetic homeless people, the wind blowing their hanklike hair; amid their vacant eyes staring off into the distance, and he was unable to take his eyes off the island he had returned from. If it was true that there were certain human coordinates, along pilgrims' trails, where a special energy collected; an unknown human force that the hopes, sighs, prayers, and desires of the masses and of each individual within the masses projected into space; if it was true that at those coordinates the air condensed into a special mist from all of those powerful desires and hopes, then the morning mists here were souls that the wind couldn't scatter, the remainder of times when millions of individuals and their wishes crowded through these narrow gates.

3

From this crevice of the world everything vanished into other spaces of memory: transitory hopes and wishes, transitory lives, his mother's, Ana's, his, everyone's. Had twenty years passed, or was it just an instant since he, Gregor, had stood just like this, a boy on the tip of an island in the middle of the Drava, in the middle of some far-off river, at the height of summer. From behind him came the rollicking commotion of a summer beach, and to both sides lapped the water of the Drava, carrying away the island's banks, time, the years of his childhood. Here, behind him, dinned a huge city, the most powerful, the most famous city, and the water was mildly agitated and carried away the fleeting time of the millions that dwelled here. A crevice, and so many lives had passed through this crevice of the world. Even some of Irene's remote ancestors, who, in the middle of this continent to their dying breath remembered some Danish river, and whose bones lay under some other earth, beneath a sky inhabited by other, Indian gods. In Indiana. And he watched a boat slowly approaching. Maybe Ana was on it, maybe she was bringing good news.

He turned around. The mountain range of skyscrapers was awash in light. The afternoon heat had arrived, kneaded with the humid ocean air. Under its weight homeless people lay down on the pavement, on benches, on the grass in the park. They swarmed around looking for scraps of food in the crevices, in the shadows of constructed peaks.

4

No bells toll here. Street traffic comes to life but never subsides completely. A tiny tugboat pulls a big ship. It projects a watery squeak across the surface. Then the dark cupola of the sky over the island again, and a narrow ray of light through it. If he were to climb up that cone, he would reach heaven, beyond, and other worlds. Screeching pigeons gather behind a tiny boat in the vast water. A dove sleepily coos on a wire fence. This is where a hint of the silence of the morning cosmos resides.

This was the cool morning silence before the hot and noisy day approaching with a rumble. Behind him was the city and behind him was a night spent in it, full of swelling crowds. This night an onslaught of windy melancholy, reaching with its toads and snakes from Blaumann's computer first into his guts, then his brains; this night windy melancholy drove him out into the solitude of human crowds, into the streets, the pubs, the concert halls with their wild lights and music that sawed through your skull and settled under your skin like some wiggling vermin. Out into the vicious mix of 42nd Street, among impatient bodies, cutting teeth, shouting oral cavities, out among jostling human beings who were forever short of space, among the swollen, wiggling crowds of the big city. Into the solitude of crowds teeming with greedy life, droopy faces luring you into dim places, into cellars with half-naked and naked bodies. It drove him out into the crazy, vertiginous vortex and out toward the edges of his own life, which could sense that this instant a life so very close to him was running out. He submerged into the rabble of the big city, into its bubbling kettle, into the smell of bodies, unwashed, scented, into the beckoning, the touching, the shoving. Into the solitude of the crowd, mindless and pointless in the evening and nighttime humidity, among piles of trash and honking cars, and then, late at night, onto illuminated street corners, toward neon-lit faces and lights that flashed over beckoning, shouting monsters, into a subway cavern and then over to the other tumultuous side, into the dark. Into the dark, into an abyss of wailing and singing mouths, to the rattle of bottles, among warlike gangs, among black, moving jaws, among dangerous movements of bared arms, into waves of physical reality, amid slander, chatter, drivel, and muttering.

Now, in the net of morning, through which he looked at the early morning glint of the wide water and a boat sailing under the shadow of a suspension bridge, all of this was behind him. Only a runner with his eyes bulging, a deranged morning jogger with taut veins and throbbing temples ran past, gasping, as though he had inadvertently strayed from the nighttime entity and wandered into an unknown region, where he was now running senselessly and aimlessly, seeking the way back to the herd, to the swarm, to the crowd, back to where the Ur-mother dwelled and held all the parts of this gigantic, movable, wiggling organism together with her invisible presence.

5

He called the doctor, who was a friend of his. An operation was needed to stop the thing at least partially. At least partially, the thing. The thing was cancer. The thing was the cancer that was consuming his mother's body. The thing was the destruction of living cells. Now the thing was moving through her vital organs and over her severely inflamed skin, looking for the part of her body where it would make its decisive attack.

6

Fred came by. He asked him if he could spare him the apartment. He and Meg didn't have anyplace to meet. He would ask him to turn a few more pages at the library. Here was a list. Or he would ask him to go to the movies.

Sam with his mangy head looked out from the bedroom.

I hope Meg doesn't mind cats, Fred said. I've never asked her.

CHAPTER 30

THE MELANCHOLY OF
PROFESSOR BLAUMANN

I

Not just his legs, but his whole body ached from walking down endless sidewalks. His femur was jutting up into his soft innards; the blunt bone was shoving somewhere toward his guts, up into the soft parts of his body, into the intestines and the vicinity of the liver and spleen on his right side, while on the left . . . he couldn't exactly say where it was jutting on the left side. At this point he could think of nothing but bed. Even if the two of them were in the bedroom. He could lie on the couch in the living room. He could turn the television on so that his presence wouldn't bother them, and he could talk with the cats. He couldn't help thinking of rest. He could stand anything at this point, even their moans, if he had to; only rest, lie down.

Even so, he rang the bell with some uneasiness: Was it impolite? Pushy? Not a sound came from inside the apartment. He slipped the key into the keyhole, but it was blocked. He returned to the lobby and sat down on the edge of a long bench where the musicians emeriti were cheerfully coughing. Maybe he really ought to go out to another movie. But at the thought of one more movie his face darkened with rage. After all, he was paying the rent and cleaning up the cats' messes. For the pleasure of sitting in movie theaters or on the edge of a bench alongside some old musicians? While Irene, and while Ana . . . ? While Fred Blaumann and his student were rolling on the same couch he could be resting on right now, and while they could at least be considerate enough to do their rolling in his bedroom. He started to get enraged at things about which he wasn't even sure. Why were they rolling on his couch? Couldn't they go into the bedroom and close the door behind them? They probably weren't even going to empty the ashtrays behind them. Half-smoked cigarette stubs stank horribly. And why did this runner, why did Fred Blaumann the jogger, smoke so unbearably much? And in the meantime his wife was pacing up and down their spacious room in the Edison Hotel.

They weren't considerate. Nobody was considerate. Gregor Gradnik belonged on the edge of the bench next to the doorman's station in the lobby of the Whitby; he belonged here and nowhere else.

"Nice day," the eighty-year-old saxophone player who had played with Benny Goodman said. Gregor nodded, nice day, even though the day wasn't visible from here, only the light that trickled into the dark lobby from the revolving doors.

"You can stay sittin' here for now," the old man said. "But later Willy's gonna come. Willy always sits here."

Before Willy arrived, the door at the end of the lobby opened. Fred cautiously poked his head out the crack.

Fred Blaumann stood in the doorway in his undershorts. His thinning hair was tousled and the skin underneath it was inflamed and red. There were dark bags under his eyes. A bottle of vodka was dangling from one hand, and bounced against his knee like a noiseless, useless bell. Inside the apartment, too, all the doors were open, as though somebody just a short time before had been running back and forth. A broken bottle lay next to the window. It was smoky, stuffy, and hot inside. It also smelled somewhat of cat shit and cat food. Both cats were perched, one on top of the refrigerator, the other on the window ledge, staring hatefully into the apartment. It wasn't theirs anymore, either; even they had been shoved toward the end of the bench, where Willy would be coming to sit down soon.

Meg was nowhere to be seen. Fred sat down amid the tousled bedcovers, sat the bottle down between his bare feet, and buried his head in his hands. Blaumann began to melancholize blaumannesquely.

"Have you got a cigarette?" he said. "I've run out."

Gregor stuck a lit cigarette between Fred's fingers, which had seized his inclined head. Fred's bald spot showed a patchy red through his sparse hair. He drew on the cigarette several times, puffing smoke out before him and saying slowly and emphatically:

"If I wrote about *this* . . . ," Fred said, "*nobody* would *ever* believe me."

2

That's incredible, Gregor thought, not without a measure of malice. He opened the window and the stench of decomposing bones wafted in. It mingled with the smell of tobacco smoke. And of marijuana. His nostrils had picked that up the instant he had walked in. It was serious with Meg, at least it had been for a while. The poison hadn't been made that her organism couldn't metabolize, there wasn't a distance she couldn't run, there wasn't a place where she wouldn't leave behind carnage as she had just done here. She just fixed her hair and went. Even if she'd drunk a gallon of hydrochloric acid just a minute before. She tucked her blouse into her jeans, combed her hair in front of the mirror, and went without looking back.

"She left?"

Fred shook his head, as though there was something he couldn't understand. He was still holding his head in his hands with the cigarette in his fingers. A length of ash broke off and dropped on his bald spot.

"Forever. She'll never come back."

"Never? With an exclamation mark?"

"Never!"

He shoved the cigarette into the glass and it hissed in the vodka. He lifted his head and looked at him with watery eyes.

"Just a while ago . . . I was on the verge of committing suicide . . . If you hadn't rung the doorbell so persistently . . . ?" Again he shook his head, oscillating it on his neck incessantly, as if he really couldn't understand this *incredible* thing that had just happened to him. So incredible that nobody would believe it even if he wrote about it. But then, reality was sometimes more real than any literature, Professor Blaumann might say in creative writing class.

"Suicide?"

3

Unhappy?
Bored?
Get no respect?
Try the one and only surefire remedy.
Suicide.
Try suicide and achieve greater success!
Suicide is a delight for the whole family!
Improve your social status only with suicide!
Real pleasure is the pleasure of suicide!
Without suicide you can never be happy in life!
So, don't delay!
Buy your own "Longing" rope and all your troubles will be over!
Your own "Longing" rope is the best insurance against fate!
Don't forget your "Longing" rope when you set out to die!
A "Longing" rope is the only guarantee of an effective finish!
Aesthetically guaranteed!
Internationally renowned!
Wide selection!
Super convenient!
Top-quality death!
Call today, "Death & Co."

"I once knew a poet," Gregor said. "He wrote an advertisement for suicide. But he didn't shoot himself in front of a camera. He turned on the gas in the kitchen. He didn't hang himself."

4

Suicide?

Well, yeah, he hadn't meant it literally. He'd meant it kind of blaumannesquely, kind of metaphorically.

"I told her I wanted her to move away from that guy. Away from that disgusting thing that she shares the apartment with. From that male-female freak."

Blaumann lit another cigarette. He blew smoke in the air and thought while his eyes darted around. The ravages of melancholy.

"Tell me, is that thing a man at all: what kind of creature is that? It isn't a man, is it?"

Slowly Gregor went into the living room and stretched out on the couch. Only now did he feel the sweet fatigue spreading out to all of his limbs. He looked at the cat on top of the refrigerator and its glowing, spiteful eyes. He didn't answer, while Fred's voice continued to come monotonously from the bedroom. He could feel that he was horribly, horribly tired, that none of this in fact mattered to him anymore, that there wasn't a single word that he could or would say at this point.

"It's not a woman, either," Fred was saying. "What is it then? Oh, I know what kind of in-between thing it is. Down in New Orleans, in the Vieux Carré, there are more of them than you can count—whole nests of them. And to think that Meg lives in an apartment with a revolting creature like that. Tell me, can that even be her?"

Seconds passed, and he could hear the guggling sound of vodka being poured into a glass. "What has he done with the cigarette butt?" Gregor thought through a veil of fatigue. "There was a cigarette butt in the bottom of that glass."

"Do you think she'd want to move out? No way! She's a

free and independent person. Free and independent! My God, what kind of freedom is that, damn it? She said she'd move out when I move out. I beg your pardon, where am I supposed to move out from? Leave Mary? My two kids? Just move out, she says. And if possible I'm supposed to go live at St. Mark's Place, sit on doorsteps, smoke marijuana, and stare off into space?"

For a few seconds there was silence. Far-off shouts from the street, the rattling of a trash can as some indigent overturned it.

"And then she left. Forever."

Suddenly Fred was standing next to him. In his underwear. With a buttless glass of vodka in hand.

"Did you hear what I said?'

"I heard everything, Fred."

"Well?"

He was looking at him, waiting for an answer. Gregor rose up and sat on the edge of the couch. Nobody would ever displace him from here again, the edge of this couch was his, and no Willy could say otherwise. Nobody could. In a while the professor would leave. In a while he could turn the television on. Go to sleep. The cat on the windowsill stirred and arched its back. It slowly moved toward the other cat, still hostilely perched on the refrigerator. With sudden vehemence Fred slammed his glass down on the table.

"Damn it, I'm going to get another fucking venereal disease."

"How? You know who you're sleeping with."

"I know," he said and started to underline every word with a bang of his glass against the table. "I know! I just don't know who she's sleeping with . . . In fact, it's even worse: I do know. She only sleeps with her friend. Fine. They share an apartment. This is New York. I trust her. I believe her. Trouble is, I don't know who he's sleeping with. Do you understand? That thing! And when he comes home at night he sleeps with her. With her! With Meg!"

The glass was shattered now. Fred Blaumann looked at his hand in amazement. One of his fingers was bleeding. This was even more improbable than literature. This was the bloody truth. Gregor offered him a handkerchief to staunch the blood. Now he felt close to tears again.

"She's so sensitive. She won't submit to authority. But she's so thoughtless, too. Why does she even live there? Do you know who lives at St. Mark's Place?"

"Marxists," Gregor said.

Fred didn't respond. He bowed his head.

"All right," he said. "Marxists. If that's what you call all sorts of riffraff sitting around on the steps. Maybe I really am a pathetic teacher. I've got my wife just a few blocks from here at the Edison Hotel, and I'm going crazy with jealousy because a student, a creature of free will, chooses to sleep with some young man at night. My God, what is happening, what on earth is happening to me?"

"Meg works at night, Fred."

He lifted his teary eyes, suddenly full of hope.

"City Never Sleeps."

"You're right."

"So if she works at night, she's not sleeping with that thing."

"She works . . . at night."

"And she sleeps by day."

If she slept at all. Gregor was certain she never slept, just like her city. But it had done the job. It had helped.

"You're right," Fred said. "When does she start? An hour from now. I'm going to apologize to her."

5

Fred took one more swig out of the bottle. He felt better. One of the cats got up and raised its tail. That must mean something; he would have to check his instructions. Its tail: the excuse was good enough even if it came on a cat's tail. Now, this instant, he was on the verge of explaining this ridiculous Slovene expression to Fred—even though he had never understood it himself—seeing as he had to accompany him through all this . . . through what? Through all this *incredible* reality that had never happened to Fred before and was more real for him than any literature. Good lord, how it stank in this room. He thought about how it stank and how his femur was pushing up through his liver, even though he was sitting. He thought about how he would have to clean up after the cats, who undoubtedly had smeared their cat food and shit all around the room in protest at having to flee in fear from the two human beasts that had rampaged through the apartment. At the thought of cleaning up, his discomfort changed to nausea. He wasn't angry; just tired of walking, tired of Fred, of his love affair, of his suffering, of reality and improbability and literature. Empty out the ashtrays; air the place out. But then he'd get the stench from the trash cans with their decomposing bones, while some hirsute homeless person with thick encrustations of filth on his hands and face rummaged through them, turned them upside down, and threw them around, talking to himself the whole time.

He took the bottle out of Fred's becalmed hands now and poured himself one finger of vodka. Suddenly he recalled the bench outside the humanities building, long ago, in February, in a rain that had done wonders to freshen the air. Fred came running across the lawn, with the water squirting up from under his running shoes. Meg was running alongside a brick building in the opposite direction. The self-assured professor was bobbing in front of him. Gregor Gradnik was his mirror: success, ease, intellectual elegance. An office in Chippendale style. An article on melancholy. An article on Joyce. A student to run with. But in this flawless image that gazed at itself in him, in his mirror, there was something hopelessly wrong. There was some flaw built into it. Now he remembered: it was that white thing, that piece of white fabric jutting out of his running shorts.

And here he was, almost a year later, standing in front of

him in his undershorts in a first-floor apartment of the Whit-by on 45th Street in New York. With red splotches on his bald spot and bruises on his body. With black bags under his eyes.

Oh, life! Oh, creative writing!

6

Fred looked at his watch nervously. His wife was waiting back at the hotel. One day she would make his life hell. Or simply leave him. One day he would have to explain why he always came back from his scholarly meetings kind of round. With bags under his eyes and red splotches on his head. And what was he supposed to do with Meg? She was even more unforgiving. She wasn't a call girl, even though you could reach her warm voice every night by dialing the phone: City Never Sleeps. She was an individual. But Fred was also an individual.

"It can't go on like this," he said and pulled his trousers on. He fell on his knees and looked for something under the bed. "And that's what I told her. I told her, didn't I?"

When he stood up again with a stocking in hand, the cat on top of the refrigerator bared its teeth and hissed.

"It's angry because I kicked it," Fred said. "Sorry."

"Apologize to it," Gregor said.

"Sorry, what's your name."

He shook a coin and a cigarette butt out of his shoe and immediately scooped both of them up. He was quickly turning into a credible man again. Carefully, adeptly he knotted his necktie. Then he remembered something and ran into the bathroom. The shower started pelting the plastic shower curtain. Fred whistled. Hello, day; hello, life. Here I come again to test your patience, to leave the imprint of my tiny, sinful presence in your cosmic surface. Fred whistled. When he came out, he tied his necktie again.

"Don't think that the shit is any less deep because I'm whistling," he said. "That's a facade."

He asked for coffee. After he drank it, spots started appearing on his face, too. It had been too much for a single New York afternoon, far too much. He brushed off his shoulders and asked Gregor to check from behind to see if any black hairs were left. Then for a long time he stood in front of the entryway mirror, smoothing down the hair on both sides of his bald spot.

"Been to any movies, moviegoer?" he asked, quietly whistling in front of the mirror.

"Three," Gregor said.

"Times Square?"

"That's right."

"Sorry," Fred said.

"It's okay," Gregor said.

He was about to open the door, but then remembered something. He turned around and looked at the toes of his shoes.

"There's a great article in the *New Yorker* about midlife crisis."

He opened the door.

"Shall I run you off a copy?" he said.

"Sure, go ahead," Gregor said.

He looked around the apartment one more time and shook his head: incredible.

"Sorry for this," he said.

"It's okay," Gregor said.

He looked at his watch again.

"I'm indebted to you."

"Right," Gregor said.

The door closed and he could hear his jaunty footsteps retreating into the distance. Outside the doorman's station he called something out to Willy, who was sitting on the edge of the bench.

Gregor picked up a dustpan and began to clean up the healthful cat food mixed with vitamins and shit.

■ □ ■ □ ■

CHAPTER 31

MOVIEGOER

I

He sat on a park bench and wrote short letters to his mother. Everything would be fine, he would be coming back soon. He wrote a long letter to Ana and thanked her for something. When he wasn't going to movies, he sat on park benches and watched relaxed people out catching rays of the autumn sun. Meg wanted to meet Fred on Saturdays and Sundays, although she could have met with him any after-noon of the week. But she wanted Sundays. As a result, Fred had to invent the most incredible scholarly excuses, and because he didn't like to lie, this caused him all the more pain. Gregor often thought with sympathy of *Tagenaria domestica,* who was a good soul and really wanted nothing so much as to spend her Sunday afternoon with Fred Blaumann. He imag-ined her sitting in their hotel room instead of their garden in New Orleans, or walking for long hours through some muse-um. He remembered her desperate drinking at Mardi Gras time. Had anyone ever paid any attention to her at all? If she were to take barbiturates and sleep two days straight, no one would even notice it.

At the beginning of October a wave of cool air drifted through the city. The foliage turned yellow in earnest now. Sudden gusts of wind eddied around him in the park. Occa-sionally people would turn up their collars. There was the smell of rot in the air.

At this point he really didn't have anything left but the movies, since the endlessly ardent, endlessly voracious lovers kept taking over his apartment. On Times Square there was a complex with four theaters, and with a single ticket he could move from one movie to the next and kill quite a few hours that way. He would munch on popcorn drenched in butter that oozed down his fingers, and sit idly among the other moviegoers between shows. At first he tried to construct some kind of dramatic, narrative system out of the movies he saw, and he took notes. Then he started confusing everything in a wild kaleidoscope of images. He started eavesdropping on the other viewers, which was sometimes more interesting than the movie itself. A woman's voice asks questions, a man's answers:

Did he really do that?

Yes.

It's awful, isn't it?

Sure it's awful, but so what?

Have you got any more?

Careful, you're spilling it on the floor.

He was a Vietnam vet, wasn't he?

So what. Everybody was back then.

Was he decorated?

So what. A piece of tin on his chest.

I feel sorry for him, don't you?

No. Maybe if it had been a real war. But not that.

That was a real one. Some good you were then.

Keep quiet. I'm here to see a movie.

At one Saturday matinee a group of young cowboys killed their enemies mercilessly. The cause had been bloody and just: they had killed their father. But the boys were shooting them in the back and stomach at point-blank range. One of them they shot while he was pissing. Another they shot in the head while he was lying on the ground. The temperature in the movie theater rose. Some young blacks in the theater were shouting and jumping to their feet more and more often. Eventually they drew the whole theater into that vortex. The shouting and guffaws at each new righteous killing became universal. This was real life on the screen—the life of the big city outside of the theater.

3

A light was burning in the first-floor window of the Whitby. He stopped for an instant, thinking he could hear their laughter. But of course that wasn't possible: the windowpanes didn't let any sound through. Or any of the air that Fred and Meg were breathing. He looked at his watch. There was still half an hour until their time was up. But it was an hour and a half until Meg started working at CNS. He could stop in and drink a glass of whiskey with them, and then, after she left, listen to Fred's melancholy postcoital laments. He kept walking west.

At the corner of Tenth Avenue and 45th Street he was stopped by the loud wailing of sirens. Smoke was pouring out of a dark brick building, girded with iron fire escapes. Bedding came flying out of a window on the second floor. Somebody was saving his belongings. A fat, awkward, obviously ailing old woman crawled down the fire escape with the help of a fireman. He looked around and saw he was standing amid a bunch of old women. One standing next to him was praying, while others watched with complete indifference as tongues of flame darted out the windows. A home for elderly women was burning. There was no wringing of hands, no apparent distress.

Silent resignation, while their pathetic last resort burned to the ground. And even he, even he felt nothing at the sight of it, no sympathy. He knew he was only here in order to kill another half hour. Next to him the woman who had been praying started to laugh. Neither prayer nor laughter seemed to have an effect on anybody. This was a movie.

He sat down on a bench outside of Macy's department store, the largest in the world. He unfolded the evening newspaper and scanned the headlines in the streetlight. Then he watched the saleswomen as they left the anthill, walking off in all directions, and then the security guards as they checked the locks after them.

Something stirred in the shadows at the other end of the bench. Someone was sitting there in the murk with his collar turned up. He was sitting on the very edge of the bench, as though he were trying not to encroach on anyone else's space. He was hunched over and his sparse hair jutted over his collar like straw out of a scarecrow. He lighted a cigarette, and in the glow of the short flame Gregor could see the cheekbones jutting up under his sunken eyes, the ravaged nose, and the white, white lips.

Gregor lighted himself a cigarette.

"Don't come near me," the stranger said. "My breath is plague-ridden."

Gregor hadn't planned on getting near.

"Don't you know this is a plague city?" the man with the white lips said.

He went on without waiting for an answer.

"I'm dying young," he said. "And that's what I've always wanted. But it's shameful to die like this."

Blaumann:

Embarrassingly graceless dying.

The other slid closer and looked at him with his sunken eyes. He passed a hand through his sparse hair.

Blaumann:

Death is devastatingly empty. Death is the empty violence of eternity.

"There's still a bed left for me," he said. "I'm going to go and lie down in it. I'll turn to face the wall and let the life run out of me. And I'll never turn back."

When Gregor turned away from Macy's display window he noticed that the plague carrier was lighting another cigarette. He turned his collar up and retreated back into the darkness.

5

Meg and Fred were just leaving. Would he like to duck out with them for a quick dinner? Not really, he'd rather turn in. Turn in? said a startled Meg, who never slept.

He was dragging that woman down the ladder. He was wearing a police uniform and suffocating from the smoke, and the woman kept sinking out of his grip. Tongues of fire were darting up underfoot. He was trying to think where he could put his expensive sunglasses to keep from breaking them. The colors of the street below quavered in the fire's heat, and police cars and fire engines were wailing. The fire surged again and he decided to drag the woman through the flames: maybe they would only singe her. He shoved the sunglasses into his hip pocket. But the woman was heavy and sick and she couldn't move. At that point the fire started to burn his eyes. He remembered the sunglasses and put them on. Now he would have to drop the woman if he wanted to save his own life. Then he began to recognize some familiar features in the old, fat, wrinkled black woman's face. There was a wrinkle running along each side of her nose, and dark depressions under her eyes. With her trembling hands the woman also put on glasses with thick lenses, which made her pupils look tiny. This face was so familiar. He looks just like her, someone said, just like his mother. It was his face, her face: familiar. The familiar glasses frame with thick lenses. Then the flames shot past their heads. He turned to look at the audience: drop her, they shouted, run.

He opened his eyes and could still feel the warm breath on his face. Glowing, green eyes were staring at him. A cat was standing at his head, sniffing. He shoved it off of the bed and jumped up. You're getting hysterical, he shouted. You're going to ruin my nerves. He turned on the television and drank long drafts of cold milk from the refrigerator.

That was on Monday morning.

On Friday he was scheduled to leave.

6

De arte bene moriendi. On Tuesday evening the elderly musicians who spent their days sitting by the doorman's station held a jam session. They brought their instruments and started to play. A few residents gathered to listen, mostly the ones who happened to be coming up from the basement carrying baskets of laundry. These lungs couldn't quite fill a cornet anymore, and the hands beat feebly on the drums. The last two members of the audience were the doorman and Gregor Gradnik. The doorman because he didn't have anything else to do, and Gregor for the same reason: nothing to do, and no one to see. He had a vacuum in his head. The vacuum expanded, emptying out all the soft inner parts, and the disjointed sounds of Dixieland, the dirty notes that these old musicians preparing for imminent death slaved over, echoed through the dead space of his cranium. But they played, and they played without ceasing. *De arte bene moriendi.* The art of a good and handsome death.

Then he went outside and took the subway to Battery Park. He stood on the tip of the island and looked at the dark water. He called Meg from a nearby pay phone. City Never Sleeps, Meg said with a voice that seemed at first like a recording. Meg, I'm leaving, he said. Is that you, Gregor? Meg said. He hung up.

That was on Tuesday evening.

On Friday he was scheduled to leave.

CHAPTER 32

THE CRYSTAL LANDSCAPE

I

The vault of the sky shook. They submerged into glowing clouds, floated through reddish, yellowish light, and reemerged each time into light blue. Home. Far below, the shimmering surface of the ocean showed, the hint of a naked, fragile ship totally exposed on its surface, a ship invisible from up here, on which somebody was traveling home. All roads lead to home. From the instant a ship shoves off from shore or an airplane disconnects from the earth on the start of its long journey, from that first instant of its perfect arc. The ship far below with the hint of dry land in its sides, in the lapping of the waves against its sides, waves that push off from the beach and run their commingling course to the ship's bow. Virgil's ship on the way to dry land, on the way to childhood, into the deathlike landscape of childhood. The hint of dry land, of ground, of earth even in the clouds around the shuddering airplane, in the clouds which are terrestrial, the terrestrial dream of his childhood reveries while lying in the grass, a superterrestrial, untouchable rainbow bridge to the unknown, to the universe, to his astonished, child's eyes, heavenly travelers never grasped. Around the airplane, on its windows, racing mists, traveling, filled with fatigue and traveler's languor, which will pour down on the earth, settle onto the meadow when he looks up and sees a skyship cutting the air sharply between them. Home. With fragmentary thoughts and whole senses, with a fuller and fuller sense of the piece of land approaching that he knows. The grass, the clouds above it; suburban streets with their familiar, mottled facades, their cracked sidewalks; humid entryways that smell of food, the stale smell of people, of garlic, rosemary, and fried onions; suburban gardens with their beds of lettuce and flowers, with cool earth smelling of autumn, with smoke from the last fires; the sun-drenched gravel of some courtyard, oil spots of some forlorn suburban train station; and on and on, to where the houses are smaller, the gardens bigger, the smell of animals and people, abandoned pastures, gray mushrooms in the forests, the smell of rotting leaves and underbrush, clematis, the snapping of broken branches, of fires, and stifling smoke in your nostrils. Scents, sounds, images, voices that inhabit the innermost soul and can never leave it again, that are renewed at the slightest touch from the outside and luxuriate, that fill the trembling of the living body, full of the sense of life. Home. Where things, places, and people have their own names, each instantly giving rise to an image, whole, complete, illuminated by the sun from various angles, overshadowed by nearby objects, radiating through the prism of numerous glass panes, full of countless meanings, shadings, intimate histories, functional in its own right, in life's right.

And when the light fades around and above the clouds, when dark space opens up above and, beneath it, mad, ever incomprehensible stars, when the memory of childhood comes, when the airplane passes over the silent coast of some nocturnal island sparsely sown with tiny lights, forgotten images encrusted with countless layers start to come to him. At evening, before bedtime, daytime images; father's voice, which he can hear clearly now from the kitchen. From the humble rooms of a suburban house, the convergence of daytime events, nighttime events, household finances, male conflicts, amorous whisperings, harsh events, hard words, gentle words, world politics, the crackling radio that he fears because it transmits something forbidden, the Voice of America. The radio of a far-off, wondrous, dazzling land, where there are relatives with crepe-paper flowers on their graves, where there are soldiers in broad helmets and where they eat chewing gum. His father's voice constantly intrudes on the crackling sounds of American Slovene, a voice that knows everything, that knows about America and Russia, about everyday business, about heating and bicycle repairs. Angrily he raises his voice, a harsh voice, a drunk-smelling, muttering voice, the coarse and hated, the coarse, beloved voice of his dead father, soaring with him now beneath the blackened sky. A voice that sees him, sees him approaching under a blanket, from the earth up into the clouds, around the airplane, that sees him amid the glimmering lights inside it, the threateningly angry, sharply commanding, ruggedly forgiving, living voice of his dead father, a voice in which vague allegories take root and to which distinct but fragmentary images of childhood return: far down below, peasants riding on a wagon, and among them a city boy sitting on a soft, smooth blanket spread out over the bare bench; the horses' heavy hindquarters shifting in front of him; and on the cart, the smell of mown grass, of everything mown, of nature cut down, of earth, of everything wrested from it, of everything still living, yet already dead.

Now he both senses and knows at once: death is a journey; the journey is death.

In the midst of this and pervading everything, his mother's face: in the village, among red-cheeked relatives, amid field scents, amid the world she came from and to which she belonged, with its happy, drunken weddings and cool, picturesque funerals, amid a meadow, amid a field, where her face glowed differently than in the city, where it was dark, and not pale as it was when she worked in the factory packaging scented soap and foul-smelling powder; it was illuminated from within and not rigid and stubborn as when she worked in the city, in the factory; it wasn't absently focused as in the evening at her old sewing machine. It wasn't pale the way it's pale now, this instant, while on the nightstand in her hospital room—that loathsome hospital nightstand that he always hated on his visits to the hospital, since it was the source of the loathsome smell of medicine and cakes, of apples and urine—on that nightstand a small lamp is burning, and perhaps she's reading a peasant tale from the last century, maybe she can barely keep the book in her hands. Maybe she is fighting the cancer cells with the stubborn rigidity common among peasants in this country, maybe the pain is hacking at her poor, pale face, maybe she is thinking about him, eyes closed, thinking about her errant son who almost got stuck somewhere on the other side of the world, and who is coming now even so, flying home through the early morning twilight, home, where once he was told to enter life, and where it is now written on the small, tired face of his mother that her time is running out and that she wants to see him one more time, before her flickering, dwindling consciousness expires. Amid the pain that medications lessen, powerful drugs that weaken her heartbeats, so that her shaking hand brings that ridiculously tiny watch right up close to her eye.

Home.

Home, over the water's surface, glimmering in the morning sun, over the approaching coastline, through the crystalline mountains and the cool light, sleepless, dreamless, with an intimation of the end, an intimation of a beginning.

2

But he both sensed and knew at once: this was where the melancholy and mocking devils were really at home. The ones that followed him to the American continent and refused to release him from their jaws and talons, that plagued him on the riverbank and the seashore, in bed and among crowds, assaulting him every lonely hour and drawing painful furrows through his soul. Here, in Alpine valleys, and there, a little farther on, in the Pannonian plains, they were at home in the wind and the air: it was impossible to elude them. They were at home in the lakes and over the mountaintops, in the crowns of trees, in the swamps and on rocky mountain ridges, in village pubs and on the desolate Sunday-afternoon streets of the cities, in the children, the men, the old folks. He both sensed and knew at once: now he was entering a landscape of suffering. A landscape that the devils of melancholy had been tormenting since the beginning of the world. A landscape where people listen to tales of suffering from earliest childhood, and understand it, even before they know what the word actually means. And nobody really knows exactly what it means, even though they constantly pronounce it. Writers and all sorts of artists utter the word *longing* with a special piety, and proudly explain to each other that nobody understands this word to the core and that it's impossible to translate this word into any other language; that it's a magical word and in some unutterable way comprehensible only to the inhabitants of this landscape. Naturally; since only the inhabitants of this landscape enjoy their suffering so much: quietly and with unstinting malice toward their own suffering and that of others. They don't smash glasses, they don't play jazz, they don't moan all that much; they just suffer and long. Suffering is neither a particular sorrow nor a particular joy for them, although they would prefer the latter; they suffer because that's how it is. Whenever poverty fails to bring them suffering, whenever life's entanglements fail to bring it, they inflict it on themselves. They inflict it on others and they inflict it on themselves. The landscape is full of natural beauty, the camouflage of melancholy devils. The more people gaze at the camouflage, the more they scale high mountain peaks and gaze at their rivers and yellow fields, the more they strike themselves and others as ugly and spiteful; and if they aren't sufficiently that way—*if they aren't sufficiently that way*—then they inflict harm on themselves and others, so that they are. And he already sensed, he already knew that he was coming to a deathly landscape. He left there with melancholy devils and death in his soul, and he could have traversed all the landscapes of the world, he could have laughed and loved, he could have roamed at will, without a care in the world, and enjoyed himself to the point of inanity, along his diagonal, along the inner diagonal that runs through his whole body, from the brain down to the genitals and the restless soul that's tethered to them, no matter: he still would have borne within himself everything that this landscape had given him from the first moment of life. From the first moment, from tenderest childhood, when he caught sight of his mother's gentle face and the premature shadow of suffering on it; from his vulnerable, poor youth to the first lines he read in urgent search of knowledge about suffering; to his encounters with people whose foremost goal in life was to injure and harm themselves and others, others and themselves, who spent their whole lives shoving each other back and forth. Here people also chose social structures that were best suited to their basic orientation toward life, to their style of interpersonal relationships, based on profound, melancholy spite. Oppressive systems worked best here: this is where the cunning, backstabbing violence of clericalism and the brutal criminality of communism both flourished. Here people could truly feel good only in those kinds of systems. Here the secret police got astonishingly good results, since it was in harmony with the essence of these people, who were in their most natural, most historically and naturally determined element when they were doing harm to, or slowly tormenting, themselves and others, others and themselves. Anyone who has spent his young, defenseless years among people waiting for the moment when they can kick each other, when they can shove a stick through the soft tissue of each other's skulls, will not find salvation on any continent, in any crowd. Good times last only a short time for him.

The instant he sensed it, he also knew: now he was entering a *landscape of death*. Here the people were absorbed in death. Here death had the appearance of a beautiful landscape: sometimes it was autumnal and cool, and sometimes it was vernal and warm. In the autumn it's gothic, in springtime baroque. Like the churches strewn thickly over the whole land like tombstones. People here liked tombstones covered with flowers, candles, and angels. Here, in mid-morning, a friend might leave open on a table a book of verses by a poet whom melancholy devils had hounded to death; and the more he understood it, the more his lucid mind understood where he was living his life and what happened in these parts, what sorts of mysterious forces ruled, the closer he came to insanity and death. Here, in mid-morning, a friend might leave a book open and go hang himself, when no one, but no one expected it. Here everyone knew someone who had committed suicide. There wasn't a family or a circle of friends without one. Everyone had his own friend or family member who had committed suicide; and everyone thought of suicide himself. Suicide was your closest companion; everyone was absorbed in suicide. A poet would write verses recommending suicide, in the form of an American-style advertisement he would write an invitation to suicide. With the title: "The Longing Rope." No, that couldn't happen anywhere else, nowhere else would that come of such a thoroughgoing disdain for life. The medieval *contemptus mundi* had been preserved here in a thoroughgoing way. The good times were brief, disdain for life was the permanent form of existence. On Sunday afternoon, when foreigners or migrant laborers would hang out on the empty city streets, puzzled at the disappearance of all the locals; on Sunday afternoon everyone sooner or later thought of a window opening on the third floor of a building where all the windows were shut and somebody throwing himself out with a rope around his neck, and dangling against the facade. All his youth he had heard stories about people jumping off some bridge into a river. Every week there was news like this. This news was a regular part of conversations, and it was told with some horror, but also with some pleasure, which at the time he didn't understand. It wasn't the kind of pleasure that came of real joy in living, the kind that says: but I'm still alive. Instead, it was pleasure in things being just the way they were, in a woman's having jumped into a river, and in the fact that things couldn't be any different. The suicide rate was one of the highest on earth, stretching from here all the way up to Humboldt Terrace in Salzburg, where in his youth a solitary Austrian poet would see corpses smashed against the sidewalk in different clothing styles, depending on the season, and from here down to the Pannonian lowlands, where Hungarian poets wrote of the anguished and mortal soul, where amid plains that were so vast, and man so small, day after day people killed themselves. Now he could sense and he also knew without a doubt: this was his only home.

CHAPTER 33

HILLSIDE, POOL

I

At first it was as though he were recognizing the features of a familiar face. Following unknown coastlines, wide fields, and nameless cities, there appeared landscapes of the lower world, bluish earthly regions over which his heart began to beat more quickly. The autumnal morning light was faint and diluted by the membranes of clouds through which the plane was flying; still, down below he began to recognize the snow-covered slopes of craggy mountains, the dark valleys between them, and then fields, and then as the skyship descended a little closer, they ceased being just familiar features of an almost forgotten face submerged in the waters of the past; this became the distinctive physiognomy of the features of a human face, the features of a landscape, and its likeness suffused the armature of his heart. And at the same time it was fun, at the same time it was a delight, because all the things of the lower world, which until a short while ago had been nameless, suddenly had their own names. That's Kamnik Pass, he said aloud, as children say when they see the ocean: that's the ocean. The Alps, he said, as the airplane's shadow glanced over the edges of jagged peaks jutting into the air. Somewhere to the left was Pohorje, a beloved, dark-blue massif overgrown with moss and trees. The moss was soft, and the trees, when you lay beneath them, roared like the huge, lumbering ocean. Sunlight glinted up powerfully from a watery strip, the Sava.

That cluster of houses was Kranj, and farther on was Ljubljana. On the hilltops were white churches with the names of saints. Every village and every hamlet had its name: if it was in a valley it was Dolič, if it was on a hilltop it was Vršič. Every field and every body of water had its name. Every street corner and every corner inside every house. Every object, smell, and sound rising up toward heaven, for a thousand years and more all of it had been named.

And hovering over all of the objects and all of the names was death. Death was hovering in this misty, yet translucent Saturday morning: the one depicted in frescoes of the Dance of Death in some chapel in the Karst, the one told about in fairy tales, and the one that nobody saw or knew.

When the airplane started to shake, when fields and the people working in them started streaking past the window. When, at eleven-thirty on some Saturday morning in October, the airplane reached its home port.

2

Ana was waiting for him. When the two of them, strangers, embraced, their bodies shuddered. It was strange and mysterious, yet so simple, with a few words about the trip and the weather. About the time difference, about joy and illness. With things abruptly put in their proper places, even if they'd been derailed, with things that said: this is the way it is. This is how you're going to live. Suddenly empty. A shell suddenly emptied after a journey.

She drove with an anxious face. He noticed the anxiety on her familiar face—the only really familiar female face in his life—and he could sense that her hands were sweaty and that she was dizzy. From the trip, from her preparations to be there, from the shadows of desire, from waiting.

The air at the edge of the forest shifted in the angular light falling from behind the clouds to the earth. To the steaming earth, the humus, the moldering leaves with the smell of putrefaction, of rot.

They lay at the edge of the forest, at the edge of a small clearing, under the still-green branches of a pine tree. On the far side of the grassy space, strewn with somber autumn flowers, the trees were bare, though some of them still bore a scattering of red and yellow leaves. The whole hillside behind them was arrayed in those colors, which shifted into each other.

Then all that remained before his eyes was the gnarled root of the pine tree, running over the surface like a thick vein of life and disappearing under the earth somewhere up ahead. The root that Ana clutched at with all her might, her white fingers locked clawlike around it. And then, then she raised her eyes toward him, showing something that he hadn't recognized at first. It was remoteness and fear at the same time, as if she were staring into a deep abyss. Her half-bared body moved greedily, as though it had a life of its own. The look came out of that motion, out of the creeping of blood-suffused, human substance, and yet it was somewhere else, too. She looked at him with far-off astonishment, as though she were looking at the dark, unknown tree overhead. As though she had suddenly started making love at the forest's edge with some passerby.

Then she spoke his name and burst into tears that mixed with spittle on her face, with the earth's dampness on her hands, with the rushing of blood, with life wanting to live, although at the bottom of that look there was terror of death, an instantaneous experience and understanding of death, of its blindness, its erratic and mysterious attraction. Of that vibration that narrows and turns into nothing, into silence.

The silence of a forest slope, a clearing, a pool, the dark mass of trees all around.

He could hear her long exhalation, his gasps, he could hear their silence.

I'm different, too, she said. He knew exactly: she hadn't stayed with him the whole time, her shell had been emptied, too. So what next? he said. What next?

On the other side of Ana's head, which was resting on his shoulder, a squirrel ran along the outline of the meadow's surface, up the slope. It stopped for a moment and looked at them, then vanished into the forest. But several seconds after that he heard it running up the trunk of the tree they were lying under. He covered her naked body with his overcoat, and now her eyes returned to him, to the things of the earth and the sky that were motionlessly poised in the vibrant sunlight. The squirrel was on a branch over their heads now, and it swayed, so that both squirrel and branch were practically in front of his eyes, within arm's reach. Ana shuddered and pulled back. This one's sick, she said, an animal wouldn't dare come this close. Then the wet little creature pushed off, soaring through space in a brief arc and landing with a dull thud on the tree trunk.

It's chilly, Ana said. It was late October, with dampness hovering over the earth. It was chilly.

4

They waited for lunch in a village pub. A peasant at the next table was coughing and wheezing, as if trying to force something out of his bursting body. Those that came into the pub brought the smell of cold air, of dampness, of the fields, of rot. Of the forest, of grass, of damply moldering wood and leaves, which the two of them had brought in, too.

He adjusted his watch. Six hours' difference, he said, I'm giddy. I'll stop by the hospital now, he said. Then sleep for twenty hours. What shall we eat after all that? he said. After all that? After all that. They started laughing emptily. Wine? she said. Lots of wine, he said. It was one o'clock when they started to laugh.

5

Even so, he asked her to take him home first. He hadn't slept in twenty-four hours, they'd drunk wine, he reeked of it. He'd splash some water in his face. When they climbed to the top of the stairs, he glanced at his door at the end of the dark hallway. A white sheet of paper had been tucked into the crevice, an envelope. He wanted to clear his throat; he thought of the peasant wheezing in the pub, and suddenly he had a black, bloody substance in his chest. He tore the envelope open.

His friend the doctor was telling him that his mother had died at one-fifteen. She hadn't suffered. He was sorry. Please contact him.

He sat down on his suitcase, looking for something. Sunglasses or keys.

■ □ ■ □ ■

CHAPTER 34

THE STROKE OF SILENCE

The bus pressed uphill along a winding road through the narrow mountains. The tires spattered droplets of mud on the rattling windows, so that the morning countryside sped past smudged, indistinguishable. Some snow had fallen at the beginning of November, but had melted fast. After a brief appearance by the sun, which shone onto heaps of wet wreaths, faded flowers, and wadded, mud-spattered mourning crepe, it got dark again. The whole time it seemed that something was about to drop out of the sky, but then the same old period of dark days came. Only now did he realize how well he knew them, these days when clouds hung over the city and lights stayed lit in the windows even at noon. A few days after the funeral he sat in his mother's apartment, at the kitchen table, under the low-hanging light with the porcelain shade, and leafed through her papers. A stack of his postcards was held together with a rubber band, and tied together with a white string on top of that. In a drawer he found an empty glasses frame. A frame designed for thick lenses, for a strong correction. The gaps in the frame stared at him vacantly. He'd seen this glasses frame somewhere; somewhere he'd seen it.

He walked down streets where the slush had left splotchy traces on the sidewalks. As always at this time of year, damp spots seeped through the walls in the stairways and halls of the old house that he came to visit every day and which he knew so well. He lay next to Ana and in the mornings stared at the ceiling while she clattered around making coffee before she left, and then he listened to her footsteps, which he could distinguish from others on the sidewalk under their window, the car door slamming, the engine starting.

Now he was here, after almost one year. And here was also this smudgy landscape outside the windows of the rattling bus. The bus stop that he left for this morning, just as soon as Ana had driven away, was black, with a crowd of workers swarming under the glimmering lights in the murk. They had sleepy faces and cold hands. Some of them stood around the kiosks, while smoke or steam poured out of them, and drank their morning brandy. Then the facades of houses ran past the windows, city streets with dark house facades on either side. Houses with empty windows, only the frames around them. Houses with memories centuries old, and with oppressive dampness seeping through their walls. From the inside out, from the cozy apartments, the oozing of suicidal dampness out into the dark November morning, cadaverous dampness that stuck to the bus windows and hovered over the silent heads of the handful of morning travelers. The road dropped into a depression and they rode through a narrow gorge. Now a hillside covered with black shrubs and moss went racing past.

He didn't exactly know where he was going. To the village where the relatives who attended the funeral came from. To be among dark, peasant faces that he somehow felt he already knew. Mornings, in front of the mirror, he recognized those features in his own face. The features of faces that, in the years of his childhood, when he would go to visit them, were still vigorous and smooth. Now the men were shaven raw, the women red-faced from the wind, and all of them had deeply etched furrows on both sides of their noses, and dark circles under their eyes. Nothing but his face, multiplied any number of times. He was going to a place where he had once lain in the grass and listened to the bell of St. Anton's. Back then he had thought of the far-off worlds beyond the mountains and the seas, but safely tucked away in books, to which the bell's peals traveled. Then he tried to think away the telegraph lines and the noise of the tractor on the next farm over. Then he had thought that it had always been like this here, always the same, motionless.

The road climbed up out of the gorge and was suddenly running alongside a pond, which they called a lake here. He got out and waited for the dawn. A young girl was pushing a bicycle uphill, with milk cans jangling on each side. The dark cupola of the sky lay over the water, and out of the distance, from out of the rift between heaven and earth a ray of light shone slantwise onto it. Crows cawed from a field. A crystalline silence emanated from that rift. Then, for about an hour, he walked toward the light coming from the crevicelike rift in the world. He journeyed, descending into depressions, and every time he climbed back up onto a hilltop the brilliance was still there. As though the sun refused to rise, or had long since risen and was now shining from some unknown region into the opening between heaven and earth.

Then he caught sight of the familiar bell tower, which seemed to be quite close; and now he knew where he was going. He walked along some muddy cart tracks and stopped next to a house. He wanted to go in. The lights were still burning in the windows of Uncle Jožef's house. He listened to the voices that came from the barnyard on the far side of the house. He didn't go in. He kept going, and when the path began to rise, he could see from the elevation people in blue work smocks and white aprons. Steam rose out of big kettles, and women in rubber galoshes brought containers across the muddy barnyard or carried them away. The men were butchering the half-living, half-dead flesh of an animal they had just slaughtered. He could hear shouts and laughter, and he thought someone had noticed him, but it wasn't directed at him. He descended along the edge of the forest, through the stubble of a harvested cornfield. On the other side of a wooden crucifix, of the pale face at its top, he entered the forest's gloom. In just a few paces he found the place he was looking for. There were tiny mounds between the trees: he recognized them precisely. As a boy he had lain here many times, looking at the sky through the trees, the sailing clouds, and listening to the far-off voices of summer. He dreamed of countries over there, far away. Near the edge, near the wall of trees with dim rays of sunlight shining through it, with the green and yellow countryside flashing through it. These were Illyrian burial mounds, the tombs of some ancient, unknown people. The locals had dug them up several times, convinced they would find coins and jewelry in them. They turned up nothing more than a few bones. Water and time kept washing away their depredations, and eventually the mounds became rounded humps again beneath piles of rotting leaves.

He sat down on the wet leaves and leaned his back against a tree. He had arrived at the graves he had known since childhood. All around there was rot, the familiar decay of wood and leaves, the smell of decomposing substance, of wet forest paths through narrow passes, of decomposing corn stubble, of worm-eaten wood and mold. This was the smell that the whole country exuded, that was in the barns and peasant beds, the smell that people brought with them into pubs and buses, the smell that inhabited city streets and hovered placidly over the landscape. The air was thick with earthiness. Behind him it settled onto the banks of the lake and crept across its bright surface, rising then in a conical sheaf up toward the sky's cupola.

Then he lay down on the wet earth. Then the light trickled down to him through the trees, coming from that gleaming rift between earth and sky. Amid jutting, black-leafed branches the broad countryside stretched all the way to the horizon. From there, from the very edge of the earth, a radiant light poured up into the rift. Lives departed upward through it, and at its most radiant point they encountered melancholy devils tumbling precipitously down.

Somebody laughed, and very close by, he thought. Then he noticed that the laughter was coming from there, from the place where the plummeting was taking place, where somebody was thinking black thoughts and gnashing his teeth, while somebody up above, even higher up, was laughing at him. The one in control was laughing, making fun of him, too, of the way he was sprawled on the damp earth, on the forested slope.

From the bell tower of St. Anton's a bell tolled through the silence. Now he could hear it distinctly. Now he knew that this sound would hesitate for an instant above his head, then float up through that bright rift on the horizon. And now he knew of himself that, just like this sound, his echo and image would also find their way toward that inexorable laughter. Bim-bam. Ha-ha.

■ □ ■ □ ■

WRITINGS FROM AN UNBOUND EUROPE

Tsing
Words Are Something Else
DAVID ALBAHARI

My Family's Role in the World Revolution and Other Prose
BORA ĆOSIĆ

Peltse and Pentameron
VOLODYMYR DIBROVA

The Victory
HENRYK GRYNBERG

The Tango Player
CHRISTOPH HEIN

A Bohemian Youth
JOSEF HIRŠAL

Mocking Desire
DRAGO JANČAR

Balkan Blues: Writing Out of Yugoslavia
JOANNA LABON, ED.

The Loss
VLADIMIR MAKANIN

Compulsory Happiness
NORMAN MANEA

Zenobia
GELLU NAUM

Rudolf
MARIAN PANKOWSKI

The Houses of Belgrade
The Time of Miracles
BORISLAV PEKIĆ

Merry-Making in Old Russia and Other Stories
The Soul of a Patriot
EVGENY POPOV

Estonian Short Stories
KAJAR PRUUL AND DARLENE REDDAWAY, EDS.

Death and the Dervish
MEŠA SELIMOVIĆ

Fording the Stream of Consciousness
In the Jaws of Life and Other Stories
DUBRAVKA UGREŠIĆ

Ballad of Descent
MARTIN VOPĚNKA